Y0-BRB-675

my sister

jill

my sister
jill

PATRICIA CORNELIUS

ST. MARTIN'S PRESS NEW YORK

 For information, address St. Martin's Press, 175 Fifth Avenue, New York, N.Y. 10010.

www.stmartins.com

Library of Congress Cataloging-in-Publication Data

Cornelius, Patricia.
My sister Jill / Patricia Cornelius.—1st U.S. ed.
p. cm.
ISBN 0-312-31228-8
1. World War, 1939–1945—Veterans—Fiction. 2. Fathers and daughters—Fiction. 3. Problem families—Fiction. 4. Australia—Fiction. 5. Girls—Fiction. I. Title.

PR9619.4.C667 M9 2003
823'.192—dc21 2002037028

First published in Australia by Random House Australia

First U.S. Edition: April 2003

10 9 8 7 6 5 4 3 2 1

Acknowledgements

For their long-term belief in me and the time and energy that they have spent on this book I thank Lesley Hall and Elvira Piantoni from the bottom of my heart.

Thanks, Arts Victoria, for funding the first draft.

Thanks, Fiona Capp and Susan Hancock, from RMIT's Professional Writing and Editing course.

Thanks for the support and feedback from Crusader Hillis, Jennifer Richmond, Andrew Bovell, Eugenia Fragos, Christos Tsiolkas, Irine Vela, Wayne Macauley, Mathew Roberts, Rowland Thomson, Leonie Roberts and Peter Cornelius.

Thanks, Judith Lukin-Amundsen, for her editorial work.

Thanks to the invaluable services provided by the archives of the National War Museum and the State Library of Victoria.

And thanks also to Anna Piantoni and my son, Lucci Cornelius.

Prologue

When I was four I knew we were shit. We moved in with my great-aunt and uncle, and my mother Martha stopped being the woman of the house and became more like a servant in another woman's house. And when I was five I knew we were shit. I wore a sundress to school and I thought I looked the ant's pants. My teacher pulled me out in front of the class. She berated me about my dress, told me not to wear it to school again. The straps were long and my nipples were there for the world to see, my poor little nothing nipples, and I knew it must be them that got my teacher going. My mum didn't know any better not to dress me in a dress like that. She was shit, see. And I knew we were shit when I was eight and we finally moved into our own house. We were all that excited and happy. We walked the two streets from my great-aunt's place to our new house. In those minutes we were talking and holding our mum and our dad's hands and laughing and jumping about and we got there, to our own new house and discovered the dump it was. I knew then for sure.

There were plenty of other things that told me. Like the way other kids dressed and we didn't. Like how we wore shoes that flapped or seeped water and sogged up our socks. How we'd wear someone else's shoes and they didn't fit and how it hurt your heels like you wouldn't believe.

I knew when I went to other kids' houses and they had things like children's books and ornaments, and brand new bikes. Their parents did things with them, talked to them, looked at them in this funny sort of way. Like they were interested in what they had to say.

My mum knew we were shit too. I'd ask her if I was pretty or if I was smart or was I really good at anything. She'd say, 'Look at us,' meaning look at her and my dad. That was her answer. I worked it out later that she meant that nothing pretty, smart or good would come from out of them.

There were other kids who were shit. I could tell by a look, a kind of grubbiness, which is a bit misleading because we're not dirty – well, not necessarily. We just have this look and mostly it takes one to know one. Worn clothes, hems that sag, held up by a safety pin, or worse, a sewing pin. Holes in elbows and bad haircuts. Shit kids belong to mothers who are too fat, have long hair, no lipstick, and high heels that are worn so far down they curl up.

But it wasn't only what we looked like. It was growing up not knowing things, or knowing bits of things. At sixteen I thought sex was unhygienic because men pissed inside you. It was being told stupid answers to reasonable questions. It was kind of believing in god but not really. Hating things because you didn't have them. Hating people because they were Aborigines or Catholic or they were black or Jews or Asian or they spoke with an accent. Not believing in anything came with shit territory. So did not belonging to anything. No clubs. No groups. No commitment to a political party. My father, Jack, resented being forced to vote. Martha voted for someone because she liked the look of him. They didn't vote Labor. They weren't workers. Jack hated the unions telling him what to do.

We had no sense of ourselves, no sense of identity, no allegiance to a class. We came from a mostly British background, a bit Scottish, a bit Welsh, a bit from Cornwall. We hoped there was a bit of Irish because they've got balls. Maybe there was a bit of something more exotic in the mix. A bit of Danish, a bit of French, any fucking place as long as it was white and could spruce up the dull and stodgy mix that we really came from.

We came from convict stock but we were told to shut up about it. It's only now that it's kind of hip to come from a poor and desperate, ignorant, ugly and mean heritage.

Knowing I was shit didn't help. I had nothing to say to anyone about anything. I couldn't talk. I didn't know how to behave, which spoon to use, whether to put my serviette in my lap or tuck it in my neck. Should I ask to sit? Was one of those biscuits for me? Was it better if I didn't have one – but I wanted one – no, better not have one. I watched myself, always afraid. Do they know that I don't know what to say, where to sit, whether to eat, if I should take off my coat? Is it polite to laugh? Should I apologise for being early? Feel sorry because someone's crying? Angry because someone snubbed me? Did I have the right? Do they know that I have no idea who painted that painting, who Puccini was, that Karl Marx was not one of the Marx brothers, that apart from the capital cities I don't have a clue where anywhere is? Do they know I'm shit?

If only I knew what I know now. My sister Jill knew. She probably tried to tell me countless times but I wasn't able to hear her. You can only go your own way, make it as best you can. Jill's way was too head on, too raging for a wimp like me. If I'd gone her way I wouldn't have made it, I'm sure. She knows that we are no more shit than anyone else. She thinks pretty much that the entire world is shit. She thinks Australia's shit, I know that, she thinks that shitness is part of the Australian character. She says that for two hundred years we've convinced the world and ourselves that it's others who are shit. You'd have to be shit to do that. She says we go on about Aborigines and the drink and the country's overrun with white fat-gutted guzzling drunks who throw down grog as quick as they can then chuck it up to drink more. We love them she says.

She says we're full of it. She never has enough to say about this. The way we bow down to authority. How we tug our forelocks at the Queen, do whatever America wants us to do. Someone's always better. As soon as that someone's back is turned we muscle up and give them the finger and say, 'Fuck you.'

Jill thinks the country's built on an easy take. We love the bloke who gets away with it. It doesn't matter who he's ripped off. Little old ladies, the easier the take the better. We took it from the Aborigine. Worked it cheap with convict labour. Kept it cheap with wave upon wave of migrants who came for their take. That's what Jill says, that's how she speaks.

She says, whenever we do anything great we don't celebrate it. It's Australians who fought for an eight-hour day and won it. Our sad piddling numbers march through the streets on May Day singing badly the few lines they know from '*The Internationale*'.

There is one thing we do feel great about though. Us and war. We think we're great soldiers, the best fighters, the bravest in battle. I was sucked in, that's for sure. Jack, my father, had been a soldier in the Second World War. Not only had he fought but also he had spent three and a half years in a prisoner-of-war camp. It's the thing that I thought redeemed us, dragged us out of the shit, saved my family and me. My father was a war hero, he'd given everything for his country, he'd endured the most horrendous conditions and survived. Surely this had to count. My sister Jill says it counts for fuck all. But I believed it did. For so long I believed it. Even now I catch myself thinking it had to be worth something.

One

Jill is born into the world screaming and it seems to Martha that for the first year of her life she doesn't stop. Anything sets her off: the rustle of a newspaper, the ring of the doorbell, the buzzing of a fly. Martha holds her, she wraps her up tight, she puts her in a warm bath, she tuts soft sounds at her. Nothing soothes her. Jill yells. And yells. Martha and Jack hand her back and forth. They are sleepless, terrified they are doing something wrong. They take it in shifts to stay up to placate her through the night. She sleeps fitfully and wakes screaming at an awful, unearthly pitch. Her bassinet walks the room from the violent vibrations. Martha constantly searches her nappy for an open safety pin. She rubs her tiny body, thinking there must be some trouble somewhere and if only she can find it she could stroke it away.

They're never sure what will upset Jill. If Jack wants a smoke he leaves the room. He rinses out his mouth before he returns. They wrap clocks up in thick blankets. They throw her rattles out. No flowers, no after-shave, no talc, these smells set her off. A stinky fart escapes from Jack's bum and starts her screaming. They laugh and her scream goes up a notch.

Martha fears Jill has got something from Jack. Something he's brought back from the war, something that would explain her baby's unhappiness. Jill's tiny body arches and writhes and blows up in rage. Martha gives up and puts her in a darkened room. She closes the door and leaves her to scream. She sits at the kitchen table but doesn't eat, doesn't take a sip of her tea. What have we brought into the world, she thinks.

Jill talks early. She is six months old and she cries out, 'No-o-o!' as Martha pries open her tiny clenched mouth to force her to latch on. From that moment on Martha feeds her children cow's milk and she is saved from the acute embarrassment she feels when she exposes her breast to her child.

Jill's intensity unnerves Martha and Jack. As a toddler her tantrums are fierce. She flails her arms about like a threshing machine. Her high-pitched squeals, which can be heard three houses away, almost pierce their eardrums.

Jack drags her into her bedroom and locks her in. Exhausted, she falls asleep snug against the door. Later when Martha goes to check on her she can't open it.

It is a common sight to see Jill standing in the centre of the room screaming, 'No, no, no, no . . .' The screams never appear to be related to anything. Martha and Jack sit on the couch and stare at her.

'God she's tough,' says Jack.

Jill continues to scream.

'We could put her out on a mountain for a night,' says Jack. 'The Spartans did that.'

'She'd frighten any wild animal off,' Martha says.

'She'd survive, that's for sure.'

Jill shifts gear and the screams move into a higher pitch.

'She's possessed,' Martha says.

'You've got that right.'

'She's got that much fight.'

'She's mine, that's for sure,' says Jack.

Jack smacks and smacks her bum. He is determined to break her will. He picks up Jill's writhing body and rushes to the bathroom. He holds her under a cold shower until she's blue and can't scream any more.

'Do something with her, for Christ's sake,' Jack snaps at Martha when she can't shut Jill up.

Jill suddenly stops screaming. She runs with all her small might and butts Jack in the legs and downs him. He grabs her, smacks her bum and puts her in her room. Jill hears Martha and Jack giggling together and her cheeks burn. There are similar attacks made over the years. Jill often finds herself alone in her room, and away from Martha.

On Jill's first day of school Martha takes Jill to the door of the classroom and gives her a small firm shove. When Jill turns around her mother is gone. She screams all that day. In the yard where the headmaster puts her she screams. The next day she screams. Again she is in the yard all day. The next day she opens her mouth to scream but changes her mind. She sits down instead. She lets out a couple of screams during the day and is promptly put out to stand in the yard. It is in the yard that she develops a technique to control the outbursts. She fixes her gaze, thrusts her head forward and holds one leg out stiff behind her. She stays like this, perfectly balanced, until she feels her rage subside.

Martha's on the bus one day, passing the schoolyard. She looks through the window and sees children playing. Jill is in the centre of the tar playground surrounded by a hundred running and skipping children. She is motionless, her nose pointed and leg stretched out behind her. Martha blushes and pulls her head down into her fake fur collar.

Martha calls it Jill's retriever act. She enters a room and sees Jill in concentrated pose. Is she practising or has something started her off, she thinks and quickly backs out again.

Martha often wonders why she went on to have more children. By the time she married Jack she was in her early thirties. She was a good five years older than Jack and his body had been undernourished and knocked about.

'It's unlikely you'll ever have children,' the repatriation doctor had warned them.

'No kids indeed!' Later they would laugh.

'We showed them,' Jack says. 'Popped out six kids in seven years.'

'The twins in one go, of course,' says Martha.

'I had plenty of live ammunition,' he boasts.

'That's for sure,' Martha says. And I'm not having any more, she thinks.

Six children have taken their toll on Martha. Some days she's found it hard to get out of bed. During her pregnancies her ankles swelled and since Christine's birth they hadn't gone down. She's tired. Her bones feel leached of strength. Jill watches her. She notices that Martha's hair is not done. She sees that her eyes are red. She hears that her voice is distant. Jill takes her brothers and sisters out. With the hood down she can fit the three little ones in the old pram. The twins squash up one end and Christine is down in the front. She puts May on a lead, a cord from Jack's dressing gown.

'Don't you let go of the pram,' she tells Johnnie.

Jill pushes the pram out the front gate. They go around the block twice so they don't have to cross a street. If the younger ones are crying she aims the pram at the bumps and gets them to sleep.

Jill can always find the comb, knows where the safety pins are, whether they've run out of milk. Christine sits on her hip as if she's grafted there. Jill changes Christine's nappies. She bathes her, feeds her and gets her dressed. She picks her up to quieten her, to comfort her, to stop her whining, to stick a bottle in her mouth.

Christine wraps her legs tightly around Jill and watches the way her big sister bites at her lip. She sees her eyes dart from Johnnie to May to Mouse to Door when Jack is in the room. She feels Jill's body, how it moves, how with jerks of her head she arranges her brothers and sisters around a room. She places them in out-of-the-way spots, beyond immediate range of Jack's attention. She prods at them to get them to move faster. She slicks back a wayward lock of hair. She indicates not to speak, to speak softly, to answer Jack's question, not to answer Jack's question, to laugh, to remain serious. The muscles in her face move at an extraordinary pace. Only Christine notices their frenzied dance. She pats Jill's cheek to calm them.

Martha disappears under piles of washed and unwashed washing.

She is lost in the steam from bubbling pots and boiled-to-death beans. If it weren't for the *thump thump* of the iron on the back porch table her children wouldn't find her. They track her down and discover her, red-faced, surrounded by unstable towers of handkerchiefs, towels, pillowslips and underpants.

'We're hungry,' say the twins.

'Where are my shoes?' asks Johnnie.

'Have you got a shilling for the excursion to the zoo?' This is May.

'Not now!' Martha cries. Jack is home and is calling for Martha.

Martha hisses at them. 'Get! Can't you see? I've got no time for you now.'

Jill sees. 'Come outside,' she suggests to her brothers and sisters in her happy, everything-is-going-well voice. 'I've got a great game we can play.'

They come to Jill when they fall over. They come to her when they want something to eat. They come and sit on her knee.

Johnnie comes to Jill damp and miserable and shivering.

Jill wakes with a start, chilled, motionless in the dark. She gets out of bed. Her feet are cold on the cracked lino floor. She pulls out a drawer. She stops still as the thump on the other side of the fibro-cement wall shakes her mirror. Her image shivers in it. She rummages through her clothes and finds some pajama pants and an old wind-cheater. She takes the clothes with her and slips back into bed. She warms them between her legs. Johnnie's whimpers become shrill. There's the sound of a slap. He never cries very loudly and only in anticipation. The moment before the slap is always the most frightening, thinks Jill.

Another slap, a bare hand against a bare leg or bum. It stops. The door of the bungalow snaps shut. Jill waits a moment. The handle of her door turns and Johnnie appears.

'Jill?'

'Take them off. Quick, it's freezing.'

Johnnie peels off his pajama pants.

'And the top. It'll be wet along the edges.'

Johnnie throws the wet pajamas out the door. Jill helps him get into the dry clothes that stick to his moist skin.

'Look! Finger marks,' says Jill.

The welts on Johnnie's bum form the perfect shape of a hand.

He climbs into bed with her.

'Can't you stop, Johnnie? He'll keep on at you until you do.'

'I try,' whimpers Johnnie. He buries his head under the covers.

'Don't take so much blanket.' Jill pulls hard to get her share. Johnnie snuggles up against her.

'Jill?' he whispers.

'Yeah?'

'Jill?' he whispers again.

'Yeah, I'm here, Johnnie. Go to sleep.'

Jill keeps track of all the children. She seeks out the twins to see what they are doing. She looks in on Christine to make sure she is not pestering Martha too much. She watches May spread the newspaper on the floor and how her eyes move from one drawing of a woman in a gown or suit or garment of some kind to another. May studies each picture, her nose almost touching the newsprint as she examines every tuck, pleat and dart. She outlines the shape of the dresses with her fingertip and cuts them out with a pair of sewing scissors that are so big she can barely hold them. Each cutout is lovingly placed into a shoebox that May keeps in the bottom of the wardrobe.

On weekends Jack gets to the paper before May. She slips between Jack and the newspaper, settles herself on his lap and waits for him to turn the pages to reveal that morning's collection.

She copies the sketches and their jaunty descriptions and begins to create her own designs. She draws them on every scrap of paper she can find. Most of the time she draws on newsprint. She stares longingly at the white tablecloth after her plate has been cleared.

Jill enters the butcher shop. Christine is on her hip and the twins are at her side. Door and Mouse drop to their knees to make patterns in the sawdust on the floor. Christine calls out, 'Hello Pig.' A pig's head hangs from a large metal hook. It smiles grimly at her in reply. Jill orders two dozen thin sausages, one dozen fat, two pounds of mince, three bits of oyster blade steak. 'Could you put it on our bill please, Mister Cox?' Mr Cox sighs. Before he can answer, Jill quickly asks, 'Would it be all right if my sister had some of your paper? She draws and she's got nothing to draw on and she's desperate.' Mr Cox looks at Jill and she meets his eye. He quickly rolls up a wad of white butcher paper, holds it together with a rubber band and places it with the packages of meat.

Later Johnnie cuts the paper into sketchpads bound by electric tape. They present them to May. Her face looks lovely with her perfect grin. May covers the pages in gowns and stoles and suits and coats and blouses.

Next time Jill comes in Mr Cox rolls up the paper before she asks for it. He puts on a posh voice and tells his wife that he is a patron of the arts.

Jill has decided to make a study of the twins. She believes she is in a fortuitous situation because she can observe the twins at any time and they will do anything she asks of them.

'It's so lucky they're identical,' she says.

'But they're not really identical,' May informs Jill. 'Mouse has a birthmark.'

'We can cover it up with makeup if it becomes a problem,' says Jill.

She designs experiments to test the various phenomena associated with twins.

'Stand in the doorway, May,' Jill tells her.

'Mouse, sit here in front of me. And Johnnie?' Jill calls out to Johnnie in the other room. 'Have you got hold of Door?'

'Yep,' says a serious Johnnie.

At a signal from May, Johnnie gives Door a well-aimed slap on the arm. May now signals to Jill the experiment has begun.

'Take your time, Mouse,' says Jill. 'Concentrate. Now where do you feel the pain?'

Mouse takes a wild guess.

'Is he right, May?' Jill asks.

Disappointed, May gives an exaggerated shake of her head. 'Try another one,' she yells to Johnnie.

This time Johnnie gives Door a pinch on his thigh. Door screams and starts to cry.

'You must have felt that, Mouse,' says Jill. 'Concentrate now. Where was it?'

Mouse is in a state. He is distressed by his brother's cries of pain and makes another poor guess. He begins to cry. Christine, who is watching from the bed, joins him. After a while the twins are swapped over and the experiment is continued.

'It's for science,' Jill explains, full of importance when they complain.

Not all the experiments are harsh. Christine is envious when Jill applies the taste test. Door and Mouse sit on chairs back to back. A spoonful of jam is shoved into Door's mouth and Mouse is asked to identify the taste. A spoonful of vegemite is next, followed by a piece of soap, a drop of sherry and a slice of raw potato.

'What about a bit of poo?' whispers May.

'Good idea,' says Johnnie.

'It's not hygienic,' Jill says.

Sometimes the twins guess right, especially when they are assisted by the smell of something familiar. Jill excitedly records it in her data book. Johnnie and May think about the fortune they will make when Door and Mouse tour the world with the act.

In actual fact Door and Mouse do think thoughts at the same time. No one notices how they stand up, or leave a room, or pick up a book and begin reading, or go to sleep – at the exact same moment. When they are parted each of them carries on a dialogue as if the other is there. But when Jack is there they are totally silent.

When Jack is home Jill sees to all the children's needs. Martha is there for Jack. His meal is warm on the stove for him, his beer is chilled in the fridge. When it's cold there's a fire crackling in the grate. Martha is at the ready for any request.

But when Jack is out the children seek their mother out, wanting something, wanting her.

Martha's body is large and bulky and looks as if it might be comfortable, warm, something to sink into. Christine attempts to get into it, to burrow herself right in, pull her mother's body around her like a coat. Martha's body has no grip. And Christine finds herself sliding this way and that, away from her.

'Hold me,' Christine whines.

'I am holding you, Chrissie.'

'Hold me!' Christine stares into her mother's eyes and sees the colour fading. She grabs Martha's arms and forces them to hold her, pushing her body into Martha's unyielding breasts.

'Get off me, Chrissie, for god's sake, you're crushing me.'

'Chrissie! Get off Mum.' Jill pounces like a cat.

Christine crawls around and over the back of Martha's shoulders where she lies like a stole. Martha groans at the weight of her. Jill pulls her off.

As soon as there's a gap May gets in on the act. 'Just because you're the baby you don't get all Mum. She's my mum too,' says May.

She thrusts a picture of a model's elegant coiffure in Martha's face.

'What about this one? You could have this one. It would make you look much better.' She dips a comb into a bowl of tepid water and sweeps back a lock of Martha's salt-and-peppered hair from her large brow. She pins the straggly bits at the nape of her neck into a sorry and bristling bun. The remains of Martha's perm spring back over her forehead. Martha mops the trickles of water that run down under her collar.

'Leave Mum alone, May. You're annoying her,' Jill says.

May's wet fingers turn the pages of the magazine. 'Oh this one. This one is beautiful. Couldn't you get this one, Mum? You'd be beautiful.'

'May, leave her alone.'

May closes her eyes and takes an exaggerated breath. She doesn't bother to look at Jill. 'It's none of your business,' she says. She returns the comb to the now cool bowl of water.

'It is my business. You're annoying her.'

May's eyes open and flare. She stares at Jill. 'I am not! I am helping her.'

Martha's laugh surprises her daughters.

Johnnie searches his body for cuts and sores and bruises to show to Martha.

'Look at this one, look at this one,' he says and shows her a bruise on his hip. When he's desperate to find something he shows her the chafing he gets between his legs. He takes her hand and flattens it and guides it across a sore knee, and as if she has some kind of healing powers he closes his eyes and breathes her touch in.

Johnnie constantly looks for an opportunity to get close to Martha. Even when he's older and his face breaks out and blackheads bead the creases of his neck he waits for Martha to sit down and put her feet up. He's there with cotton wool and a bottle of methylated spirits in his hands. In a moment his head is on her lap and she's squeezing his skin. A good slosh of metho on cotton wool is administered to red and swollen ruptures. A hiss escapes from Johnnie's clenched teeth. 'Love it,' says Johnnie. The cotton wool is thrown into the fireplace where it explodes. Sometimes Jill steps in for Martha but she doesn't squeeze hard enough for Johnnie's liking. 'You haven't got the touch,' says Johnnie.

The twins have each other. When they do seek Martha out it is usually for a kiss or a quick cuddle. As long as she kisses each one in exactly the same spot they leave her alone. Sometimes Martha sits on the couch with one of them either side of her, their heads under her armpits, their hands held together across her belly.

Jill gave up touching her mother a long time ago. She can't remember when she last kissed her or laid her head on her shoulder. There are too many others pecking at her. She wants something from her mother but she doesn't know what it is. She suspects it is something that Martha cannot give.

Two

Jack spends a lot of time at the Club. It's the place to go when he can't go to the pub. He spends a lot of time at the pub too. There's no obligation for Jack to come home, no rules for him to follow, he comes and goes as he likes. He tells Martha, 'I'm going to the Club,' and he goes. Sometimes he might not even say where he's going. He might just say, 'I'm off now.' There's never any argument. Martha nods or says, 'Cheerio.'

It is peaceful when Jack is not there. Squabbles are over and done with in a moment. They laugh, tell silly jokes, talk. Someone might even sing a song, or leave the wireless on. Martha is a different woman. She laughs more, puts her feet up, chases one of the kids with a wooden spoon.

At dinnertime Martha takes no nonsense. She expects order. She sits at the head of the table, the bread knife to one side of her. A bent back or an elbow on the table cops a smack from the flat of the knife.

'Get your head out of that plate,' she yells at Door as she gives him a whack.

Martha brings in the hot plates from the tiny lean-to kitchen and passes them around.

'Not Irish stew again,' says Johnnie.

The grey meat threaded with grey fat swims in grey water with grey potatoes indiscernible from the lumps of fat. Thick slices of carrot bring colour to the plate. The stew is greedily shovelled down and chunks of soft white buttered bread wipe the plates clean. The children eat in silence except for slurping sounds and Jill's jaw, which clunks when she eats. She had once taken an elbowing from Johnnie in a race to be first in at the beach. Mouse licks his tongue across his plate and Martha is on to him and the knife comes down with a *thwack*.

The children are always hungry and interested only in feeling full. They rarely complain about Martha's meals but there is one thing they hate. Martha serves pumpkin every chance she gets.

'It's good for you. And it's cheap.' She is unsympathetic as she drops sloppy pieces of pumpkin onto their plates.

Christine sits squashed between Door and Mouse – The Twins, as they are called most of the time. She feels them join hands behind her back. One of Jill's plaits trails through the gravy and Christine watches it draw a pattern on the plate. She looks at May, who is off in some fantasy; she's got a pinkie out as if she's sipping from a tiny cup. Johnnie, head down, is eating at a ravenous rate. He looks up and gives Christine a wink.

'You'd better hurry and eat up, Chrissie,' he says.

Christine looks down and five pieces of pumpkin have appeared on her plate.

Sitting on a bench seat between the twins is risky. When Door leaves his seat the bench lurches dangerously to the right. If Mouse leaves or even lifts his bum for a second the bench lurches to the left. Christine is put in the middle because it helps with the balance and Martha thinks the twins need to be parted occasionally. It was Jack who called Mathew or Matt, Door, as in doormat. The name stuck. Michael was called Micky, which naturally became Mouse. The twins look identical but there is no problem telling them apart. Mouse has a strawberry birthmark along the line of his jaw. They are inseparable and stand together as if attached.

'You're not Siamese, you two. Stand apart,' Martha reminds

them. They step apart until Martha turns her head and then step in again.

The twins didn't speak until they were five. They appeared to understand enough, so Martha didn't worry. She secretly felt relieved. There were enough voices without two more to add to the din.

After they've eaten they all talk about their day. Johnnie is in his element. He is a terrific liar. Every night he tells a story and every night he convinces each one of them that this time it is the absolute truth. 'No bull,' he says. The lies pour effortlessly from his mouth.

'Paulie Briggs fell down as he was crossing Hampton Street today. He tripped on a piece of iron that had come off a truck. He fell and this other truck didn't notice him because it was driving so fast. It hit him. I never heard anything so horrible in all my life.'

Johnnie's eyes fill with tears because he can see it as if it's actually happening and feel the sorrow of it. The twins join Johnnie in a cry. Christine sits goggle-eyed wishing she'd been there to see it. May and Jill are a bit suspicious and ask Johnnie a stream of questions.

'Is he dead?'

'Which hospital is he in?'

'Do his mum and dad know?'

'Is this really true?'

Johnnie answers each question convincingly until finally May says, 'Oh my god, poor Paulie.'

'Got ya!' says a jubilant Johnnie, as he does every night.

The stories are always about Paulie Briggs and his misfortunes. He's had four legs broken, been mauled by a mad dog, ravaged by a shark, inflicted with some deadly disease, lost an eye, all his teeth, an arm, a leg, and died over and over again. Paulie Briggs is Johnnie's best friend. He's a lovely boy, a large smiling boy with enormous confidence. His father takes him everywhere: to the footy, fishing off the pier, camping, to the pictures.

When Jack is home Johnnie tells no yarns. They sit up straight at the dinner table, they eat their pumpkin, and not a single chair is scraped. As soon as possible they leave the table.

'Can I be excused, please?' Jill cues the others to clear out.

'What's your hurry?' replies Jack.

'No hurry.' Jill sits still and stares at her hands clasped in front of her.

'Why's everyone so quiet?' asks Jack.

No one answers.

'Cat got your tongues?'

Christine laughs. Jill flashes her a look and she cuts it short.

Jack is hungry and it's not food he's after. Martha brushes invisible breadcrumbs from the tablecloth and the children follow the motion of her hands. It is fatal to have eye contact.

'A man comes home to his family after a hard day's work and wants to sit around his table at dinnertime and have a lively conversation about any bloody thing, but that's not possible, that's asking for too much. No, I come home and am surrounded by a bunch of morons. Talk, for god's sake. Talk!'

But when they do talk Jack listens too closely. He searches for something he can grab a hold of and shake. Mouse asks May to pass the salt and Jack pounces. 'Must you whine?' he asks Mouse. He whines out the question and the others nervously laugh.

Occasionally Jack is the best of company. 'You'll never guess what happened to me,' he starts, and Martha and the children learn of the horse that came in or the wager he won and the dozen bottles of beer that came with it. Or he slaps a tray of meat down, won in a raffle at the pub. 'And not just sausages, Martha. There are chops and a bit of steak, and look at the size of that liver.'

Whatever time Jack comes home his meal is always hot. It's kept warm under a saucepan lid on a simmering pot. He loves a curry. He breathes out the heat in a succession of noisy pants. He fans himself, screams for a beer and drinks it down to quell the blaze. His children watch, transfixed. They are in awe of his bravery. How can he eat the stuff? Why does he endure such agony? When Jill is fourteen she dares to taste Martha's infamous 'curry of fire'. She waits for the wave of heat to overwhelm her but nothing happens.

When Jack eats tripe the children stare at the thick white slabs of sheep's stomach lying heavy on his plate. Steaming white parsley sauce disguises its peculiar texture. They watch Jack chew and chew and eventually swallow it down. 'Here, who wants a bite?' He holds out a white glob on the end of his fork and the children scatter.

Every few months Martha cooks him steak, rump steak with a beautiful thick yellow rind of fat. They watch him eat. Six mouths water and swallow when he swallows.

'As tender,' he says, 'as tender as the ripest plum. Or . . . a baby's bum.' He gives Christine's bum a pinch and she shrieks.

They watch the juice spread among the bristles on his chin, until all that's left on his plate is a great slug of fat, and whoever's turn it is to suck on it sucks with delight. May dreams of the day when she will eat steak big enough to cover her plate.

'How come Dad's the only one to eat steak?' she wants to know.

'Because he's the breadwinner,' says Martha.

When Jack comes home late he's always drunk. They hear him drive the car up on to the lawn. 'Night Mum.' 'Night Mum.' 'Night Mum,' the children file out and head for bed before he puts his key in the lock. There's no hurry. The paintwork bears a myriad searching scratches because he's usually too drunk to find the keyhole and that gives them time to clean their teeth.

When the door opens at last, he nudges one side of the doorjamb. 'Oops a daisy, here we go,' he says. He nudges the other side. 'Right oh . . .' He centres himself and stumbles through the doorway. He sees Jill. She has taken too long to get to bed and he's in the mood to talk.

'And I told him, yes I bloody well told him, who do you think you're talking to you bloody, you bloody bastard, I told him. Yeah I told him. I told him all right, the bastard. Yes that's right, I did all right.'

He sits in his armchair by the fireplace and Jill is caught, forced to listen to his barely comprehensible ravings. He is quickly argumentative and maudlin, self-obsessed and paranoid. But he finally falls asleep. She stands up and he nods himself awake. 'And then I told him . . .' and back he falls to sleep. She takes a step towards the door. 'I told him all right.' His eyelids close. She makes it to the centre of the room. 'Where are you going? I haven't told you . . .' Jack wakes and snorts or belches or farts, punctuating her every step.

Later when he wakes he is at his most dangerous. He wakes mean. His head pounds from countless beers. His mouth is dry, putrid from the constant dragging on the butt of a Craven A. He calls for his dinner. He's ugly as he looks about him to take a piece out of someone. When he's almost sober there's an edge to him, a way with words, which cuts to the quick. Over the years he has sized up his children. He knows where they are the most vulnerable.

With Johnnie it's simple.

'You're stupid, Johnnie, you're so stupid. Thick as a brick, Johnnie. You haven't got a brain in your head. You're an idiot.'

'You're the one who's stupid!' cries Johnnie.

'You're so stupid I feel sorry for you,' says Jack calmly.

'I'm not stupid. I'm not. I am not bloody stupid,' Johnnie finally blows his stack.

The twins are easy. 'Shrimps, the both of you,' says Jack.

There's no pleasure in getting a rise out of Christine, she'll always be the baby and besides she's the only one who talks to him.

He tries to get at May. She is pretty and her hair falls in thick black curls around her heart-shaped face. Johnnie too is pretty, with the longest lashes that sweep up, but Jack perceives this as an immense flaw, something close to an abomination. When he looks at Johnnie he feels somehow disturbed. When he looks at May's face he feels soft and warm. She imitates the rituals of older girls. She sits and files her nails or paints them with Mercurochrome. With the mirror perched on her knees, she picks and prods at her face. She sets her hair in large rollers to reduce the curl. She pretends to pluck her eyebrows into the thin lines she's seen arched in magazines. May is truly lovely, especially when she smiles. She is the most difficult kid to get to smile. She very rarely laughs. Perhaps that's why she is so lovely when she does.

'Give us a smile,' says Jack.

'Why?' answers May, taciturn.

'Come on, a little one.'

'No, I don't want to,' says May.

'Come on, smile for your old dad.'

'No.'

'You better. Because I won't leave you alone until you do.'

May sighs and parodies a smile that could kill. Jack laughs his head off.

'That's the best one yet, May.'

He enjoys these interludes. Not only is May pretty but she has a toughness he admires.

But it's Jill he likes to fight. When she blows she really takes off. She's a challenge. He has to keep his wits about him to remain on top. So now Jack nabs her at the door as she's about to make a run for it.

'Where are you going?' His words spring up at her like an old brown snake.

'I'm going to finish my homework.'

'No you're not, you're going to sit here with me and we're going to have a talk.'

Jill sighs and makes one more attempt. 'I have to finish some sums.'

'Fuck your sums.'

The poker is in his hand. He jabs the Mallee root burning in the fire. Reluctantly Jill sits opposite him in a matching armchair. The fire crackles and spits between them.

'All right,' says Jill. 'What do you want to talk about?'

In profile they make a formidable sight. Heads thrust forward, they stare reptilian-like.

'Well,' says Jill, 'what do you want to talk about?'

She watches him watching her as he looks for something to hold her there.

'Your hair. Your bloody hair. Your mother and I want it off. It's in your eyes, it's a mess. If you could keep it nice then it wouldn't matter. But it's matted up like a bloody dog's.'

Jill is silent. She tries hard not to let him get at her, to let it ride over her. But the words escape her. 'It's my hair and I like it long.'

Jack's grip on the poker tightens. He jabs at the log and sparks fly. Jill's face fills with contempt but Jack is intent on having his will.

'Is that so?' says Jack. 'You think so?'

'Yes I think so.'

'Well I'm not so sure.'

'Well I am sure,' asserts Jill.

'You're bloody sure are you?'

'Yeah I am.'

'You are.'

'I am.'

'Sure are you?'

'Yes. Sure. Sure. Sure, bloody sure,' Jill cracks.

And it's on. Jack scrambles for her hair. His fingers entwine in it and she screams. He roars and pulls her hair towards the fire. She angles her head and butts him in the belly and he falls to the side. He grabs at her hair again and offers it like straw to the smouldering coals. The ends of her hair snap and singe and when the acrid smell reaches Jill's nose she uses all her strength to pull, and leaves Jack with a handful.

Outside the lounge-room door Johnnie stands shuffling from foot to foot, cursing Jack under his breath. 'You bastard. You bloody bastard.' Back and forth he shuffles. 'Bastard. Bastard.'

Martha lingers in the lean-to kitchen. The dishes are done and benches are wiped and she looks for something to keep her there. A batch of rock buns, she thinks. But there are no sultanas. Maybe some Anzacs, she thinks. Get them chewy, Jack likes them like that.

If she intervenes it sends him over the top. He becomes more cruel, more savage. Once she saw a pit-bull terrier and thought of Jack. The dog had grabbed some poor old mutt by the scruff of its neck and held on. The owner tried everything to make it let go, kicked it, hit it with a steel pipe, yanked at its genitals, gouged its eyes – but still it held on.

And Martha's tired, she yearns for peace. She hears the fly-wire door crash back on its hinges. There goes Jill, she thinks. And there goes Jack bellowing after her.

'They're going to wake the little kids,' Martha mutters. She folds the damp tea towel. It's Irish linen, a present from her aunt. It has a sprig of wattle splashed across it. She's saving the one with the waratah for last.

Christine lies in bed, her hands over her ears. 'Why can't you stop? Just shut up for once,' she whispers, fuming at Jill. Across the room May groans in her bed and pulls the blankets over her head. Why can't Jill just leave him alone, Christine thinks.

At times Jack seeks out the kids. He rushes them outside, excited, almost childlike in his pleasure. He shows them where the first sign of a bean shoot is lifting its hooded head. He shows them the miniature apricots, the size of peas, clustered around a branch. Signs of life excite him. 'Look at this, look at this,' he cries. 'Isn't that marvellous? And look at these, look at these. I only planted them last week.'

The children hate these moments. They find the intimacy excruciating. Their responses are stilted, dull and don't match his. They irritate him and he feels cheated. They prefer the cranky Jack, the drunk Jack, maybe not the raging Jack but not this man trying to be friendly. They don't know how to be friendly back. Inevitably it ends in tears or in a rage.

It's to Martha, in her kitchen, that they come.

'I hate him,' Johnnie cries.

'Don't hate him,' replies Martha.

'How could you have married him?' Jill sneers.

'He wasn't always like he is.'

'Must he drink so much?' May is frowning.

'Yes, he must.'

'Why can't he leave us alone?' The twins sob.

'Try and keep out of his way.'

'Why is he like he is?' Christine wails.

'Remember what he's been through,' says Martha in heavy, loaded tones.

Christine could kick herself. She forgives him instantly. 'Of course, the war, that's why he's like he is.'

Three

'Changi, Changi, Changi,' Christine chants quietly under her breath.

It's Anzac Day and her chest is loaded with Jack's medals. She loves the weight of them. They slap on her flat breast as she marches around her primary-school quadrangle. The children come to a stop and the chant fades like the rhythm of a train disappearing in the distance. Her head tilts proudly upwards and the flag is lowered to half-mast. The old crackling public address system plays the Last Post.

'Lest we forget,' she says.

Christine is ghoulish in her appetite for details of the infamous Burma Railway. She never tires of hearing about the thousands of half-starved, sick and exhausted prisoners of war who perished there. She imagines herself with them, in the wet, in the mud, exhausted by the heat. She couldn't find Burma in an atlas if she tried. What she knows are the stories she can wangle from Jack when he's half-whacked. She loves them; they fill her with pride. She loves the fact that Jack survived. She loves the names of the diseases – beriberi, pelagra, malaria, dengue fever – and how Jack had them all and pulled through. She sees him lying on the bamboo slats of his bunk shivering and shaking, his joints swollen and aching. His skeletal body wears only a white loincloth; he's an angular and awkward baby writhing in agony. She loves the respect when she announces that her father had been a prisoner of war.

'A POW,' she says reverentially.

Jack talks about the war, about his three and a half long years captivity in a Japanese prisoner-of-war camp, and Christine sits watching him. Her breathing is shallow, her heart beats slow as she transports herself into his stories.

'Tell me again about the man whose balls got bitten by a scorpion and how they swelled up as huge as the spread of your hands?'

'Slept stacked in bunks up to the roof of the hut. The scorpions were in the thatch and they'd come down and scuttle across you in the night.'

Christine squirms. She's certain there's one inside her shirt.

'This guy gets stung between his legs. He goes mad. He flings himself down and around and jitters and jumps. His balls are swelling all the time. I mean watermelons. He's screaming that he wants to die. It takes eight of us to hold him down.'

Then Jack's back is bent and his arms hooked around invisible legs while he tells the story of him and his mate Bob racing for the jungle during an air raid. Bob's feet were swollen and split and couldn't support him.

'He rode me like a jockey,' says Jack. 'He had this stick for a crop and he'd bring it down on me and yell, "Run you bastard. What are you trying to do, get me killed?" Then he'd laugh like a mad bugger as we high-tailed it for the jungle.'

Christine rubs her belly when Jack talks of how little they had to eat. Her mouth waters when he recalls the taste of the luckless chicken that had wandered into their hut.

'Its neck was as long as a snake, it had that many hands screwing it,' he says.

Christine can't help it, she feels sorry for the poor chicken.

'We were that hungry we'd pick at each other like monkeys,' says Jack and he pinches at Christine's scalp and pretends to put a juicy louse in his mouth.

'Live off that one for a week,' he says and laughs at her because she believes him.

He talks of sores pouring with maggots, of the smallest cut ballooning into a raging wound.

'The bloody heat, and the bloody wet, always in a sweat. Nothing dry or clean. It got you down, made it hard to give a damn.'

Jack leans forward and punches his fist into the palm of his hand.

'But we didn't give up. It was the officers who caved in. Weak shits. Men who had no grit. Couldn't save themselves if they tried. Namby-pamby private-school boys who never knew hardship. You see, when it comes down to it you have to have it in you to survive. They died like flies.'

Thankfully she and Jack share the same blood, Christine thinks. Whatever's in his is in hers and it will see her through, it's tough stuff, like him she'll be there at the end.

Christine relishes the stories of Japanese brutality and waits patiently for Jack to work his way to the best bits. He tells of the men forced to stand for days in the hot sun.

'For nothing more than looking sideways,' says Jack.

Christine licks her lips and tries to imagine her mouth without spit, her lips blistered, her legs buckling in the searing heat. Her body tenses as Jack begins to talk of the fate of others, those who attempted to escape.

'They brought in three blokes, two Australians and a Yank. They'd only been gone a week. They were on their way back, in fact. The jungle had been too tough and they knew they wouldn't make it. The Japs assembled us to watch. The three blokes were made to kneel. They told them to bow their heads. They raised their swords. And down they came.' Jack's arm slices the air. Christine sees three heads roll in the dust and come to a stop.

There's never a hint of a tear, no sudden silence while he struggles with his emotions. Christine listens for a tremor in his voice, watches for his eyes to close, shutting out the horror, for some sign that the experience has touched him. There's none. Sometimes he catches her out.

'Shut your trap and stop gawking at me,' he says.

And she's immediately alert, because once she's got him started it takes all her skill to keep him going. She can never lose herself entirely. Encouragement and not too much of it and just at the right time is vital. She's learned to flatter him, to gasp, to look solemn, to laugh on cue.

'It must have been awful being forced to watch those men die,' she says, her voice a serious monotone.

Jack lights up a smoke. 'I didn't feel much like wandering off, I can tell you.'

'Tell me the story of you on the raft.'

Christine has patiently and painstakingly endeavoured to bring Jack to this story. Instead he begins a litany, calling the names of survivors, conjuring up the faces of the men in his battalion who made it safely back home. In a drone Jack sings them up.

'Henderson, Somers, Weaver, Langridge, Leadbatten, Laurie, Lewis, Danielson, Harding, Roberts, Farquerson, Jackson, Johnson, Mackenzie, Bleasdale . . .'

There is no hurrying him, to interrupt him would mean the end of the storytelling. Christine folds her hands to keep them from signalling her impatience. The names are brought to attention and they stand for a moment before they drop back. She watches Jack, only his mouth moves, he is poised, concentrated, as if to forget someone would bring about their death.

'Lamberts, Campbell, Smythe, Smith, Smith and Smith, Symonds, Clark, Clark and Vanderstone. What am I talking about?' Jack interrupts himself. 'Vanderstone didn't make it. He died in the second year. It was Vandstone. Vandstone made it!' he says jubilantly, as if Vandstone had only that moment been saved. 'He was picked up in Japan,' he adds.

Jack rests for a moment, satisfied.

Christine tries again. 'And you on the raft?' And immediately he starts.

'We were sent from Java to Japan to be put to work in the salt mines. We never made it. They put us on a Japanese ship and luckily for us the hold wasn't battened down. An American submarine torpedoed the ship. Immediately the sub rushed off to another battle without realising the mayhem it left behind. We scrambled to get off the sinking ship. Japs filled the lifeboats. Rafts were thrown overboard and everyone dived into the water. The ship was foundering and the sea was aflame with spilled oil.'

Christine leans forward to take in every glorious word so that she can remember it in detail later. She is there with him at every moment, in the ship's hold, in the water, on the raft, holding on, desperately holding on. It is a story that has seeped and settled in her.

'Men swam around and around. Swimming from one Jap to the next using all their strength to hold them under. A frenzy of killing.'

Christine rubs the chill up and down her arms.

'Fools!' spits Jack. 'Left no bloody strength to save themselves.'

He nods at Christine and taps his head with his finger.

'Others were smarter and would beckon the Japs over to their rafts, all friendly like as if to save them, and then knock them on the head, or push them under.'

'Did you do that?' asks Christine.

Jack hesitates. He drums his fingers on the arm of the chair. Christine holds her breath, afraid her interruption has risked the best part of the story. Jack ignores the question.

'Shorty's in the water. He's looking for something to hold on to and he hears a baby crying. He thinks he's going mad. There before him like a miracle is a baby. It's buoyed up by its swaddling clothes. He thinks he's really flipped his lid now. He swims alongside the baby, cooing at it. Then he hears a woman screaming hysterically. She's lost her baby. And Shorty's found it! He swims, pulling the baby towards a lifeboat where the woman is wailing. It's filled with Jap soldiers and this one crying woman. Shorty holds the baby up to the mother. Great, he thinks, they'll take me aboard. He reaches out his arms.'

Jack lifts his arms and spreads them plaintively. He snorts with laughter.

'And what did they do? Took the baby and pushed him off!'

Jack is on a roll.

'There were hundreds of rafts. We tried to keep together at first, but eventually drifted apart. There were twelve men hanging on around the edges of mine. Couldn't all get on or it'd sink so we took it in turns. The sick ones would have to stay on. When they died we replaced them.'

Christine looks to see if there's a glimmer of grief. None.

'The Japanese were picked up by their frigates but they left us to die,' says Jack.

Jack stops to light up a fag. He appears to have forgotten Christine and the story.

'It was the oil that saved you, wasn't it?' she says quickly to keep him on track.

'The bloody oil. Inches of thick sludge all over us. In our eyes, stinging like we'd been bit by bees. We couldn't see. It covered everything, made it slippery, impossible to hold on. Blokes would slip off and we'd help them on and they'd slip off again until we couldn't do it any more and we'd let them go. Later they told us that the oil saved us. Kept us warm. Kept the water out. Made us buoyant. But I saw plenty that sank.'

There are many parts to the story but only a few get told in one sitting. Each time Christine responds to Jack's mood and keeps him going for as long as possible. She loves the new details that emerge in each telling. She thinks she's there in the water with him, covered in oil, and her knuckles are white with holding on. She's holding on, just as Jack held on when so many about him let go.

Some went crazy drinking salt water, seeing things. One of them dived down for an imagined blanket and never came up. Some bit into others wanting to drink their blood.

'Had to let them go,' says Jack.

The first time Christine heard this story she revelled in its tragedy. No one had the strength to help these men.

'Let them go?' She pushes Jack closer to the truth.

'Kicked the mad bastards off. Beat at them until they let go their grip.' He has no sympathy for their weakness.

Jack drags on his smoke. 'It's the ones that gave up I hate the most. The ones who wished you luck and waved as they let go. And mates, who'd go in pairs, couldn't go on without the other. They lowered morale, made it harder to fight, made you sink in your guts,' says Jack.

But it's these men Christine loves. The ones who care for someone else more than themselves. Those who can't face the inhumanity. If only Jack . . . but of course if Jack had been like them she wouldn't be here. Christine frowns.

After six days on the raft there were only two of them left, himself and a man named Doug. He and Doug were almost unconscious. They were worn out, starved, dehydrated, naked, their rags disintegrated. Their bodies, soaked in thick black oil, were tiny and racked with pain. They were sunburned, covered with sores and ulcers large enough to fit a fist. Their tongues were swollen and their minds were wandering. These two men had held on, tenaciously, single-minded in their desire to survive. The time had come to die.

'I didn't want to,' says Jack. 'But the sea was choppy and the wind was blustering, a typhoon was on its way. It looked like I didn't have a choice. I thought we were done for. Then we were spotted.'

Men attached to debris were sighted by plane. An American submarine scoured the water.

'The very one that had bloody sunk us,' says Jack.

A solitary man standing on his raft floated past the submarine crew and they almost didn't see him until they heard his miserable call. His pus-filled eyes had blinded him and his call had merely been a cry of despair.

The crew were silent as they watched empty rafts float past. And floaters, the bodies face down, their arms and legs submerged, forsaken, drifted by. They were rewarded occasionally by the sighting of half-submerged black figures, almost too small to see. The crew dived into the increasingly surging water and roped them in.

On board the crew stood in awe at the bodies that soon lay at their feet. They tentatively touched the men's soft, soft skin, fearing it would come away in their hands.

Jack and Doug were picked up last. Two men sitting miraculously on top of the water, their raft unseen inches beneath them.

'I can't tell you,' says Jack. 'I just can't describe to you how that felt. Lifted out of that bloody foul water, off that stinking raft.'

Each prisoner of war was designated a buddy, a member of the crew, who bathed them, fed them, watched over them. When Jack woke up in his bunk, thrashing his arms about in a frantic effort to swim, his buddy was there beside him telling him, 'It's all right, you've been saved, you've been saved.'

'I loved that man,' Jack says sentimentally. 'I can't remember his name but I loved him. I still love him. People can say what they like about the Yanks and they're probably right but I love them.'

And the story's done. Christine is exhausted by it. She and Jack sit quietly for some time.

Jack wipes his dry mouth. He goes out to the Club, to his mates, to sink a few too many, to drown the memories conjured up by his youngest child.

Jack's stories satisfy Christine for weeks. She is with Jack in the camp. She is in the hold of the ship on the way to Japan. She is on the raft, alongside Jack, valiantly holding on.

Four

Shrieking, screeching, whooping, the Wheatley children bolt from around the corner of the house. Out into the street they run, disappearing behind parked cars and fences. Christine presses her back up against the house boards and watches the others run past her. The edges of the boards cut into her back and her legs shake uncontrollably. The children run from Jack. He bursts out from beside the house, a wild beast, his chest barrelled, sweat running down it into his worn-thin underpants. He is carrying a plastic bucket full to the brim. Martha can hear him from the kitchen where she is washing up the lunch dishes. The heat of the day and the hot water in the sink make her sweat and the trickles tickle her as they run between her breasts and collect at her waist. Jack spots Christine. He stops and is about to douse her.

'You're too easy,' he says looking around him. 'Where's those other brats?'

Christine nods her head toward the street.

'Come on kids, game's over. Come on. The bucket's empty,' he calls sweetly as he walks along the footpath. 'Yes, come on my little suckers, come to daddy,' he chuckles.

Jack's enjoying himself. Relieved, Christine leans against the wall. Safe from Jack. The sounds of laughter now draw her onto the street. Jack spots the twins huddled behind a fence. He creeps up and holds the bucket over them. Their eyes are shut tight, they have no idea he is there.

Suddenly Jill comes out from behind a car. 'Na nee na nee na na,' she sings and dances a gangling dance to attract his attention. Jack turns, swings the bucket and hits Jill splat in the back as she attempts to escape. Christine giggles wildly at Jill's drenching. Jill will always save us, she thinks.

When the children are little, Jack likes to play with them and they like to play with him. He's fun, terrific fun. He does things no other father does. He chases them, wrestles them and squirts them with the hose.

'Geronimo!' he calls out as he jumps on Mouse and pins him to the ground.

When other kids come to play Jack tosses them around. He bellows and snorts and tries to buck them off. 'Your dad's the best,' they say. Christine beams with pride. The older children give a nervous smile.

Jack plays hard. The children love it but their shrieks of joy are slightly hysterical because they know the moment always comes when the game gets tough and unpredictable. If they try to drop out altogether Jack is merciless.

'You've spoilt everything, you brat,' yells Jack when Johnnie refuses to spar with him and runs off.

Jack likes to tease his children. 'Good-natured teasing, what could be more harmless than that?' says Jack to Martha when one of the kids takes off sobbing.

'Who's got the fattest arse in Melbourne?' he asks Jill as she walks past.

She doesn't answer.

'Who's got the fattest arse?' he insists. 'Come on. Who? Who do you think?'

'Me,' says Jill to get him off her back.

'Who thinks she's better than us?' he asks May because she's quietly drawing in one of her sketchbooks.

'Me,' she says, quick to answer. 'Much better.'

'You're no better, young lady, no bloody different.'

'Couldn't have got two kids more plain,' he says as he looks at the twins who are happily binding two sticks together with string.

'What did you say?' he asks Christine, who is playing a game with pegs that she's dressed in bits of rag. 'What did you say then?'

'What?' says Christine.

'What word did you use then?'

'What word?' she says, thoroughly confused.

'La di da,' he says.

'What?'

'Darnce, is it?'

'What?'

'And I suppose you're going to Frarnce where you'll prarnce around with Grarnt?'

Christine laughs.

'Talk properly, for god's sake,' he snaps.

'You got makeup on?' he says to Johnnie, who is laughing with Paulie over a comic.

'No!' Johnnie is outraged.

'Yeah you have, I can see it.'

'I haven't got bloody makeup on.'

'Don't lie to me, I can see it.' Jack purses his lips. 'You look beautiful. Doesn't he, Paulie?'

'Fuck off!' says Johnnie.

'What did you say to me?' Jack smacks Johnnie over the head and Paulie takes off.

Holding back his tears, Johnnie runs to Martha. He whispers feverishly in the lean-to kitchen. 'I hate him.'

'Remember what he's been through,' Martha sighs.

'I don't care, I hate him. He's mean.'

'It's the way he was brought up.'

Martha and Jack's bedroom feels unlike any other room in the house, thinks Christine as she sneaks in the door. It's as if it has a special light, a different smell. It's mysterious. There are secret things hidden in the drawers that take her to faraway places. She is transported to elegant rooms in which heavy brocade curtains fall, to open thatch huts with bamboo floors, to dark places in which occur unspeakable acts.

All sorts of valuables are stashed beneath the underwear in Martha's top drawer. Old rings that once belonged to Martha's grandmother, a pair of soft suede gloves for dainty hands, old photographs with scalloped edges. There's a photo of Martha's mother Ada and her sister Agnes looking dour and respectable in dresses of lace and tulle and muslin with cameos tied to ribbons at their throats.

'Are you sure they didn't have lots of money?' Christine asked when Martha first showed it to her. 'They look rich to me.' Martha picked at a crusty spot on her cardigan and smiled. Fine lines splashed across her pale face. She exhaled a short puff of air. 'Not likely,' she said, dashing Christine's hopes.

Under the photos are medals in velvet cases, brooches and imitation pearls, loose and on a broken string. There is a heavy crystal bowl with pink powder in it. The puff feels like it is made from someone's skin. There are letters on fine paper, newspaper cuttings, recipes, cards and a menu from the reception of someone's wedding. In small envelopes is a lock of each of the children's first hair.

In a blue square envelope there are three small photos. Tiny figures of emaciated men stand in blinding sun. There are palm trees and huts where others lie, their sharp knees and elbows beetle out, long stick legs extend from white cotton loincloths. Christine searches for Jack but the faces are too small and wear the same angular hunger. 'Like old men,' Christine breathes her disappointment. She imagined them proud and upright. Still handsome. Not these frail birds with gaping holes for mouths. She thinks that Martha should not keep these photos, that she should burn them. It's not right, Christine thinks. It shows them at their worst. No one should be able to see them like this.

Christine picks up a larger photo of Jack in uniform. He's young and handsome. This is the look, she thinks. He stares directly into the camera, so self-assured. His eyes have cheek and his mouth is curled in a crooked smile. Christine clasps the photograph to her chest and closes her eyes. 'Good luck, Jack,' she whispers. She salutes this man in the photo who is about to take up arms and go to battle.

Christine lifts white lace handkerchiefs and sees a beautiful hatpin with a green glass grip. The sight of it sends shivers down her spine. 'Oh god,' Christine gasps. She tries to hide it again but the hatpin flips up and lies on top of Martha's white cotton pants. Christine shoves the drawer shut. On top of the chest of drawers sits a photo of Jack's mother and her sister Amelia. Christine looks at the tiny women, not quite five feet tall.

'Why did she have all those babies if she didn't want them?' Christine wonders.

Amelia never told Jack how his mother died. It was a secret for women's ears only. Amelia told Martha who told Jill and May. Christine heard her sisters talking and quickly covered her ears, but she'd heard enough to feel burdened by this terrible secret kept from Jack.

At forty-five Jack's mother cannot face a thirteenth child. She takes off her underwear, folds a sheet and puts it in the centre of the bed. She lies down and plays for a moment with the tassel on the cord that ties the curtains. The light through the window masks her in lace. She bunches up her dress, lifts her knees and spreads them wide and sighs. She has done this before. She picks up the hatpin, draws a deep breath and directs it in.

When Jack's mother dies he is two years old and he is sent to live with Amelia. The smell of mustiness in her house overpowers him. It is in the wood of the floor, on the benches, in the drawers and cupboards. The kitchen table is furry. Tiny strands of wood have lifted with the severe scrubbings, it is like Amelia's face that is covered in short soft hair. Amelia wants to kiss Jack but he's not used to kissing. He's afraid of her. Her fingers dig in too deep under his arms.

Jack doesn't have his own room. He sleeps in whatever bed is empty. Amelia takes in lodgers, a stream of men, down at heel, down from the country, down on their luck. They pay for a bed for a night, a week, a month at the most, and move on. Jack only remembers them by smell. There is Citrus man who works at the back of the fish-and-chips shop and washes his hands in lemon juice. There are the Sherry men, the Metho men, the Tobacco men, the Piss men and the one who smells like lavender.

Amelia likes to drink. She drinks with her husband Bob in long sessions that sometimes last a week. When Jack's big enough he helps his aunt. He runs errands, airs mattresses, pushes heavy and twisted sheets around the copper with a wooden spade. From the age of ten he collects the rents and does the shopping. He helps with the meals and gets his drunken aunt to bed. Jack comes to love his aunt. He rubs her feet, he changes her when she pees herself. When she's sick he cleans her up. He gets a job selling newspapers after school. He brings home treats for her, a chocolate heart or a packet of sherbet.

When he's a teenager Jack tells her, 'When I make it, when I'm rich, when I own my first house you will never want for anything.' Amelia laughs a drunken laugh. 'It's true,' he says. 'I promise you. I'll buy you fox furs. And good shoes for your feet. I tell you what, I'll take you dancing every night of the week.'

Jack's father rarely visits. When Jack is twelve he comes. He spends an afternoon drinking beer and eating scones straight out of the wood stove. Jack is outside playing footy with some boys down the street. Nobody thinks to call him. After the game he comes in, his jumper tied around his waist and the sweat cold on his cheeks. His aunt is washing up the plates at the sink. 'We've had a lovely afternoon with your father,' she says. 'You just missed him –' Then, as Jack runs out the door, 'What's up with him?'

Three of Jack's brothers drop in. They come with paper bags full of beer bottles and a flagon for their uncle and aunt. Jack is keen for these men to like him. He listens wide-eyed to their stories, he laughs too loud at their jokes. He wants to talk to them but he has no stories to tell. They talk a lot about footy but they argue among themselves. When there's a gap in the conversation he jumps in and tells them how well he is doing at school. He thinks they'll be proud of how smart he is.

'I came top in mathematics,' says Jack.

'Good for you,' says his eldest brother.

'And I'm the best in literature by far.'

'Whacko,' says the brother with a bung eye. They begin to talk about catching the tram.

'I'm good at sport. I'm fast. I can run the fastest in my class.'

His brothers shift uncomfortably in their chairs and ignore Jack and start their usual comfortable banter.

Jack perseveres. 'I'm always picked first. They all want me on their team.'

'Put a sock in it, would you, Jack,' says the brother who rarely smiles.

Jack tries desperately to hold down the rising colour in his cheeks and laughs loud and hard as if it's all a joke.

They walk to the park to have a kick. Jack tries to be tough, to be one of them. He swears and they tell him to watch his tongue. He jostles them, shoves them, pushes them in the back. He corks his eldest brother too hard on the arm. 'Fuck off!' he says and clips Jack over the ear, and he brings the game to an end.

His brothers like to drink. Back in their aunt's kitchen they settle in for a solid session. They swallow a glassful of the amber stuff in a single gulp. They give Jack a glass of port and urge him to scull it. The sickly pink reappears with his dinner on the lino floor and they groan with disgust.

When they go Jack lies on his bed. He feels sad and left. He thinks of his mother in the only photograph he has. She is with Amelia, dressed to the nines. My mother was a lady, he thinks. She was fine, so fine. 'Why did you give me away?' he whispers and the words hang lonely in the dark.

Christine picks up the photograph from the chest of drawers. She quickly puts it down again as the image of her grandmother's death seeps in.

'Poor Jack,' whispers Christine. She is working herself up to a point where she might be able to shed a tear, when she is interrupted by a high-pitched scream.

Jack has thrown a rope way up into the jacaranda tree. He has made a loop and May has her foot in it. Jack pushes her and she shrieks, her curls wheeling out behind her as she scoops through the air. Jill, Johnnie and the twins are jostling each other to be next in line. 'Me next!' they cry.

Christine joins them as May's foot is extricated from the rope and Johnnie takes her place. He wants to sit in the loop.

'Stand up,' says Jack.

'No, I want to sit,' says Johnnie.

'What are you afraid of?' says Jack.

'Nothing, I just want to sit.'

Jack pulls Johnnie back as far as he can and lets him go. Johnnie swoops and lets out a whoop. Jack pushes him again and again each time his bum comes past. He flies higher and close to the trunk of the jacaranda.

'That's enough,' yells Johnnie.

Jack continues to push. He pushes with all his weight behind him now and Johnnie soars up into the sky and back, scraping along the trunk. The other children are quiet and watch their brother streak past them, the rope too tight squeezing his legs. Johnnie calls continuously, 'That's enough. That's enough.' His voice cracks and he cries out when his body hits the tree trunk hard.

Jack lets Johnnie swing down to a stop. Tears fall down Johnnie's cheeks. The rope is hurting, he's scratched his leg and there's a fury that screams through him.

'You big shit. You big stupid shit,' he yells at Jack.

'What? What's wrong with you?' Jack says in mock surprise. He steps back and leaves Johnnie struggling with the rope.

'Pull yourself together, you dope,' says Jack.

Five

'You're so fucking stupid!' yelled Jack the first time he raised his voice at Martha. She blushed. She looked around to see who had heard. It was as if he'd slapped her but Jack would never slap her. He believed hitting a woman was despicable, cowardly. He knew a few men who slapped their wives, men he had thought were decent. 'I showed her who's boss,' they'd gloat over their drinks at the Club. Jack sipped his beer and thought, You're nothing but weak pricks.

The words shot from Jack's mouth and just as he was about to ask Martha to forgive him, Martha said, 'I'm sorry, Jack.'

Jack accepted her apology. She must have done something to make me shout at her like that, he thought and the prickling discomfort he felt went away.

The next time Jack shouted Martha didn't apologise. She was very quiet.

The potatoes boiled dry and he yelled at her again. 'I can't believe how stupid you are,' he shouted.

He shouted when his dinner wasn't there in front of him the minute he wanted it. 'I can't believe it, I can't bloody believe it. What are you doing all day? I'm starving and you're sitting around on your fat arse the whole bloody day!'

He shouted when he couldn't find her. 'You're deliberately hiding from me,' he yelled when he found her out on the back verandah swallowed up in the ironing.

Martha learned to stay silent under his assaults. 'You think you're so superior,' he'd say. She wouldn't respond. 'You sanctimonious bitch.' Martha would continue to ignore him. 'You think you're so bloody fine,' he'd shout.

Jack's shouting got worse with the delivery of each child. The list of insults he directed at Martha grew and the tone was always angry. By the time Christine was born Martha was used to it. She shrugged her shoulders, rolled her eyes and remained quiet. She carried on with whatever she was doing. She ironed, put the clothes through the wringer, cut up beans, made beds. If I stopped still every time he shouted I'd never get anything done, she thought. She started a game when the twins were born. While he shouted she matched the names of flowers to the letters of the alphabet. She tried to name as many as she could before he stopped shouting. The letter Q was a hard one. She looked it up in the Yates gardening book and came up with the word *quince*. But that was really a fruit.

Jill cannot tolerate Jack's tirades against her mother but she has learned control and mostly she stays quiet. She waits for him to leave the room.

'Why do you let him speak to you like that?' Jill lifts her head from her homework and scowls at Martha.

'Oh, he doesn't mean it. He's full of hot air,' Martha replies. 'You have to remember –'

'What he's been through.' Jill finishes the sentence in full mocking tone. 'I couldn't care less!' she yells.

Jack yells and rants and raves at Martha. He smacks his hand down hard on the table. He jumps up and throws things about. Jill seethes. She sneers. She takes short breaths. She digs her fingernails into her palms. She mutters menacingly under her breath, 'You're a shit, you're a shit, you're such a shit.' Christine doesn't hear him. She thinks Jill is mean to Jack. 'Stop picking on him,' she tells Jill. When he shouts at Martha from another room Christine continues to talk to her mother as if it's merely the radio blathering on in the background.

'Did you love him from the first? Did you fall in love with him the moment you saw him?'

'No and no,' says Martha.

'Did you think he was gorgeous? Did he think you were gorgeous?'

'No and no,' says Martha.

'When did he ask you out? What did he say? What did you say? Where did you go?'

'I don't know, I can't remember.'

'You must remember.' Christine is interrogating.

'Well I don't,' says Martha.

'Why don't you remember?' Christine says loudly. 'What about when he asked you to marry him, what about then?'

Martha sighs. 'He asked and asked and in the end he wore me down. So I said yes.'

'Why won't you tell me properly!' Christine screams.

'You, young lady, can go to bed.'

Martha first met Jack at work. She didn't like him. The way he strutted in, the way he looked at her as if he knew her, as if he had a right to look all he liked. She'd been working there for years as a stenographer. He had been put on as a junior clerk and it was as if he owned the place. He was so sure of himself, going to have it all, he was, going to do this, going to do that. He bored her to death with his big-noting. He never came too close though, not like some of them, married or not, who stood right up against her chair. He looked all the time but it wasn't the sort of look that made her crawl. It was a lovely look, like he was looking at something worth something.

He was a boy when Martha first worked with him. She didn't take any real notice of a lovesick boy. He was an embarrassment.

'Did you cry when he went to war? Were you afraid he'd die? Did you tell him to be careful? Did you write to him all the time?' Christine is at it again and Martha is irritated at the way in which Christine brings her back.

'No Christine, I didn't. I don't think I wrote to him at all. I barely gave him a thought the entire bloody war!'

'Will you write to me?' Martha remembers Jack asking her when he announced at work that he'd been called up.

'I'll see what I can do,' she said. 'I've got a few to write to before you.'

Martha did write. The letter arrived in Puckapunyal a few days before Jack left the country. A second letter arrived in the Middle East. He could scarcely believe it when he opened them. 'You'll never guess what? Martha McDonald has written to me. To me. To me, mate. Martha has written to me.' He sang it as he danced about.

The letters were as good as a promise to Jack. In those pages he felt something of her fineness pass through his fingertips into him. He kept the letters until they disintegrated in the heat and wet of Burma. There wasn't much in them to romanticise about. The letters were matter-of-fact, full of information about others they knew. There was not one personal reference. I'm going to marry you, Martha. That's all there is to it, Jack thought as he lay with his bony body against bamboo slats. He knew it and so would she when he got home to tell her.

At the end of the war a small strange man walked into Martha's work. He stood in the middle of the room and looked about him.

'Can I help you, sir?' asked the manager.

The man's face spread with a grin as he said, 'I'm beyond help, mate.'

The manager clapped the man on the back and shook his hand.

'Welcome home, Jack,' he said.

Martha stared at him. She knew it was Jack, of course it was Jack, but she could barely recognise him. All the puff has been let out of him, she thought. She started to cry.

Later when she left work she found him waiting for her.

'Can I walk you home?' he asked. Silently they walked to Martha's house.

Most nights Jack met Martha and walked her home. He did all the talking. She never asked him to come in. They stood outside while he talked. 'I'm going back to school,' he said. 'The army's paying. I'm going to learn bookkeeping. I'm sure to get on.'

One night he asked her, 'Will you marry me, Martha?'

'No,' she said.

But Jack wouldn't give up and every night he'd ask her again.

'No. It doesn't feel right,' she said.

One night he was not there and she felt disappointed. She was surprised. The next time he asked her to marry him she smiled and said, 'When?'

Martha rang Agnes, her aunt in Ballarat. 'I'm getting married,' she told her.

'But who is he, Martha?' Agnes shouted, believing Martha couldn't hear her down the phone.

'He's been a prisoner in some camp and he's just come home.'

Martha sits shelling peas at the dining-room table. Jill and May are helping her. Christine's peeling potatoes that float in water in a green enamel bowl. They listen to the pinging of peas in the aluminium saucepan.

Jill and May sit either side of their mother. Jill gives May a conspiratorial nod.

'Do you love Dad?' Jill says nonchalantly.

Martha is silent.

'Do you, Mum?' May smiles sweetly.

'Come on, Mum, what's wrong? Do you love him? That's all we're asking.'

'That's all,' May concurs.

Martha sighs and throws down the pods she holds in her hand. She folds her arms and leans back in her chair.

'Why?'

Jill laughs a light happy laugh, which raises Christine's head from the potatoes.

'We're just asking. We want to know.'

'Why?'

'You do or you don't. It's simple.'

'You don't,' May says.

'You couldn't,' says Jill.

Christine pipes up. 'Yes, she does.'

'How could you?' says May ignoring Christine.

'She could.' Christine is determined.

'It's not possible,' Jill says. 'Unless . . .'

'What?' says May.

'He's good in bed.'

Jill and May fall about laughing. Martha, despite herself, giggles with them. Christine pouts. She doesn't get the joke.

'Is that it?' laughs May.

'Is he?' laughs Jill.

'What?' Christine says.

Martha laughs.

'Must be,' blurts out May.

'He'd have to be,' says Jill.

Martha smiles smugly and stares straight ahead. She says nothing.

'Whatever they're saying, Mum,' Christine says, 'don't tell them a thing.'

Jill can't let go. She leans forward and with all the joy gone says, 'Because why else would you stay with him?'

Agnes helped Martha pack a small suitcase for her honeymoon. Martha and Jack were off to Sorrento for three days. Martha put in her togs. 'We'll have a midnight swim,' Jack had said. Martha looked forward to this exciting and daring moment. She waited for Agnes to tell her she'd catch a cold but Agnes was more concerned with her flannel pajamas. 'A nightie is more suitable and less embarrassing,' she explained to Martha.

While Agnes packed, sadness overwhelmed her. It was as if Martha was going away and never coming back. The moment Agnes had seen Jack she knew he wasn't right. She could see he was bright enough but he held Martha too tight and he watched her too much. If his gaze had been all-love-sick Agnes wouldn't have worried. It was the look of fear that concerned her. He seemed afraid that Martha would disappear if he couldn't see her. She had tried to pretend to like Jack but he was on the alert. He knew she thought he wasn't good enough for her precious Martha.

Martha lay on her back in a darkened room at the Sorrento hotel. Her heart raced. The white cotton nightie with its blue satin ties was still scrunched up around her waist. She didn't want to pull it down. She didn't want to move. I wish Agnes had told me this was going to happen, Martha thought.

In fact nothing much had happened to Martha. Jack had had too many drinks. Without warning he rolled on top of Martha and pushed his almost limp penis somewhere between her thighs. Moments later he rolled off and instantly fell asleep.

The next morning Jack tried again. This time his penis was up and about but he couldn't find what to put it in. Martha had no idea what he was looking for. She started to giggle. Jack laughed too. They laughed on and off for an hour. When they came down for breakfast the other honeymooners broke out in applause. Jack and Martha ate their eggs and bacon avoiding each other's eyes. A glance set them off and their shaking bodies rattled the tea service on the table.

That night at around midnight they held hands, shivering in their togs, at the water's edge.

'Let's take them off,' Jack said.

'What?' said Martha.

He peeled his bathers down. Martha thought his bum was lit up by someone's torch but it was only the moonlight reflecting off it. She stripped off.

'You are so beautiful, Martha, so unbelievably beautiful,' Jack said.

Martha tried to smile. Her teeth chattered madly and her breasts danced comically with the cold. She looked at Jack and felt sad. He was still so thin. Flesh had deserted him. He looked tiny as he moved from foot to foot to keep the blood flowing through his veins. I've married a boy, thought Martha. His body was blotched with the shadows of old sores. The moonshine picked up the pattern on his legs where sea lice had eaten into his flesh.

'I love you, Jack,' she said.

'I told you you would, didn't I?' he replied.

The twenty-second dip in the shining black sea had frozen them through. In bed they wrapped up in each other's arms. They whispered goodnight and kissed a salty kiss. During the night Martha woke. A light peeping in through the crack of the door gave Jack's eyes an unnatural shine. 'It's too cold,' he said. Martha pulled the blanket up to him. 'It's too cold.' Martha offered to cuddle him. 'It's too cold.' She saw again the way his eyes shone, and then knew he was fast asleep and couldn't answer her. 'It's too cold,' he said over and over again and then cried out in a miserably pale voice, 'I can't hold on.'

Martha shivers. She picks up the saucepan and rattles the peas. 'Are you cold, Mum?' asks Christine.

Jill and May have changed tack. They lean in close to Martha and buzz at her with steamy questions.

'Did you do it before you got married?' Jill asks.

'Did you wait for your wedding night?' May asks.

'You didn't, did you?' Jill's mouth drops in disbelief.

'Did you do it with someone else?' May asks.

'What, on her wedding night?' Jill asks May.

'Did you like it?' May asks, shuddering at the thought.

'Not likely,' says Jill, grimacing.

Martha looks at Jill and May and says, 'As a matter of fact, he's very good in bed. Very, very good.'

Jill and May run screaming from the room.

Christine looks at her mother. 'What's he good at?' she asks.

'Never mind,' says Martha.

After the honeymoon, once or twice during the night Jack climbed on top of Martha. He poked about a bit and then rolled off. They no longer laughed like they did in Sorrento. It had become a serious endeavour. Martha tried to accommodate Jack and open her legs as wide as she could. One night she thought to pull her knees up and in an instant Jack found his way in. He came immediately and Martha was shocked. So that's what all the poking was about, she thought. Jack slipped from her and turned his back. He started to shake in convulsions. He sobbed silently and dreadfully and Martha pulled him round to her. He sank easily into her arms and wept out loud. 'Shush now, shush,' she said, rocking him.

Martha liked the feeling of Jack's body on hers. She liked to listen to Jack's breath as it gathered and crashed finally in a long hiss. She found it uncomfortable when his penis was pushed far inside her but she learned to control this by tilting her pelvis. She liked how grown-up it made her feel. Who would have ever thought I'd be doing this, she marvelled.

She'd never imagined she'd have a double bed. She never thought she'd have a husband lying in one beside her. She had always expected to live with her aunt. They would have gone on walks and talked about what bulbs were up. They would have done the sales together and rejoiced at the good manchester they'd got.

When Jack fell asleep, Martha let her fingers trail over her stomach. There was warmth there, just within reach, but she never reached. She bit her lip when she thought of it.

It took Martha a few months with him to sleep through the night. She felt awkward, conscious of every move she made. She had never been aware of her body before, never taken any notice of it really. Not once had she stood in front of a full mirror and looked at it. Her body was strong, and as long as it served her well then there was no reason to know it more intimately. But now she was married she felt her body as if it was a new one and that she'd just shifted into it.

She was acutely aware of Jack's body. Sometimes she woke to Jack sleeping soundly, one of his legs stiff and upright and pointed at the ceiling. She gently placed her hand on top of his thigh and pushed it back down on the bed. She pulled the discarded bedclothes over his body and he grumbled in his sleep. He pulled an arm out and up. It reached for the ceiling. She brought down one limb only for it to be replaced by another. Once, all four limbs faced upwards, a pitiful dead beast offering itself to the gods. It disturbed her terribly. She wondered if he had brought some exotic bug back with him from the tropics. Perhaps he'd always been like this, she thought. A man with a yearning, some terrible wanting for something he could never reach.

Martha described Jack's odd sleeping positions at a barbecue for returned soldiers.

'Sometimes I think I'm in bed with a beetle,' she said.

'Oh that,' said one woman. 'My bloke does that.'

'They all do it. They've been cramped in huts for so long,' explained one of the wives.

'They were so squashed they'd take it in turns to lift an arm or a leg,' said another.

'I suppose it'll stop when he stops dreaming about it,' Martha said. She quietly giggled at the thought of these women and her sharing their beds with these men and their protruding arms and legs.

Martha had hoped she and Jack would do a lot together once they were married. 'We'll get to know each other,' Martha told Jack. But a lot of the time she finds herself alone. Jack goes out without explanation. The phone rings and he rushes out the door. He comes home hours later, drunk and maudlin. 'A mate is doing it hard,' he explains. Another mate disappears. 'I have to find him,' Jack tells Martha. One time Jack answers the phone. 'I'll be there in a minute,' he says. 'It's Hughie. He's got a bad case of the jitters and I can't leave him alone,' he tells Martha. Two weeks later he rushes out and calls to her, 'Harry, the bloody idiot, has blown his top in a shop. Couldn't wait for them to serve him.' Max Martin slits his wrists and Jack and his mates rally. They sit by his hospital bed. 'The bastard just won't talk,' Jack says. But it is Billy Stokes Jack cries for. 'He was just a kid when I met him in the camp. He was sixteen. Shouldn't have been in the bloody war. I thought he'd be all right. He went home to Horsham to his mum. Then what does he do? He goes out to the chookpen and shoots himself.' After Billy dies Jack and his mates meet at the

Club every day for a week. They drink and drink, trying to wash away their sadness.

When Jack is home he can't leave Martha alone. He follows her from room to room. He calls for her when he can't find her. 'Come and help me put the garbage out,' he says.

When he buys cigarettes she has to go to the shop with him. He always has a cigarette between his fingers. He draws back hard and fills their house with smoke. It settles in a canopy over their bed at night. 'I've missed out on so much.' He blows smoke rings above them. 'I've got to catch up,' he pleads. 'I'm too far behind.'

'You will,' she says. 'You will.'

'But how?' he asks her.

Martha often lies awake in bed at night and listens to a sleeping Jack call and wail and chatter non-stop. He sits bolt upright, eyes staring into a nightmare that she can never know anything about. On the coldest nights she wipes sweat from his forehead, bathes him as if he has a fever. His dreams are in Burma where he lies hot and bothered by insects and vermin and wishes he was home in clean white sheets. She feels such tenderness for this tormented young man, this stranger with whom she shares her bed.

'When I got back from the war there was no warm welcome. No fanfare, I can tell you,' whispers Jack one night into the dark. 'What we needed was family and friends. All they were interested in was lists of the dead. No one asked us how we felt. They didn't give a damn.'

Martha wants him to tell her about the war but she is afraid. 'Don't let him talk,' the doctors have said. 'It's better for him to forget.' Everything about him seems to cry out, she thinks. He's got terrible things locked in, but who is she to let them out, and what would she do with them once they were free?

Jack's car pulls up on the front lawn. 'Oh god, there's Jack and I haven't got tea on,' Martha says, and rushes out to the kitchen.

Six

In Heidelberg nobody cared what you looked like. Everybody had too many kids in Heidelberg. Everybody was broke. And no one whispered behind your back. If they had something to say they'd say it to your face. Martha wonders if everything went downhill when they came to live in Brighton.

Jack and Martha started out in an old ramshackle house in Heidelberg. Agnes had arranged it for them. The house belonged to a distant cousin and he was happy for Martha to live in it until he got back from overseas. And Jack too, of course. Jill and Johnnie loved the house in Heidelberg. It had a big backyard and a shed with a pole to slide down. And they went to a school with a pool.

But Martha's cousin had come home and they had to find somewhere to go, and there was no money. Jack had lots of jobs with long spaces in between. The jobs came via a mate who knew someone who knew someone else who needed his books done. Jack would be good for a while then not turn up or finish the task. Often he'd go to work drunk. Occasionally he'd score a big job at a pub and work long and hard and after work he'd share his dreams with the barman. Money was always short. Jack borrowed as much as he could from everyone he knew. He ran out of people to ask.

'Ask your Aunt Agnes,' he'd tell Martha.

'I can't.'

'Ask her,' demanded Jack.

'We didn't pay her back the last time,' Martha said.

'Try her one more time.'

Martha rang Agnes. She shut her eyes to close in her shame.

'There will be no more loans,' said Agnes.

Jack sat in the dining room. The kids were finally in bed. Martha bit her nails. Jack stubbed his cigarette out in an ashtray overflowing with butts.

'What else can we do?' Jack said.

'No!' said Martha.

'What choice have we got?'

'You could get a full-time job . . .'

'Don't start,' said Jack.

'You go. I'm not. I'll find some place somewhere else.' Martha was firm.

'You and Martha and all those kids!' Amelia squawked. Amelia and Jack's Uncle Bob were living in a house in Brighton. The house was divided into two and there had been a couple who lived in the other half. Amelia got rid of them. 'She had Mondays to do her washing,' Amelia exclaimed. 'She washed every bloody day.'

Martha and Jack arrived to two warnings. 'Monday and only Monday is washing day,' Amelia told Martha, who tried to smile but it got stuck. 'And you have to pay rent don't forget,' she growled at Jack.

From the moment they moved in Amelia would watch Martha work in the main kitchen. Jack had offered her services to do the cooking. 'She won't ask us for as much rent,' Jack had said to convince Martha.

'Don't take off all the fat!' Amelia would snap when Martha trimmed the four quartered chops. 'Too much salt,' she'd say giving the wooden spoon a judicial lick and quickly dipping it back into Martha's pea-and-ham soup. 'What on earth is that sad-looking thing?' Amelia sneered at Martha's collapsed cake.

'I'm under her evil eye,' Martha whispered to Jack in bed at night.

'She's all right.' He'd turn over and show her his back.

Amelia engineered it that she and Martha would work side by side.

'Then I can help Martha out,' she told Jack.

They cleaned, laundered and kept house. Amelia sniped at Martha every chance she got. 'Oh my god,' she'd say, 'who brought you up?'

'Not like that, not like that,' she'd snap at Martha's way of folding a sheet.

'Oh, for god's sake!' Amelia shoved Martha aside and finished ironing Jack's shirt.

In bed Martha whispered to Jack's back, 'She pulled up the mint I planted and put it in a tin.'

'Because it'll take over,' said Jack.

Martha turned her back to his.

Bob was a big silent man. He got home from the Port Melbourne gasometers at four each afternoon. He had his Gladstone bag in one hand and the other gripped the neck of a flagon of port. He and Amelia would settle in, pouring glassful after glassful of the thick red drop down their throats. 'It's what you're thinking that I don't like,' Amelia said to Bob in a slur. Bob would put down his glass and give an exaggerated sigh. She'd set in on him. 'It's disgusting what you think. You're filthy, you are. Dirty, shameless, a disgrace.'

Jack and Martha sat in the backyard leaning against the fence listening to Amelia making accusations against Bob.

'I can read your mind, you filthy old bugger,' they heard Amelia shout.

'How does she know what he's thinking?' Martha asked.

'Who knows.'

'I know what you want. You make me sick,' yelled Amelia.

'It's shocking the way she talks to him,' said Martha.

Jack snapped. 'Stop bitching about her, would you?'

Martha kept her mouth shut. She did her work, she ignored Amelia's insinuations, her insults, she didn't rise to Amelia's snipes. Not until three shillings went missing.

'Johnnie's a rotten little thief,' Amelia accused. She smacked Johnnie's legs. 'Confess or I'll take a bullwhip to you.'

Martha exploded. She grabbed Johnnie from Amelia's clutches. 'I'll take the bullwhip to you first, you nasty old bitch!' They stared at one another a full minute then Amelia left the room.

'But Mum,' Johnnie whispered, 'I did take it. It's in my shoe.'

'I know, but don't tell anyone,' said Martha. She held out her hand and Johnnie fished the coins out of his sock.

Amelia erupted again and again, always over something the children had done. The twins cut out the flowers in her bathroom curtains and she chased them from the room with the straw broom. She pulled Johnnie's hair because he forgot to say please. She pinched Jill because she didn't like the expression on her face. She called Christine a dirty brat and took to her with a scourer because she had cake crumbs on her face.

'Amelia never liked kids,' said Martha to Jill when Amelia erupted over someone leaving the lid off a tin.

'What about Dad?' Jill asked her.

'Now she likes him, but not then. Not really,' said Martha.

Amelia fawned over Jack. As soon as he opened the door she offered him a beer. 'Would you like something to eat, Jack?' she would ask.

'That'd be good, Aunt,' Jack always said.

'Hurry up and get Jack his tea,' Amelia yelled at Martha.

By the time Jack came home Amelia was half-whacked. She was all droopy and syrupy and she'd pat him on the bum. She stroked his face and flicked back his hair. 'Oh my beautiful boy, my gorgeous young man,' she said.

After Jack had got back from the war he'd entered his aunt's kitchen and Amelia screamed. She'd thought he was dead. But there he was, her Jack walking through the door. Jack picked her up off the floor and held her in his arms. 'It's been so hard. It's been impossible to make ends meet. So unbelievably hard,' she wept. Jack abruptly put her down on her feet.

Amelia did not like children and in particular she hated May. She watched Jack wrap his arms around her and give her a cuddle. 'You're not his favourite, you know,' she whispered to May when Jack was out of hearing. 'He told me that.'

Wherever May was Amelia wasn't far behind, her eyes narrowed and her mouth pulled tight. 'You are so spoilt,' she'd say. She intervened when May asked for something to eat: 'You won't get everything you want just because you ask for it, you know.'

May never acknowledged Amelia. 'You're an uppity little thing,' snarled Amelia. 'Look at those horrible curls.' And, 'Don't give me that, that's not real,' she'd say when May's face brightened with a smile. 'Put your legs together, you're showing your pants,' she growled whenever she got the chance.

Martha was furious when Amelia attacked May. 'You're the loveliest thing to look at, May,' Martha would tell her, to compensate.

One day Martha decided to cut the twins' tremendous mops of hair. 'Together,' they insisted. She sat them up on stools and cut Mouse's fringe, then she cut Door's fringe. She cut one side on Mouse and then the same side on Door. Finally she went over both heads with the clippers.

May was sitting up at the kitchen table drawing on a brown paper bag. Martha blew the specks of hair off the twins' necks and smiled at May. Then her smile faded.

'May, what have you done to your hair?' May's beautiful curls were gone. Martha heard a snort behind her and saw Amelia doubled over, convulsed in laughter. 'It was in her eyes,' laughed Amelia. 'She couldn't see. Thought I'd help her out.'

Martha moved swiftly across the room. She took the scissors from Amelia's hand and snipped three times into her bun. When Jack came home everyone was wailing. Once May had seen what Amelia had done, she hadn't stopped crying. Amelia was in her bedroom, long strands of grey hair in her hand, screaming like she'd been stung. Martha leaned against the back fence; her arms were crossed and her chin was sticking up. She watched Jack walk across the lawn towards her and drew the scissors from her apron. 'Do you want me to cut yours for you too?' she said.

Not long afterwards Agnes loaned Martha the money for a down-payment on a house. 'Now you can get away from that dreadful woman,' she said.

Martha and Jack had been married for fifteen years. Now at last they had their own home. They bought a house, two streets away from Amelia and Bob. 'We don't want to hurt her feelings,' said Jack.

'I'm going to plant azaleas and rhododendrons and lavender and gladioli bulbs and edge with lobelia. I'm going to pull out the mirror bush and put in a lasiandra,' said Martha, standing in front of their new house. She saw the disappointed faces of her children.

'It's a bit rundown, that's all,' she said.

'It's got no front fence,' said May.

'That's nothing,' said Martha, 'Jack will build one.'

'It needs a paint,' said Johnnie.

'You and Jack, you'll give it a lick in no time.'

'The carpet's worn thin,' said Jill.

'Oh, we'll replace it, it's first on the list.'

Martha's excitement could not be doused. She was away from Amelia. In her very own house. She thought it resembled paradise. Jack dug in a vegetable garden and fastidiously edged it in brick. He did battle with the long and treacherous tendrils of couch grass. He showed Martha mounds of the stuff. 'I think I've won,' he said. He dug a hole for the compost. He pruned the apricot tree. He fixed a hole in the back fence – and then ran out of steam.

He never got to the front fence or the paint pot. The carpet remained on top of the list. Martha stuck in an occasional cutting but most of the time the garden remained untouched. 'I'll do it. I said I'll do it, didn't I?' said Jack when Martha nagged him about the light switch in their bedroom after it gave her a fierce shock.

Their house stands out in the house-proud street of Brighton. On weekends the roadway is lost in a mist of motor-mower fumes.

Edges are cut, hedges shaped, boughs lopped, creepers trimmed and tied back. There is nothing out of order, no weeds in the lawn, paths are swept clean. There is no peeling paint, no rusted gutters, no dripping taps, no windows propped up because of a broken sash. Nobody parks their car up on the front lawn. Our house would look no different from any other if it was in Heidelberg, thinks Martha.

The Wheatleys' grass is always long. The motor mower died the day Jack bought it. The edges trail untidily over the path. The lawn is stained in oil where Jack parks his car on it. The hedge has grown back into a tree. Their nature-strip is full of dog shit. It accumulates in mounds and Jack refuses to remove it.

'Don't you clean it up,' he says to Martha.

'But it looks so awful, Jack,' she says.

'They can stick their noses up,' he says, 'but it's their dog shit, never forget that. We don't even own a bloody dog.' He stands at the lounge-room window and looks out onto the street.

'Look, here she comes, the old bitch,' Jack hisses. He watches Mrs Knox leave her manicured lawn. She crosses the road with her dog. She stops and waits while her dog shits on the Wheatleys' nature-strip.

'If one of the bastards tells me one more time that the house could do with a paint I'll scream,' says Jack.

Now the house will never get painted, thinks Martha.

'I reckon they'll be bringing around a petition next,' he says. 'With all their names on it, asking us to piss off.'

When Mrs Knox puts out her rubbish Jack takes out the bin in his underpants. 'She's so bloody up herself,' says Jack. 'It does her good.' He makes a great display of putting out the bag full of empty bottles for the bottle-o. He thumps the bag down so that the clink of glass sounds out. 'Let them all know. I don't give a stuff,' says Jack.

Mr and Mrs Goldstein live next door. On their first meeting Mr Goldstein hangs over the back fence and asks Jack to keep the children quiet.

'My wife is trying to sleep,' he says.

'It's the middle of the day! What are the kids meant to do? Go around with cotton wool in their gobs?' Jack snaps. 'Bloody Jew,' he mutters under his breath. What right has Goldstein got to ask me anything, he thinks. Then he notices the tattooed numbers on Mr Goldstein's arm.

'I could have cut my bloody tongue out,' he later whispers to Martha. 'After all they've been through and here I am not giving him the time of day.'

The children rarely see the Goldsteins. They're afraid of them with their thick accents and their dark pained eyes. Jack smacks the children when they go near the Goldsteins' fence.

'Stop making so much bloody noise,' he whispers.

One night Jack comes home late and his headlights pick up Mrs Goldstein in the street. She's cowering up against a fence. He parks the car and calls gently. 'It's Jack,' he says. 'Mrs Goldstein, it's just Jack from next door. Will you let me take you home? Will you let me do that?' He moves slowly toward her and she whimpers like a small child. 'Come on. I've got you now,' he whispers and he guides her in the direction of her gate.

The whisperings come and go as Mrs Goldstein disappears for months at a time.

'An ambulance took her to the loony bin,' says Johnnie and collects a slap across his ear from Jack.

One Christmas Mrs Goldstein sends in a present for Martha. It is a box of chocolates with liqueur centres. Martha doesn't go much for dark chocolate but she's tickled pink.

'And they don't even believe in Christmas,' says Martha.

'Don't they?' the children call in unison. They marvel at why anyone would give a present if they wouldn't get one back.

On a Sunday afternoon the whisperings are thick and fast and have poured out on to the street. A police car and an ambulance are parked out the front of the Goldsteins' house. Neighbours mill about in small groups. Martha bites her lip, but not because she wants to cry. She doesn't quite know how she feels. She's never experienced this sort of thing before. She feels strangely responsible but doesn't know what she could have done to help. Jack weeps. His children are astounded. 'Why couldn't you hold on?' Christine hears Jack cry.

'Is Mrs Goldstein off to the funny farm again?' Johnnie asks.

'Get inside,' growls Jack and gives his ear another clip.

'Mrs Goldstein put her head in the oven during the night,' whispers Martha.

The street is full of whisperings. Neighbours hold their hands over their mouths when Martha walks past. They stop and stare and put their heads together when Jack pulls up and staggers out of his car. They whisper fast hard words when Jill turns on them: 'What the hell do you think you're looking at?'

Christine hears snatches of their whispering from her hiding place in the jacaranda tree.

'I've seen him in his underpants!' says Mrs Knox.

'And what about her? Have you seen her shoes?' says Mrs Jones.

'He's never home,' says Mrs Knox.

'Does he work?' asks Mrs Jones. 'And do you hear him shout?'

'And those children,' says Mrs Knox.

'Poor things,' says Mrs Jones. 'Got to feel sorry for them.'

'Unruly, horrid brats,' says Mrs Knox.

Mrs Knox bakes cakes and stores biscuits in tins. She has a doll with a huge lacy layered skirt sitting in the middle of her bed. She has a son who plays football for a league team. He sometimes gives Johnnie a lift in his car and when he shifts into top gear he runs his fingers along Johnnie's thigh.

The Joneses have a son in his last year at an exclusive private school. He wears a blazer and a straw hat. 'He looks a right prat,' says Johnnie. His parents drive a Mercedes-Benz. 'They're loaded,' says Jack. When it rains the son strips off his clothes and stands naked on a pillar of his front fence. Laughing, Martha, Jill and May squeeze under the umbrella and go take a look. 'You're not old enough,' Martha tells a pouting Christine.

Martha hears the whisperings, they're loud enough to rustle the leaves, she thinks. She sees the twisted mouths, the cupped hands, the sharp hungry eyes. She smiles sweetly when she collects the post, she waves when she takes the spade and scrapes the horse shit off the road. Her perm is holding on to the very tips of her hair but she doesn't care. 'I don't give a damn what you say, what you think, what you know,' she says quietly as she bends down and picks up the rubbish-bin lid. 'I know enough about you to sink a ship.'

Seven

Every year Agnes sends Martha a parcel. It's big and bulky and there is always something inside for each child. The children sit in a circle around Martha and wait for her as she slowly unwraps it. She takes an age to untie the knots in the string.

'You could just pull the string off, Mum,' Johnnie suggests.

'I know that, Johnnie, thank you very much,' says Martha and continues to pick at a tiresome knot.

As she takes off each layer of paper she smooths every sheet and slowly folds it. Jack sits back in his armchair pretending to read the newspaper.

'Quick Mum,' whispers Door.

'Quick Mum,' whispers Mouse.

'What's the hurry?' Martha laughs.

'Do you think there's something for me?' Christine asks, shrill with excitement, clasping at some imaginary treasure in the air.

'Sure to be,' says Martha.

The last layer of paper is smoothed and folded flat. The contents sit in enticing shapes in tissue paper. Martha rips the tissue around something soft and flat and pulls out a large dusk-blue scarf that is see-through and has minute black beads sewn around its edge. 'This is for you, Jill,' she says. Jill takes it and wraps it dramatically around her head.

Martha tears the next bundle and hands Johnnie a tool. 'I don't know what you're meant to do with it,' she says.

'I do,' says Johnnie and he runs off straight away to use it in the shed.

'He doesn't know how to use a tool like that,' mutters Jack and shifts uncomfortably as if a spring in his chair is attacking him.

'It's obvious who these are for,' says Martha.

'Us,' say Door and Mouse. She hands the twins two red and yellow metal trucks.

'Oh, look at this,' gushes Martha. She hands a brush, comb and mirror set to May. May runs her finger over the ornate silver handles, which are delicately inlaid with mysterious mother-of-pearl. 'Perfect,' she whispers.

'You'll never get her head out of that mirror,' says Jack, not lifting his own head from his newspaper.

'Where's mine?' Christine is almost in tears.

'Here,' says Martha. She gives Christine a little découpage box. Fat naked cherubs holding ribbons fly about on its lid. Inside the box, coloured glass beads, cut like gems, glitter up at her ecstatic face.

'And the rest must be for me,' says Martha. There are a dozen other things. Some that have meaning from the past. Some are brand new. She pulls out glass jars for this and that, a fine knitted cardigan in teal green, a colour her children have never seen. She unfolds a delicately embroidered damask tablecloth.

'What are you going to do with that?' asks Jack, full of scorn.

'What about Dad?' Christine suddenly remembers him. 'Isn't there something for him?'

'No, there doesn't appear to be,' says Martha, terribly matter-of-fact.

Jack pouts and petulantly tosses his paper aside. 'What would I want from that old bat?' he says.

*

Martha turns the corner of the street. Her feet ache. The circulation in her fingers is cut off by the weight of her shopping. She carries bottles of milk, butter, white sugar, jam, Vegemite and a double square loaf of white bread. It's our staple diet, she thinks. It's all I ever buy when I go to the shops. Food disappears at an extraordinary rate in the Wheatley household. Milk and bread are delivered but always run out. Martha believes that somehow she economises by never getting enough in the first place.

Thank god I went to the shops alone this time, thinks Martha. When the children are with her the trip is a nightmare of endless chants and games of 'I spy'. Johnnie constantly wants to talk, to tell another story about how his friend Paulie came close to losing his life. Christine leans into her, wanting her body to fit right in warm against her mother's, and Martha has to stop and prise her out. 'Christine! You're pushing me over, Christine!' May nags at her the entire way: 'But why can't you buy that dress for me?' Jill is always surly: 'Why did I get nine and a half for the test when there was nothing wrong so I should have got ten?' The twins dawdle way back, holding hands and chatting away, no time much for anyone else. 'What did Dad tell you about you holding hands all the time?' yells Johnnie. 'Leave them, Johnnie, they're not doing any harm,' Martha always says.

Today her trip is peaceful. Patterns from the leaves of silver birches play across her face. She is assaulted by the vulgar, overblown camellias, crimson blooms composting at their feet. The wattles are a dazzling yellow, the daphne pungent. The sun on her back feels beautifully warm. She sits on a low brick fence and gives her aching fingers and feet a rest.

A lemon-scented pelargonium flowers beside her. When she was a child she and her mother visited her Aunt Agnes in Ballarat. They always returned with a cutting of some kind. Often they were pelargoniums. 'Leave them in the tin until it has almost rusted through,' Agnes would say. 'It makes the colour richer.'

She gave them cannas, chrysanthemums, carnations and dahlia tubers knotted in a handkerchief. Martha's mother Ada loved carnations. 'Look at that,' she'd say to Martha. 'Who could imagine such a beautiful flower could come from a plant looking like that?' They'd gaze at the straggly grey stalks pulled together and tied to a stake. When Martha's father died Ada had bound carnations together to make a simple wreath for his coffin. Martha was seven and thought that the flowers were beautiful as she watched them disappear under the dirt shovelled into the grave.

Fuchsia bells dangle shadows across Martha's hands and she rubs her skin as if to brush the shadows off. Look at my hands, she thinks. They're the hands of an old woman. Her knuckles are large and misshapen. Each finger points in a different direction. Her mother would be shocked. Ada had taught piano and her students played their pieces beautifully for their proud mothers and fathers. Martha's clumsy fingers fumbled along the keys, causing her mother to blush ever so slightly. 'We will persevere'; her lips thinned as she whispered in Martha's ear. These days there was no way Martha's fingers would stretch an octave.

When Martha was young she wondered if she would always be a disappointment to her mother and aunt. Theirs had once been a family who had made their fortune in gold in Ballarat. Ada and Agnes's father had spent it as easily as he had made it. He left his two daughters with the look of money only: an uppity tilt to the chin, a sophisticated way of putting up hair, a brooch on a ribbon, always a nice touch to the throat. Martha was never quite sure what colours went together, whether the feel of cloth was fine or coarse. Her hair fell from the tightest clasp, her skirt creased when she sat. Her mother and aunt were educated women and held high hopes for Martha. But Martha found it difficult to concentrate on her studies. She was vague, easily distracted. For a while she applied herself wholeheartedly to tiny pen-and-ink drawings of eagles. They were not good enough to show, she thought. They were copied and there was no real talent in that.

Ada had been sickly and often spent weeks in bed. Agnes would come to stay and all flowers were removed from the house. A student would come to the front door with a gift of roses for the ailing teacher. Agnes would march the bunch through the house and out the back door and deliver them to the bin. The fragrance caused Ada to cough, so Agnes believed, and once she started she found it hard to stop.

Martha remembers Ada lying behind a screen on a makeshift bed in front of a blazing fire. The shadows frightened Martha. Agnes hurried past with a green enamel basin filled with blood. She listened to the *hack-hack-hacking* cough coming from behind the screen. She did not approach her mother. She found it difficult not to retch. She feared Ada might see her disgust and this caused her great shame.

When finally Ada coughed her last cough Martha was twenty-one. When you looked at Martha's face this was hard to believe. Not only did she look young but she appeared disconnected. She focused inches in front of her as if she were concentrating on the fine lines of her drawings and not on the world about her. Conversations would happen around Martha. She rarely participated in them. She would faze out, like a child waiting for the adults to stop talking.

Nearly home, thinks Martha now as she crosses the street. That blasted dog barks every time but still she jumps out of her skin. She can see the nature-strip outside their house, unmown, a handful of assorted weeds growing angrily among the mounds of dog shit.

Until Martha married Jack, Agnes had always visited Martha in Melbourne once a month. Most weekends Martha had caught the train to Ballarat. They liked each other's company. They enjoyed the simplicity of their conversations. There was the war to talk about, the rations, who'd been called up, who was shirking their responsibility, who'd got shot, what the newspapers said. Martha always read the papers from cover to cover on her trip up.

Outside the house Martha stands still, her baskets on the path at her side. She takes one last rest before she lugs them in. She thinks of a hot cup of tea and longs to put her feet up. She looks at the enormous jacaranda tree. The tea tree and hibiscus are woody and leggy. Should have been cut back seasons ago, thinks Martha. The mirror plant takes over one side of the house with its thick glossy foliage. Martha had planned to take that mirror plant out and grow something pretty in its place, a lasiandra with its velvety purple petals perhaps. At least there's something green, thinks Martha.

From the lounge-room window the children peer out at Martha. Their faces are stricken with guilt.

'Quick,' says Jill. 'Mum's home.'

They look at this year's parcel from Agnes. It arrived while Martha was at the shops. It was large and lumpy, having been wrapped in layers of thick brown paper and trussed in miles of coarse string, knotted and knotted again in a dozen places.

MARTHA WHEATLEY (NÉE MCDONALD) was written in capital letters on it. The six of them had sat and stared at the parcel, willing the string to undo and reveal its prizes.

'She's taking such a long time,' said Johnnie.

Christine said, 'We could just take a peek.'

'Don't,' ordered Jill.

'There's a small hole,' Mouse noticed.

Door agreed. 'There is.'

'Don't touch it,' Jill said.

'We could wrap it up again,' said May.

'Wait,' Jill commanded. 'Mum will be home soon.'

'She'd mind, wouldn't she?' Door said.

'She would,' agreed Mouse.

'She would.' Jill was emphatic.

They had all agreed.

They had tried to ignore it. It was a big parcel with mysterious bumps and points. There were soft bits and hard bits and it was gorgeously heavy. They did their best to keep away from it. They left the room but, unable to stay away, they eventually came back in and surrounded the parcel. They edged toward it.

'Maybe she won't mind,' said Jill.

It was the cue they were waiting for. They jiggled the string over the bundle and tore the paper and snatched at what was inside. Door grabbed a wooden box with mermaids carved into its lid. Out fell six black elephants, each smaller than the next, all linked trunk to tail. Johnnie pounced and one elephant's trunk was snapped off. May snaffled a shawl so soft she shuddered at the touch of it. 'I think it's silk,' she breathed, enraptured by the elegance of its design. Brilliant yellow irises streaked across a purple background.

Each treasure was grabbed at and pawed over. 'Who's this for?' asked Johnnie. He picked up a leather writing case. The children were silent, unable to work out who should get what. That was Martha's job and Martha wasn't there. They felt heavy and unhappy and ashamed.

Martha rubs her sore hands, they still sting from the weight of her baskets. She vows to do something about that mirror plant. A snowball bush would look lovely there beside the house, she thinks. If she cut back the tea tree and hibiscus now they would be leafy and full of bud for the spring. Tomorrow, she thinks. Tomorrow I'll be out here and watch out, nobody will recognise the place.

Martha fills the kettle, lights the gas and empties the teapot. She begins to unpack the baskets but suddenly stops. There's something wrong and she is instantly afraid. It is quiet.

She opens the lounge-room door and picks up on the atmosphere at once. She thinks that someone's hurt or bad news has been brought. On the floor she sees the parcel, or what remains of it, the brown paper ripped and strewn around.

'Was that parcel addressed to me?' Her voice is dreadful, each word is frail and about to break.

'Yes,' her children say.

'And who unwrapped it?'

'We all did.'

Martha leaves the room.

The children listen to the terrible silence in the kitchen. They sit, their heads way down. May bites her fingertips, the twins snivel a bit. Christine sticks out her bottom lip, Johnnie looks afraid and Jill's face is screwed up in pain.

They hear the back door open. Jack is home. Their stomachs collectively swoop. Martha's voice is soft and flat in the silence. The children wait in dreadful anticipation. His footsteps resound as he walks towards the lounge-room door. His face is thunderous and he stands and looks at them for a while. His stare moves from face to face.

'You rotten little shits. Grasping, greedy little shits. That was your mother's parcel, as if you didn't know it.'

He stops for a moment and his children look up suddenly, wanting, desperate for a beating.

'Look at you. Pleased as punch. Got your booty? Got everything you want? Happy now?' He steps closer with each question and threatens to relieve them of their shame.

'Go to your rooms,' he hisses.

They are surprised. They had expected greater punishment than this. Without a word they disappear into their bedrooms.

Jack is unable to find the level of bile that spills over in a moment at other times. He smiles. He is pleased with their crime.

Eight

Christine spends her childhood missing, hidden in special places, or inside her head.

She curls up her legs and buries herself snugly in dozens of threadbare towels. She concentrates on not moving, on barely breathing, on listening. She is in training. Her senses are honed to detect the slightest noise, the gentlest vibration. Is that a footstep in the hall? Is that someone leaning against a wall? Is that someone's breath that she feels so lightly lift the hair on the back of her neck?

She is Anne Frank and the Gestapo is searching the house. They are calling her name. As if she's going to fall for that! The towels smell of Velvet soap and tickle her nose. She must not sneeze. She manoeuvres the towels away from her mouth so that she can breathe. Her eyes close but she must not fall asleep. She's been having nightmares and if she calls out someone might hear her and she will endanger lives. There are many families hiding in the secret rooms and cupboards of the house.

Christine wakes in the dark and for minutes she lies still. Terrified, she has no recollection of where she is. She has no sense of which way is up or whether she is upside down. She thinks she's dead. Then she hears her name called over and over and the anxious voices finally locate her and she responds. She pushes the bathroom cupboard door open with her foot.

'I'm here,' she calls.

May finds her first. 'You're in for it,' she says.

The twins push each other aside to look at Christine. They throw her an identical reproachful look. Christine's head is all that's visible under the mounds of towels on the shelf.

'I was asleep,' Christine explains plaintively.

May sneers in disbelief. 'We've been calling you for hours. Mum's gone looking for you up the street. She's frantic. She's sent Jill and Johnnie down to the park.'

'Why didn't they take me?' whines Christine beginning to pout.

'They're looking for your dead body, you idiot!' May says as she walks away, the black curls trembling as she shakes her head.

Blood stains the sand. Blood bleeds through the water. Blood pours from the mutilated bodies that bob hideously beside her. She cannot sob, she cannot call out her anguish. She wants to stand up and scream at the murderers who span the beach, with their deadly rifles in their hands. Her lungs burn with the ache to breathe. She cannot lift herself out of the water. Not yet. She must let her body sway to the rhythm of the warm waves. She is Vivian Bullwinkel, the sole survivor of a group of military nurses gunned down in the waters of Indonesia. She raises her head and like Lazarus pulls herself up from the dead. The Japanese soldiers have moved on and left her alone with the torn and bloody bodies that were once her friends.

Christine lies spread-eagled, face down in the shallows at Dendy Street beach. Her head suddenly bursts out of the water, her fringe like a blindfold over her eyes. She gasps desperately for breath and down her head goes again. She stands to begin again. Her nose spread white with zinc. She faces the shore, her body suddenly shakes as if a demon dances within her and she drops into the water and floats.

'What's she doing?' a shivering Johnnie asks Martha as they watch Christine from under an umbrella on the beach. He peels down his wet shorts. Martha has to bring at least four pairs of shorts to the beach for Johnnie. When they're wet he can't stand them on his skin. A skimpy bath towel reveals his pink bum.

Martha looks at Christine. Her face pulls up out of the water and her eyes are scrunched and her mouth is pulled in agony. She lets out a groan of misery. She is striped bright pink and floral blue in her two-piece bathing suit. I must remember to dab those pink stripes with cold tea tonight, Martha thinks.

Christine rushes through the water searching in a frenzy for something precious. She suddenly drops to her knees and howls sadly at the sky. A man has stopped on the beach and looks about him in concern, uncertain whether to intervene and placate this demented child.

'Who knows?' Martha sighs.

A young girl makes a dash to a tree and throws her back against it. She waits. The sound of tanks rumbling past is deafening. Time is imperative. She must keep on the move. Her name is Marie-Louise and if she doesn't get a message through enemy lines, her village will be levelled. She makes a dash to the next tree. Its trunk is barely wide enough to give her cover. She rushes to an older and more substantial tree. She squats down and catches her breath. She leans out to watch the progress of the Nazi platoon escorting the tanks. She snarls, she despises these animals who have murdered her father. Streams of bullets imbed themselves in the tree trunk. She's been seen. She runs to the next tree then to the next. Bullets ping past her. If only she can make it to where the forest is thicker. She must. All depends on her.

She sees May up ahead ambling along, her school bag casually swung across her shoulder. What's she doing? The fool! Doesn't she realise the danger? Only she, Marie-Louise, can save the girl.

'May! May, get down! Zee soldiers, zay ave guns,' Marie-Louise calls.

'Christine, that's the most ridiculous French accent I've ever heard,' says May.

'Run I beg you. Zay vill kill you.'
May rolls her eyes and runs away from Christine.

The jacaranda tree is at the front of the house, which is up on a hill. An excellent spot. Anyone coming in has to pass beneath the tree. Suspicious activity can easily be sighted. Details of numbers, weaponry, comings and goings of troops can be reported without fear of detection. A lean muscular girl who looks a lot like a boy sits motionless high up in the branches. The jacaranda's delicate fronds form a dapple across her face, the perfect camouflage. She shimmies along one of the larger limbs and waits. A line of ants continues its passage across her hand but she does not move. The slightest motion may bring discovery and possible death, or worse, torture, unbearable torture, slowly, cruelly inflicted to make her talk. She has endured days of grinding interrogation, tied to a chair, starved of food and water. She has endured the most horrendous violations, unspeakable acts. But she doesn't talk. She will not give up her brothers and sisters. She is Mademoiselle X! The information she has could devastate the entire partisan movement. She scarcely breathes as a patrol of Nazis pass beneath her.

Jack parks his FJ Holden on the front lawn at the top of the hill. Martha and the children can always tell how drunk he is before he comes into the house. If he's very drunk the wheels spin on the grass and he revs the engine so loud it seems it's about to bust. He has been known to come too far up the hill and give the house itself a nudge.

Christine watches him get out of the car, his Brylcreemed head beneath her. She thinks for a moment of dropping her spit. Jack spreads his legs and unzips his flies. He pisses for an age. The constant stream steaming up in front of him astounds Christine.

'*Rat-a-tat-tat*,' Mademoiselle X points her machine-gun at his back.

In dreams, salt stings Christine's mouth. She swims up towards the surface. Her lungs scream for breath. Flames burn black above her.

She bursts through and gulps at air. Disconnected voices and discordant sounds surround her. She churns the water desperately, searching for something solid to grasp. She must rest, clear her stinging eyes and mouth of salt and oil. Two identical figures black with sludge float past her. They hug each other and sink beneath the waves. A raft miraculously appears, bobbing ridiculously only an arm's length away.

'Take my hand,' a voice calls to her.

She grabs at the hand but it is covered in oil and she slips from its grip. She grabs again and slips. And again, and she slides down in the water. Like a stone she drops deep below the surface. Someone swims up under her and takes her in their arms and together they break through the water.

'God no, let me go, you'll drown me,' she splutters and writhes madly to escape them. But the arms hold her tightly and she is propelled along and onto the raft. She is saved. When she turns her saviour has disappeared beneath the waves.

The raft drifts and shamefully she blocks her ears to the pleas for help from out of the sea's darkness. It is some time before she realises she is sharing her raft with a black-oiled man, the white of his eyes shining ludicrously against his skin.

'Hold on,' he says. 'Hold on. You'll make it if you can just hold on.'

Christine wakes and thinks she's safe, she's wet through but she's home. She has pissed her bed.

There is no peace for Christine. Everywhere is a war zone. Any moment there is the possibility of an attack. On the way to the shop, walking home from a friend's house, the rustling of a shrub reveals an ambush in waiting. There is nowhere she can relax. Her own home is not safe. She checks behind the door when she enters a room, there is an assassin lying in wait for her under her bed. When she comes home she expects her mother to be dead. Martha is constantly rearranging the lounge-room furniture that Christine has pushed back hard against the walls. In sleep she is exhausted. Her perpetual swimming, the desperate seeking to find something to hold on to, overwhelm her. There is nowhere safe.

The woodyard is her only haven. She goes there at dusk. It is in the far corner of the backyard. A shed covered in Morning Glory with its blue trumpet-like flowers and an overgrown privet hedge hide it from view. The boys go to the woodyard. They whine about whose turn it is to cut kindling and chop wood. Johnnie also goes there to smoke cigarettes he steals from Jack.

It is in the woodyard that Christine's reveries take on a strange and peculiarly violent shape. She doesn't understand them but she isn't afraid. Far from it. In the woodyard with its smells of fresh split wood and black rotting wood-dust she stands absolutely still and is exultant. She waits for her body to change itself. At first it's a warm feeling, which trickles thick and pleasurable like hot wax, and it begins in her chest, which gradually expands, and changes shape, it barrels out. The pressure on her skin is so intense she feels she is about to cleave down the centre like an over-ripe peach. It is deliciously painful. She closes her eyes and breathes deep. Her body opens gradually and with each tremendous contraction Christine is swallowed up. Her skin peels back and reveals him. His coat is fine and sleek. He twitches and sheds her from him. His head is held high and stretched forward as if straining at the bit. There is no harness to withhold him. This magnificent stallion is highly strung, temperamental, and the containment to the woodyard maddens him. He needs to run, to gallop, to travel across great empty spaces. He yearns to stretch, to work his powerful flanks, to race great distances. He would take on the world, given half the chance. She lets him out a little at a time, reeling him back in when it looks as if he might bolt. 'Whoa,' she whispers. 'Whoa.' She's sorry she can't let him go. It's cruel, she thinks, a dumb animal needs to be let run.

Christine is standing still in the woodyard at dusk and everything is grainy and faded in dusk's gorgeous light. She relishes the peace, the smells, the orgasmic aftermath of the visit from her steed. Her small body aches from the weight of him, the power he exerts has drained her. She is a girl again and is limp and frail, with no authority.

Johnnie enters and for a split second Christine believes he is the enemy. He's come to spy on me, she thinks. Johnnie doesn't see her. He thrusts his head into the hedge and his headless body heaves. He's sick, thinks Christine. She is about to run for Jill when he begins to sob loud and dreadful sobs. He's having me on, he's pulling my leg. He must know I'm here. Any moment she expects him to turn around and grab her, lift her up and dance her round.

Johnnie turns. He sits on the chopping block and cries like a baby, his nose streams snot.

Christine is shocked. Please Johnnie, not you, not you crying, not my brother Johnnie crying like a little kid. She moves across the woodyard and touches him lightly on the back. He's hot and steamy and the tears have soaked him through. She retreats a step.

'Johnnie?' Christine whispers.

His face darts around and seeks Christine out in the semi-darkness. Desolate, he thrusts his head down between his legs. She doesn't recognise him. It is not right, a big brother blubbering like this. Be brave, she thinks. Be bold. She wishes she could share her stallion with Johnnie to give him strength.

'Stop it, Johnnie,' she snaps then. 'Stop crying, you big sook.' Christine crosses her arms and stamps at the ground with her foot.

'Stop it, Johnnie!' she yells this time.

Johnnie staggers up and past her and is gone.

'Good,' says Christine. 'Good.'

Nine

Tom Thumbs crack and snap and leap about. Threepenny bungers explode mid-air and the twins cover their ears. A Catherine wheel whizzes on a nail on the fence. It sprays blue then pink then red. A Roman candle shoots coloured sparks and goes bang just when it seems it is dead. A skyrocket launched from an empty milk bottle shoots into the night. Gold dust falls and then disappears. There are shrieks and squeals and ahs and ohs and calls of, 'Watch out! Watch out!'

'Get down, get down,' Christine mutters quietly in an American accent. She's in combat. A flare explodes overhead, exposing her and her men. Don't move a muscle, she thinks. The slightest movement makes you a target and then you're dead.

Johnnie is dancing a wild dance, his knees lift high and he holds a bunger and it's lit.

'Throw it,' screams Jill.

'Throw it,' screams Martha.

'Throw the bloody thing,' screams Jack.

Johnnie laughs like a maniac. He lifts the bunger to his face, then with a flick of the wrist he throws it up and it goes off. He lights another one and chases May around the apricot tree. May squeals and thrashes about, crazy like she's covered in fleas.

Christine slowly feels for her knife. This mad German is terrifying these innocent village folk and he's not going to get away with it. She inches her way closer to her prey.

Johnnie puts two bungers together and they go off loud in everyone's ears. He lights one and then the other and throws them up together. *Bang!* And *bang!*

'Go easy, Johnnie. What's your hurry?' growls Jack.

Johnnie lights and throws and lights and throws. One of them falls back into the box and the whole lot goes up.

Like a grenade, thinks Christine. The box lifts high into the air and moves suddenly to one side and then another. As if someone's in it, Christine thinks. It fizzes and farts and finally explodes, showering down thousands of sparks.

Door screams. His hands cover his face. Mouse joins his scream, staring all the while at Door who can't stop. Martha looks for the matches to light the candle. Jack aims a kick at Johnnie's retreating bum and scores. He pulls at Door's hands.

'Let me look, for Christ's sake, let me take a bloody look,' he says.

Door and Mouse continue to scream.

'Shut up, Mouse,' says Jack.

He lifts Door up in his arms and takes him inside the house.

Johnnie has scaled the back fence. The others follow Jack and crowd round Door who is sitting on a chair refusing to take his hands away from his face.

'Give us a look,' says Jack. 'Door! Give us a bloody look.' He pulls Door's hands down and they all peer in at Door's face. It's burnt in red and raw splotches down along his jaw.

'Well, I'll be,' says Jack. He looks at Mouse and back again at Door.

The pattern of burns mirrors the port-wine splash of Mouse's birthmark.

'Well, I'll be,' repeats Jack. 'Now we'll never tell you apart.'

*

A bunger going off behind you, no warning, that's Jack. Martha and the children creep around the house. The slightest thing might set him off.

'Turn that fucking thing off,' he says when he comes home and finds Martha listening to talkback radio. 'Turn off that music,' he yells at Jill. 'Get out of those pajamas right now,' he yells at the retreating heels of Door and Mouse. And when there's no one around to have a go at, he explodes because no one's home. 'I will not have my children wandering the streets any time of the day or night,' he shouts.

Johnnie makes himself scarce and is rarely home. His mates call out to him from the street and he escapes. The twins spend entire days away from home hanging on the railway-crossing gates in Hampton watching the trains go by. Christine is with her platoon lying in ambush, behind a shrub, up the jacaranda tree, in the long grass, waiting for the enemy. May's head is down, she's filling her sketchbooks. Or it's stuck in a Georgette Heyer novel and she is lifted onto every horse, pirated on every ship, whisked across the continent by each dark and handsome hero. In the margins she draws pictures of the gowns Heyer describes. 'I love Empire lines,' she sighs regretfully. When she's not helping Martha with the housework, Jill studies. She has her textbooks out at the breakfast table. She reads them on her way to and from school and way into the night.

When Jack catches Jill reading it's like a spark landing on dry grass. 'Get outside, get some fresh air, for god's sake,' he explodes. Late at night he peers in through the slit of her door. He turns the light off and leaves her complaining in the dark.

It's not that Jack doesn't read. He reads long into his restless nights. He reads Zane Grey, Alistair Maclean and Maurice Walsh. Walsh's book, *The Small Dark Man*, had done the rounds of the prisoner-of-war camp. Jack reckons he's read it a hundred times. He likes westerns and crime and the occasional adventure. He would love to share them with his eldest daughter if she was inclined. It's the textbooks that set him off. Jack picks up Jill's books and throws them in the bin. She gets them out and wipes them clean.

'You think you're so smart,' he goes off again. 'I don't know what use you think it is to you. You're not going to become anything. You're wasting your time, you know. Not much point in all this education when you're working behind a counter or in a factory.'

The threats don't perturb Jill. Jack is like tinder waiting to be lit but Jill thinks of Mr Oyston, a man much scarier than Jack, and she is unafraid. Mr Oyston likes her brain and that sustains her. Mr Oyston, a most formidable teacher with an accurate eye when it comes to the placement of the cane, told her she was smart and there were few women with brains like hers. 'Don't waste them,' he said. He visited her in the library at least one lunchtime a week and left her books on philosophy or geometry or mathematics. Once he left her a copy of *Gulliver's Travels.*

Jack had dreams of becoming many things – a lawyer, an architect or a doctor – but he left school as soon as he could. He felt obligated to pay his own way. Jack had been a clever boy but not where it counted. 'Can't hammer in a bloody nail,' Amelia and his uncle Bob would say.

Jill rushes through each page and constantly looks to see if Jack is creeping up behind her. She stops to listen for his car, she hears him outside her door. Her books regularly disappear and he won't tell her where he's hidden them. She's jumpy and jittery and it's like she's got shellshock. She becomes more and more frantic as she tries to cram it all in, until she looks at the page in front of her and nothing goes in. The numbers and the diagrams come to the surface and float off the edge. Perhaps Jack is right: Is there any point or should I give it in, she wonders. She chews the inside of her cheek and makes it sting. She gives herself a bash to the head. She gets up and goes out to the woodyard and sobs against the hedge.

Jill wonders how she will ever do her best. In her class there's a girl who is better than her. She tops Jill by half a per cent. Jill wishes Maria would get sick or go back to Italy, just not be the best. When Maria starts to cry in class there is nothing stopping her. She sits at her desk and the tears flood and she saturates her books. Jill is flabbergasted. Why is Maria crying, she wonders? She's the smartest in the class.

Various teachers and students try to placate Maria. When nothing helps they grow awkward and annoyed and leave her to cry. One morning she doesn't turn up. A month later she walks into the classroom, sits in her usual seat and smiles. That day they have a test. Jill knows it's not kind but she looks forward to getting a better result. Maria beats her by half a per cent.

After school that day Jill helps her mother prepare dinner. She hangs out the clothes on the washing line and cleans the ashes from the hearth in the lounge room. She weaves in and around Martha, waiting for a chance to speak to her. Martha puts her feet up for a minute and Jill's there. She tells Martha about Maria's return.

'Where's she been?'

'At home,' answers Jill.

'What's she been doing?'

'She's been in her mother's bed.'

'That's a bit odd, isn't it?' Martha's brow knits and she looks stern.

'Her dad got out so Maria could sleep with her mum,' Jill says. 'And she slept there for a month in her mum's arms until she stopped crying and felt better again.'

'Why are you telling me this?' asks Martha.

'I don't know,' answers Jill.

'Well, they do things like that and we don't.' Martha is irritated by the story.

When Jack looks at May he comes close to exploding. May is twelve and is changing shape. Jack can't bear it. It hurts. He feels furious when he sees the lovely roundness of her body.

May has been keen to grow up and things are happening at last. She pushes her foot against her bedroom door until she hears it click. Leaning into the mirror she examines her lips, lowers her lids and flutters her eyelashes. I'll have to practise, she thinks. Widening her smile she places the tip of her tongue between her teeth and laughs. She stares solemnly at the mirror and, colluding with her reflection, she gives herself a nod. She shimmies one of the straps off her shoulder. Her reflection smiles a secretive smile. The second strap is shimmied down. The singlet falls to her waist.

'Breasts,' May whispers. 'At last.'

She pulls up her singlet and stretches the fabric to make a strapless gown. It's a gown in light blue satin, edged in white lace. A diamond necklace nicely picks up the delicacy of the lace. She smiles across the table to a man she has just met. He offers her some wine and she answers him with the slightest nod of her head. There are candles in candelabra. A splash of colour from flowers in a crystal vase spray across the white damask cloth. The red of wine in long slender glasses shimmers in the light.

The door of her bedroom opens and a hand holding a wide, white sanitary pad appears through the crack. 'Here May, put this on. And don't forget, not a word to Christine,' says Martha.

Jack feels it is his duty to keep an eye on May. She is about to head off to school and he sees the lipstick she's plastered on her mouth. He grabs at her and smears it with his hand. He grabs her by the elbow when she walks past and hisses in her ear, 'Don't walk like that.' He has never driven his children to school. On miserable rainy days the children used to get Christine to ask him but he'd laugh and say, 'What's a little bit of water going to do to you?' All of a sudden he wants to drive them. May sometimes declines and walks. The others sit very quietly and he fumes and splutters like he's alight when he sees her. She deliberately sashays her bottom as they drive past.

In the week leading up to the visit from Doug Jameson, Jack is like a string of bungers set off. 'You'll never guess, that was bloody Dougie Jameson,' he tells Martha after hanging up the phone one Sunday afternoon. 'I haven't seen him since we got picked up.' He is both excited and nervous, awful states to be in for someone like Jack.

'He's coming to see me,' says Jack.

'He was the one on the raft with you,' Christine claps with delight.

'The very one,' says Jack, his mouth tight over a forced grin.

'You kids be out of the way so that Jack and Doug can talk,' Martha tells her children as she makes rock buns and pikelets with jam. She wants everything to be just right.

With the older children there's no argument. There is no desire to be anywhere near this reunion. 'I can tell you now,' says Jill, 'it will end in a fight.' She sees how Jack's body is delicately poised, as if any movement would cause him to detonate.

'Can't I stay? I won't say a word. I'll just sit there. Please?' asks Christine, desperate to be included.

'It's got nothing to do with you, Chrissie.' Martha is adamant.

Christine can't believe it. It has everything to do with me, she thinks. She crosses her arms and pouts. How dare they not include me when I've been there, on that raft with them, covered in oil, desperately holding on.

When Doug arrives Jack hurries to open the door. He and Doug stand there silently for a few minutes staring at one another. Finally they step forward and, for a second only, they embrace. Christine peers around her bedroom door. She catches sight of Jack and Doug in each other's arms. Satisfied, she spends the afternoon lying on her bed dreaming about her two heroes. Two men bonded for life, and in her house. She is exalted.

By that evening Jack has gone off like a rocket. He rants and raves as he paces up and down the worn floral carpet in the lounge room.

'I never liked that bloody Doug Jameson. He was always a lying snake, a bloody big-headed, over-rated shit. I should have pushed him off the raft when I had the chance. And I had plenty of chances because unlike bloody Doug-lying-Jameson's version of the truth it was me who kept my head. It was me who stopped Doug from wandering off.'

According to Doug, Jack had become delirious on the raft. 'He wanted to go down the street and get a cup of coffee,' said Doug. 'In the end I had to knock him out,' he laughed.

Martha is worn down by Jack's remonstrating each time she enters the room. 'I know what the truth is,' he says. 'There's only one truth and I know it. I don't think much of a man trying to change the truth on me. I know the truth. Don't you believe me?'

Martha opens her mouth to tell him that of course she believes him – but there's no need.

'He can have his opinion, he can stick his opinion up his bum, an opinion isn't what actually happened. You can't just change how things were because you have an opinion, can you? Well, can you?'

'No Jack,' says Martha.

Christine listens from the safety of her bedroom. She frowns at May who is lying on her bed giggling. 'I wish he had gone and got himself a cup of coffee,' May says.

Perhaps Jack had had a mouthful or two of salt water after all, Christine thinks. She is entirely sympathetic. She had tried to go without water for a day and hadn't lasted the morning. She thinks of Jack and Doug on the raft, staring at each other and wondering which of them would last.

'It must have been too painful to be in each other's presence,' she says.

When Christine and Jack talk about life in a prisoner-of-war camp, or about Jack bobbing about for days on a raft, about ticks and snakes, scorpions and rats, about men who made it, and men who didn't, then Jack is calm. It's as if the talk defuses him.

Jack asks Christine to go for drives in the car. He wants the company and none of his other children will go. Martha would go but she is never asked. Christine says yes but she is anxious. She is rarely totally alone with her father, and not in such a small and captive space as the car. It isn't the right atmosphere for talk of war and she knows no other way to calm him. She treats the outings as some kind of training for her, like going on bivouac. It's a test of her nerve, she's in close quarters with a bomb that's ticking and she can't fall apart. She is never sure where she and Jack are going as she sits in the front and listens to his commentary.

'Look at that huge arse squeezed into those bloody slacks, would you? My god!' says Jack.

'What have we got here?' Jack has pulled up at a red light and he and Christine watch the pedestrians cross. 'Fucking wops! Whose country is this?' Jack is sent into violent spits and splutters: 'Who . . . who . . . who do they think they are?'

He points at a woman in a sari. How beautiful, thinks Christine.

'If they're going to come here then they've got to fucking well fit in!' says Jack.

An older man and woman are ambling along the footpath holding hands. Christine sees them through the window. How sweet, she thinks.

'Jesus Christ!' says Jack. 'Have a bloody look at them. Nothing makes me more sick. How pathetic is that?'

They drive further afield and cross the river into Melbourne's inner city. Jack points out a solitary woman sitting on the path with her back against a wall. His face distorts into a sneer. 'Who'd live here?' he says. 'Bloody Abos everywhere you look.'

Christine stares at the woman, who seems to be relaxing in the sun. She looks around to see the other Aborigines Jack is talking about but there is no one.

It's the sixties and men wear beards and beads and Jack sees a young man with long hair. Quickly he unwinds his window, sticks his head out and wolf whistles. 'You fucking great girl!' he yells.

He pulls right up alongside another young man whose hair is on his collar, and mincingly says, 'Hello gorgeous.' Then he yells bullishly, 'Get a haircut, you poofta!'

Christine marvels at the lather Jack works up. He thumps the steering wheel, blasts his horn, curses, grunts and groans in a peculiar agony. The world is changing and change irritates Jack. He splutters and spits, his fuse is short. His children are growing up, going out, filling themselves with bullshit ideas, he thinks. Getting high opinions of themselves, thinking they're smarter than everybody else. Jack is about to crack and there's no keeping the world and its irritations out.

Ten

Johnnie falls asleep anywhere. He falls asleep with his head in his hands, he falls asleep in a second to the vibrations of a motor car, he falls asleep in the middle of conversations. 'Johnnie!' cry his exasperated brothers and sisters as they shake him awake. They've grown tired of waiting for him to answer their question. He falls asleep the moment he sits at his desk in school. He wakes to the whack of a duster or the sting of a well-aimed piece of chalk. Martha has seen him drop, fall flat on his face and immediately wake wondering how he got there. He falls asleep in the middle of board games.

'Wake up, Johnnie!' shout the twins in unison.

'It's your turn,' whines Christine.

'Are you playing or not?' May huffs a curl out of her eyes.

'Go to bed,' says Jill.

'I'm awake, I'm awake. I'm still playing, I was thinking about my next move, that's all,' says Johnnie.

When Johnnie is asleep on the lounge-room floor, Christine, never letting the opportunity to torture him pass, tickles his nose with a stray straw from the broom. She inserts the straw far into his nostril without touching the sides. He wrinkles his nose, suddenly snorts and wakes with a start. He sees the retreating and giggling Christine and grabs her foot.

'Got you. Now you're in for it!'

Johnnie turns Christine over and straddles her. He pins her shoulders down with his knees. 'There's a letter I've been meaning to write,' says Johnnie.

Christine shrieks in anticipation. 'No Johnnie, no Johnnie, no, no, no.'

Johnnie feigns a business-like seriousness. He uses his two index fingers to type out his letter on Christine's chest.

'Dear Christine,' Johnnie jabs.

Shrieks and hysterical giggles burst from Christine.

'How . . . are . . . you . . .' he continues to type.

Jack comes in and quietly stands behind Johnnie. It's as if he's seen maggots, or rats, or a leech hooking in. He pulls Johnnie off Christine and slams him against the wall. Pulling him up by the neck he shouts into his face. 'Don't you touch your sister again. Do you hear me? You don't get on her like that again.'

Jack's hand squeezes too tight. Unable to speak Johnnie nods his head.

Johnnie does the early-morning paper round. Three nagging clocks wake him. Paulie's dad helped him fix an old bike. It carts him and his load of papers around the streets. Every night the back verandah is littered with bike bits and tyre tube patches. A bowl of water reveals the bubbles from the latest troublesome leak.

That year the winter is so cold it burns the buds of the hardiest plants, water freezes in the pipes, the ice on windshields has to be chiselled off. It rains. It drizzles. The sun never shines. Johnnie stuffs his pants and jumper with newspapers. He wears a balaclava over his head. He cuts the fingers out of some woollen gloves and binds his shoes in canvas strips. He gets to school late and peels off his gear. His shoes, trousers and jumper steam. He constantly sniffs back snot. Finally his bike gives way. The frame almost folds in two. He leaves it on the footpath and continues his rounds on foot.

At the dinner table Johnnie is holding up his head and his hair comes away in his hands. Great hunks of hair fall out and he places them on the tablecloth in front of him.

'What's happened to your hair?' cries Martha. 'Your beautiful hair.'

The clumps of hair form a long row of furry caterpillars and the bald patches on Johnnie's head shine.

In the morning Jack rises early and he goes outside to warm the car. He puts his head in through Johnnie's bedroom door. Johnnie is sitting on the edge of the bed looking like death. 'I'm driving you,' Jack says.

A couple of hours later they return soaked to the skin. Johnnie stuffs down a piece of buttered toast and runs cheerily out the door. Martha raises her eyes and looks at Jack who rubs his head with a towel. 'I told him that's it. He's not delivering any more papers. He's to give it in,' says Jack. Martha fills the kettle to the brim.

At fourteen Johnnie is apprenticed out to learn a trade. 'He's good with his hands and there's nothing going on up there in his head,' says Jack. There is no question of him staying on at school.

The three nagging clocks get him out of bed at four in the morning. He walks, takes a bus and a train. He reaches Jolimont railway depot at six. He's assigned to the boiler-making section. Most mornings he stands asleep at his workbench. The blokes surround him and when the siren sounds the dinner break they laugh as he wakes with a shock.

Johnnie's used to waking up in fright. He wakes during the night to Jack rummaging through his jeans. 'Leave me my fare, would you?' Johnnie asks groggily.

But there's no reasoning with Jack. He's nasty, desperate for a drink, and guilty, which makes him nastier. He takes the lot.

Martha looks up when she hears Johnnie cough as he passes under the window. She smiles. He coughs to let her know he's arrived home. He doesn't know he coughs. Only she knows. When she hears him she puts on the kettle.

'There's Johnnie,' Martha says.

'How do you know?' says Christine.

'Magic,' says Martha as Johnnie walks in.

When Johnnie is late Martha imagines he's fallen asleep at the bus stop or on the train. 'I guess he'll wake up when the cold seeps in,' she says.

Sometimes the men take him to the pub after work. They swill down as many beers as they can before closing time. They slip Johnnie an occasional pot and laugh at him when he's drunk and can't stand any more. They laugh some more when he vomits down his front. He finds his way home, sick and falling over. Martha puts him to bed.

'Hi there, Mum.' Johnnie opens a bleary eye for a moment.

'Hi there yourself, Johnnie.' Martha rolls him over and gives him a smack on the bum.

One Sunday Johnnie isn't out of the house quick enough.

'Dig the dirt out of the incinerator and spread it on the lawn,' says Jack.

Things tend to break the moment Johnnie lays his hands on them. The rusty incinerator crumbles with the first touch of the spade.

'Can't ask you to do one bloody thing without you making a mess of it,' hisses Jack. 'You're bloody useless, weak as rat's piss.'

Johnnie recognises the twitch in Jack's fingers as he berates him. He needs to make a run for it. Jack hasn't had a drink for at least twelve hours and is feeling the strain.

'What's that bloody look on your face meant to mean? You think it's funny, do you? You think – Hey, where are you going? Come back here or I'll . . . ' calls Jack.

Out in the street Johnnie slows down. He lights a cigarette. Time for a quick smoke before he joins Paulie. Johnnie spends most Sunday afternoons with Paulie. The Briggses were the first to get a television. Paulie and Johnnie lie on the floor and watch the wrestling. Killer Kowalski is their hero and they take it in turns to impersonate him. They wrestle each other for hours on end.

Johnnie has Paulie in a Nelson, Paulie pulls Johnnie's head over his shoulder and breaks his grip. Johnnie throws Paulie back and pins him down, chest on chest. Paulie's lips are large and soft. Johnnie looks at how red and soft they are. So soft. He leans toward those soft lips for a moment until his lips are touching Paulie's. What am I doing? thinks Johnnie. Paulie is not pulling away. He presses his mouth hard against Paulie's, crushing his mouth against Paulie's soft lips. His hands are behind Paulie's head and he keeps his eyes shut tight. He doesn't know how he can ever open them, how he can look Paulie in the face again. He pushes himself away from Paulie and glimpses the blood running in a trickle from his lips to his chin. He runs. He runs out the door, out of the house, into the street, and doesn't stop until he slams his own bedroom door behind him.

He sees Jack out the window. He is tying up tomatoes with Martha's old stockings. In a flash Johnnie is out there beside his father. He picks the largest of the tomatoes, still too small and green to be touched. Jack bellows. He slaps Johnnie. Johnnie swears at Jack and kicks out at the tomato bush. Jack kicks Johnnie. Johnnie swears at him again. Jack picks him up by the collar and knocks him to the ground. Johnnie is silent and still and Jack pulls back his foot as if he might kick Johnnie, but he goes inside instead. Johnnie lies and feels the warmth of the sun on his back. 'I'm just going to lie here,' says Johnnie.

Johnnie starts to mix with a rough crowd. He meets them at trade school. They carry iron bars in their coat pockets. They drink and don't get sick. They go out with girls and touch their breasts. They can fight; in fact, their main preoccupation is with fighting. They spar, jump on each other's backs, trip each other up, put their heads in locks. They shove and thump and cork each other's arms. There's barely a moment when someone's not being touched. There are serious fights too. Someone's too big for their boots and needs to be taken down a peg or two. Someone else is a ponce or a poofta, doesn't swear, and didn't laugh at a joke. There are others who need to be shown what's what. Johnnie learns to split lips, to splat noses, to head-butt, to lay them out flat. He keeps up with the best of them. These tough boys like him. Johnnie is not full-grown yet. He still foams up his face every morning and night to control it from breaking out. They don't mind. He's funny and can spin a yarn that's almost as good as the flicks.

Johnnie often stays out late. On weekends he's never home. He crawls through windows when he comes in at night. Jack locks the doors when he goes to bed. 'If you can't come home at a reasonable hour, don't come home at all,' he tells Johnnie, who's knocking at the back door. Jill sometimes sneaks out to the back verandah and unlocks the door for him.

Johnnie comes home less and less. He no longer sees Paulie. That weak prick makes me feel sick, thinks Johnnie.

The phone rings in the middle of the night. Christine is up first and answers it. It's the police and they want to speak to her father. Jack and Martha look at each other in alarm and Jack takes the phone.

May emerges from the bedroom with her curls flattened under a bathing cap. Christine bubbles with excitement. 'It's the police, it's the police,' she whispers. May looks mortified.

'I see,' Jack says down the phone. 'Yes, I see.' He sighs dramatically. 'What do you recommend?'

Christine watches Jack intently.

'Keep him in then, teach him a lesson,' says Jack.

Martha lifts her hand to her mouth. 'Oh Jack,' she quietly utters.

Johnnie goes to prison for the night. He is kept in the remand section with about a hundred men. There are men he has never seen the likes of before, mean men with large dark tattoos in indistinguishable patterns, angry men swearing at the ceiling, men looking at him with half-smiles, drunk men and silent men with their heads in their hands. There is a cage in the centre where a warder sits and occasionally lifts his head to survey the scene. Johnnie doesn't sleep a wink. He resists the temptation to wrap himself in a grey blanket for fear of becoming warm and falling asleep. All he wants to do is sleep, he loves his glorious sleep, and usually he's safe when he's asleep. He sits upright, his eyes darting in all directions. He looks like a scared rabbit but he doesn't care. He is scared, and he wants to go home. He wonders if he could be someone else, another boy, someone with a different head. He's been worried that he doesn't feel deeply about anything. He thinks of Martha. I love Mum, he thinks, and then shakes the thought from his head. Jack might hear it and then he'd never hear the end of it.

His spit tastes venomous all of a sudden. Jack. He can't bear to think of him and instead thinks of how he's going to punch Spud on the chin.

'It's going to be a humdinger,' Spud had said. 'There's booze and a big spread and lots of girls, just waiting for us.'

Johnnie and his mates had caught the train to Frankston and wandered the streets for hours looking for the party. 'It's O'Connor Street,' said Spud. They walked for miles, arguing all the time. Then Spud remembered, 'It's O'Toole Street!' And they walked some more. 'Shit!' said Spud, 'I think it's O'Brien Avenue.' They all groaned. They gave it up and decided to go home but it was late and the trains were stopped for the night. They hot-wired a car. They took a Holden, a cinch to get into and this one started without a key. They were careless, noisy and angry at Spud for ruining their night.

The cops were behind them before they drove out of the street. Barry was driving and his brother Martin told him to gun it. Although Johnnie felt sick with fear he also urged him to ignore the siren and race it out. When the back windshield shattered Johnnie didn't know what was happening but he instinctively slumped low in his seat.

'Pull over, pull over, they're fucking firing shots at us,' screamed Spud.

Barry immediately pulled into the kerb. The cops yanked the four boys out of the car and gave them a beating on the spot.

At the police station three fathers came to collect their sons and take them home. A crying Spud walked past Johnnie with his father silent at his side.

Johnnie waits for Jack. When Jack gets here he'll be off his head, thinks Johnnie. It's peculiar but he finds some comfort at the thought. He shuffles his feet and looks around for a clock. He wonders what's keeping Jack. 'I wish he'd hurry up and get here,' thinks Johnnie.

Eleven

'I'm cold,' Christine says.

'We're cold,' say the twins.

May shivers. 'Me too.'

'Mum, we're cold,' says Jill.

It's late at night and they're sitting in the car with Martha. Jack's nicked into the Club on the way home. There's no money for a taxi. There's nothing to do except wait for Jack to return.

'Just drop in for a moment,' Jack had said.

How many times had they heard that before! Jill leans over and toots the horn.

'Don't!' Martha slaps Jill's hand.

They couldn't join him even if they wanted to – no women or children are allowed. Now they have been waiting in the cold for hours. With feigned joviality Martha tells stories of things she might have done, places she might have gone.

'I always wanted to go to some place like Cairns,' she says. 'Where there's sun.'

They walk up and down the street and try to bring life back into their dead feet. They stare in shop windows, put in a bid for things they're never going to have. 'I'd like that pop-up toaster,' says Martha. They linger there outside the hardware over the electrical goods. They take the risk that he might return and erupt in fury when he sees they're not there.

'It's bloody cold,' says Martha and the children giggle because their mother rarely swears. It's the cold and the wind and the hope that Jack has drunk his fill that has brought them back to the car.

Christine looks out at the Club and says, 'At least at the pub he might have brought us out raspberry lemonade.'

Suddenly Jill's out of the car. She walks across the lawn towards the Club like she means business.

'Jill! No!' calls Martha, quickly rolling down the car window.

Jill opens the heavy wooden door and walks into a small wood-panelled alcove. The walls are covered with names inscribed in gold. All the dead, I suppose, she thinks. There is a tiny hatch. She takes an enormous breath and knocks on it. A man with a bald head slides open the doors. He looks at her suspiciously as if she's someone with a dagger behind her back. Or a spy maybe. Jill feels his disgust. It gathers on her like dust. She has contaminated something sacred.

'Could you please tell my father, Jack Wheatley, that we're ready to go home now.' The doors snap shut.

The car swerves and screeches around the corner. The kids on the inside of the swerve push the others back. Jack's pissed. The lights are red and he isn't slowing down. They're through them and the twins look out the back windscreen and see them turn green. No one says a word.

If anyone speaks, thinks Christine, I reckon we're dead. She looks at Jill who shines for a moment as a streetlight spots her out. You are dead, for sure, she thinks. She's glad Jill went and got Jack and she's glad she's going home but it's colder now than before. The car is filled with an icy chill and Jill is picked out again in the lights and Christine sees Jill is breathing short smoky breaths and her bottom lip is trembling. She knows, thinks Christine.

'I was talking to a man about a job. Well, thanks to your sister you can say goodbye to that. I hope she's proud of herself,' says Jack. The words come hard and fast and fill the car with dread.

He's silent for a moment. Then in a voice that scares Christine, a voice down low like an animal's growl, he says, 'And you know without a job there's no bloody money and without money it's very hard for us to keep you all at school.'

He means Jill. Everyone else would happily leave school. Jack always threatens to take Jill out of school. Jill stays frozen but her heart palpitates and she thinks that everyone can hear it.

He's full of bull, he doesn't mean it, she thinks.

Jack is silent and his driving settles. I'll fix the little bitch, he thinks, once and for all.

Jill rings the bell on the door of a square brick house. A small man with a red face opens the door. Tufts of hair stick straight out of his ears. Suddenly Jill sees him as an angry cartoon character. She thinks, Why did I come?

Her words topple over: 'I know it's not my time, I'm sorry, I didn't know I was coming, I just came, I had to let you know I won't be coming again.'

Now her face is red. She puts a nail-bitten finger inside her collar and gives it a tug. She feels the old impulse to lift her foot and to shoot her head forward.

'Come in,' says Mr Oyston and steps aside.

When Jill first entered this room she didn't know it was called a study. She couldn't speak but he didn't seem to notice. He was too busy talking about formulas and how to apply them. The first time she saw the books in the shelves behind him she thought, There's thousands of them, and in his own home. While Mr Oyston talked she had smelled the pages and the leather that bound them.

'I'm leaving school,' Jill says.

'Why?' he asks simply.

'I don't think there's much point in me going on.'

'Nonsense,' he says.

'I think I'd rather get a job.'

'Don't be ridiculous. You are one of my finest pupils and I have not invested my time in you so that you can leave school and get some job,' he says contemptuously

'I know. I'm sorry but I've got to go and I wanted to let you know.'

Mr Oyston leans forward and looks at Jill. He drums his fingers on his desk. He quickly scratches his forehead at an idea that's itching. Jill holds her breath. Any chance at grasping it is shattered as he brings his hand down and slaps it on his desk. He rises in his chair in one fast and frightening move, and says, 'Yes, you'd better go.'

This is not what Jill means to happen. She wants to say, save me, save me please. My father's forcing me to leave school. Tell him that I've got to stay. Insist that I remain at school.

Mr Oyston leads her out. On the step she turns to show him her tears. But he has closed the door.

Jill knocks on the door of a large rambling old house. Her only school friend Emma Lubransky lives here. Emma's mother opens the door. Her breasts are enormous on her tiny frame and in an instant Jill finds herself enveloped in the warmth of them. She sobs. Mrs Lubransky sways and makes strange comforting sounds.

Inside the warm kitchen Jill is fed. She usually refuses Mrs Lubransky's offers. The tastes are strong, too unfamiliar, but today she is hungry. She eats the chicken soup with matzah balls, two potato latkes, a stuffed cabbage roll, and even the chopped liver finds its way down. She is full but Mrs Lubransky has put a piece of poppy-seed cake on her plate so she eats that too. Emma and Mrs Lubransky sit with Jill around the kitchen table looking sad. They don't talk much. Their words are tired and offer no condolence.

Emma's father and two brothers are normally crowded around this table. There is great exuberance that Jill often finds overwhelming. They sing, tell stories, make jokes, gossip mercilessly, and argue. They argue about books, about films, about religion and politics. Above all else about politics. It took Jill a while to see that the arguments in this household were not going to end in fury or in tears or frustration. The heat in the Lubranskys' arguments was a very different heat from that in the Wheatleys'. Jill didn't understand what they argued about. She didn't know the people, the books or the issues. Emma and her brothers held strong opinions and they fought for them. Their parents expected no less.

'They are Communists,' Martha had said.

'Don't be afraid, Jill, we will never get under your bed,' Mr Lubransky once told Jill. She had laughed, but it was a nervous, shallow titter. She was unsure what he was warning her against.

'What are your politics?' he asked when they first met.

Jill didn't know what the word politics meant. She looked it up in a dictionary later. She was glad she didn't know because she would have had to answer him and she didn't have a clue.

Now, downhearted, Emma and Mrs Lubransky look at Jill with matching doleful eyes.

'What can we do?' Mrs Lubransky asks the kitchen.

'Ring him up, Mum,' says Emma. 'He'll listen to you.'

'No!' Jill exclaims loudly. 'He won't listen to you or anyone else. It would make him worse.'

Jill gets up suddenly. She changes tack. 'Oh well, it will be all right, I'm sure.' She's all breezy.

Emma and her mother smile but they don't believe her.

'I'd better go,' says Jill suddenly. 'See you.' She hurries out of the house.

In the woodyard at dusk Christine's stallion is out. He rears and strains to be released. He desperately wants to be let go, to gallop across an endless expanse. The urge to run is irresistible. His hooves pound the ground. His flanks are wet with sweat and his nostrils are flared.

It has been a week of bloody battles, of roars and screams, of tussles, tantrums, table thumping and door slamming. Her father and Jill screeching like two cockatoos have been at one another the entire time. Christine is exhausted by the emotions spent, she's skittish, her skin twitches – to be enveloped by her stallion saves her. She wants to let him loose, to leave Jill and Jack and their squabbles behind her. Christine finds it difficult to understand why Jill feels so much. It can't be that bad, she thinks. All she's doing is leaving school. She snorts annoyance.

But now Jill rushes in and buries her face against the hedge. Christine withdraws into the shadows near the fence. The noise Jill makes frightens Christine. It's a high-pitched moan that rides on the strength of her breath. It dips and falters and comes from somewhere deep. It reaches across to Christine, who is cornered. She wants to block her ears. She doesn't want to hear Jill's weird and dangerous song, it will draw her into turbulent waters. She is about to make a run for it when Martha arrives.

'Jill? Jill?' Martha calls.

Jill turns toward her mother. Her face is stretched in a tortured pull. Her silent scream is deafening to Christine's ears.

'Oh Jill.' Martha steps toward her, arms out, wanting to scoop up this eldest daughter.

Jill thrusts her hand out to stop Martha's advance.

'What am I going to do?' wails Jill.

Martha is silent.

'Tell me. Tell me,' insists Jill.

Martha covers her mouth with her hand.

'Why can't I work part-time and still go to school?'

'He seems to have made up his mind,' says Martha.

'What am I going to do?' Jill repeats.

Quietly Martha says, 'Something will come up and, you never know, you might like it.'

'I won't. You know I won't,' says Jill loudly. Her tears completely disappear.

'You might,' Martha says.

'I fucking won't like it, Mum!'

'All right, calm down.'

It is quiet for a minute. Martha hugs herself. Jill covers her face with her hands.

'It's not fair,' Jill says then.

She drops her hands from her face and looks at Martha.

'It's not fair. Is it? Is it, Mum?'

Christine too waits to hear the words from her mother.

'Say it. You know it. It's not fair, is it?'

'It just is, Jill,' says Martha. 'That's all.'

'No!' Jill sobs. 'Help me, help me, Mum. Please.'

Now Martha mumbles: 'It will work out, just wait and see . . .' And she leaves.

Jill sits on the chopping block.

Christine has pins and needles so bad she thinks she's going to die.

Jill picks up the axe. She chops up an old fence paling into kindling bits. She makes a tidy pile.

Good, she's over it, thinks Christine.

'Okay,' says Jill.

She knew I was here all along.

'Okay,' Jill says again.

Christine is about to come out of hiding.

'If that's the way you want it, that's the way you'll get it.' Jill lifts the axe and splits a bit of wood in two.

Twelve

'Ratsak in his whisky.'

'Ground glass in his beer.'

'Explosives in his tobacco.'

'Acid in his face.'

'Slit his wrists when he's pissed.'

'Knife him.'

'Disconnect his brakes.'

'Garrotte him.'

'Push him off a cliff.'

'Pillow over his head while he's sleeping.'

'A brick at the back of his head.'

Jill and May are lying on the carpet on the lounge-room floor and it's May's turn to come up with a way to kill Jack.

'Can't you think of any more?' says Jill.

May lifts her hands and flashes her nails. 'Rip him apart,' she says.

Christine is appalled. 'Remember what he's been through,' she says outraged.

Jill and May look at her. May rolls her eyes and gives an exaggerated groan. She and Jill cackle together.

'Grow up, Christine. Just hurry and grow up,' says Jill.

*

Everybody else is growing up fast.

Jill is working and has already had a number of jobs. The moment Jill feels her first pay packet in her hand she feels a surge of growth. She's sixteen but she's a full-grown working woman. She pays board. She hands over almost all her pay to Martha every week. She gets herself jobs, she gets herself to and from those jobs, she meets new people, she learns how to do the work, sometimes in about five minutes. She learns how it is on the factory floor, who to trust, who to give the time of day to, how to keep in good with the boss.

In a couple of years she's worked in most of the factories around Moorabbin. She stays the longest at a paper-bag factory because she starts fucking a machinist during the lunch break and she can't remember ever feeling that good. This young nuggety man with tight curls and a taut body, he did something with his fingers one lunchtime as they hungrily kissed behind some machinery. After that, nothing in the world can stop her from meeting him in the car park. They've spent two weeks looking and smiling and buzzing with the shocks whenever they accidentally and purposely touch. By the time she climbs over into the back seat with him all thoughts of saving herself for marriage have slipped away and she falls greedily to giving up her virginity.

Two things keep her rapaciously abandoned in this pursuit. The first is the boredom of the job. The second is the intense pleasure she feels. But she is yet to orgasm. She knows there's more to be had and she is determined to discover what it is. And of course there's something in there about Jack that she is mildly aware of but she refuses to give it much attention. If he could only see me now, she thinks as she straddles the mechanic. Wouldn't he be proud?

The toilet breaks are timed but Jill is cornered by the three women all named Pat who work the same conveyor belt.

'We want a word with you,' big Pat says, pushing open the cubicle door while Jill has a wee.

The other two Pats standing behind her solemnly nod their heads.

'Don't think we don't know what you're up to,' continues big Pat.

'Because we do,' chips in Pat number two.

'What we want to know is if you've got any brains,' says big Pat.

Jill has stopped weeing but is too embarrassed to get up.

'Well? Have you?' Pat number three calls out.

Jill is flabbergasted. 'I don't know what you're talking about.'

'Contraception,' big Pat says. 'Are you using it?'

'No,' Jill whispers and immediately pees.

'Oh my god!' Pat number three throws back her head and makes a quick mumbling prayer at the ceiling.

At lunchtime the three Pats head Jill off as she makes her way to the car park. They sit her down.

'You're Protestant,' says big Pat. 'So we're letting you know what you can use.'

'We don't use any of it,' Pat number two says. 'We want to make sure you know that.'

'We're Catholic,' says Pat number three. 'So we don't have sex at all.'

They throw their heads back and howl their laughter like wolves.

They tell her about condoms, about a thing called a Dutch cap which Jill imagines to be something like the white-pointed hats girls wore in nursery rhymes. The most important thing they tell her about is withdrawal.

'Pull out. Don't let him go off inside you,' each of the Pats tells her.

This education encourages Jill, makes her feel older, more responsible. The thought of becoming pregnant makes her brain shudder. It would wreck everything, she thinks. From then on, each time the machinist's glove box is opened condoms pour out. The machinist complains at first. 'It's like having a shower with a raincoat,' he says. Jill smiles – the Pats had predicted he'd say exactly that.

But it's not long before her nuggety young man becomes moralistic about her voracious appetite. Her insistence unnerves him. And he doesn't like how she wants him to pull out. Eventually even he can't save her from the tedium of endless hours of packing paper bags.

Jill gets Martha a job at a cannery on the highway. It is winter and she and Martha have to walk past the high school, a mirage in the grey early morning light breathing smokily into the cold air. Jill doesn't look at the school. She stares determinedly ahead and ignores the ache she feels in her heart. School is where she's meant to be, sitting up in class, getting top marks. And one day I will be, she thinks. Just you wait and see.

At first Jill doesn't think anything of Martha and the older women working on the conveyor belt outside. They work under a tin roof on concrete floors, where vegetables are washed before they go inside to be cut and canned. They wear raincoats and rubber boots but they end up drenched. Their hands are constantly in the cold water and they are frozen through minutes into starting work.

'It's the bloody wind,' Martha complains to Jill when they're eating lunch. She can barely get the sandwich to her mouth. 'It cuts right through you.'

At the end of the first week she and Martha compare pay slips. Martha is paid less. She is also getting sick and two weeks later she's in bed with pleurisy. Jill walks into the office and says, 'Stick your job up your bum.'

She also works in the public bar at a pub for a couple of hours each evening. She helps with the rush before the pub closes at six. She's had this job since she left school. She loves it. It's fast and busy and some of the regulars give her tips. And she's used to drunks. The publican knows she's too young to work in a hotel. 'Didn't you tell me you were twenty-one? I'm sure I heard you say twenty-one,' he says.

Jill is decking the bar with towels to soak up the swill when Jack comes in. He's drunk, broke and looking for a free drink. She gives him a pot. And another one. And then he demands a third.

'I can't,' says Jill.

He's cranky and mean and he starts a scene. 'You can't even shout your father a bloody beer.'

Jill ducks to miss the ashtray that comes hurtling at her and dusts her in ash. In a moment the publican and his two burly sons put Jack out on the footpath. They never say anything to Jill. It's like it never happened.

Next time Jack comes in he's all charm. He talks to the men who threw him out the week before as if they're old friends. They laugh and talk footy and Jill shakes her head. I don't get them, she thinks. I just don't get them.

Johnnie's hair scrapes the top of the doorway when he enters a room.

'You better not grow any more,' says Martha. 'You'll knock your head off if you do.'

He's taller than Jack, has been for a while. He likes to sidle up to his father and make the most of it. 'Guess who can see the top of your head?' he asks Jack.

Jack gives him a playful shove that edges on too hard.

'And he's filling out,' Martha says.

Johnnie's turning into a man. His lashes are still long and gorgeous and his skin has almost cleared up although he occasionally breaks out.

'There's no doubt about it, he is truly lovely to look at,' Martha whispers to Jill.

'Half the girls around Melbourne think so too,' Jill says.

Johnnie is besieged by girls. They see him, they meet him, they want him. 'It's because he talks,' says Jill. 'If he were only good to look at they wouldn't bother with him.'

Girls ring him on the phone all times of the day and night. 'No, he's not here,' snaps Martha, who thinks girls chasing boys is not right.

He gets smelly love letters in the mail. 'He can't read the bloody things, they're that saturated in scent,' Martha says.

They come to the door and demand to see him. 'He's not here,' Martha lies while Johnnie clambers over the back fence.

Most of the time Jack says nothing about the girls. He has mixed feelings about Johnnie's popularity. He feels proud of him but believes it's not right. He thinks that Johnnie should only have one girl and be serious about her but he's not sure that he wants that either. He doesn't want anyone apart from his family coming into his house.

One day Jack's home and the phone is ringing and all the calls are for Johnnie. The doorbell's buzzing and all the callers are for Johnnie. Jack feels a kind of disgust. He rises suddenly from his chair. 'That's it!' he bellows. He grabs the phone out of Johnnie's hand and slams it down. He answers the door the next time it buzzes. 'Johnnie's not home, do not call again,' he yells at the lovesick girl in front of him. There's a group of her friends not far behind and Jack also yells at them. 'Clear off, all of you, he's not in.'

The twins too are growing up. But they remain the same size as one another.

'Thank god,' says Martha. 'I can't imagine what they'd do if one was taller.'

They are still inseparable. 'The only time they're apart is when one of them is in the dunny,' says Jack.

The school decides for no reason at all that it would be better to split them and put them in different classes. They stop going to school.

'If you don't go to school I'll send one of you to live with Aunt Amelia,' Martha threatens.

'If you don't go to school I'll take you both outside and belt the living daylights out of you,' says Jack.

The warnings go unheeded and the twins continue to skip school.

Martha is serving dinner and she calls to Door and Mouse to come to the table. When she sits down finally to eat she sends Johnnie to go and find them, but he comes back alone.

Jill clears the table. Two full cold plates sit there untouched.

'Has anyone seen the twins?' Martha asks.

No one has.

'Were they at school?' Martha asks May.

'I don't know.'

'I haven't see them,' Christine says.

'Where are they?' wonders Martha.

When Jack comes home late that night Martha is shrill. 'I don't know where they are, I don't know what's become of them, I don't know how to find them, I don't know whether they're alive or dead.'

They call the police. For two weeks there is no word. Martha stops cooking and cleaning house. Jack stays home most of the time. The other children tread softly, afraid the noise they might make could do more harm. They all harbour the same fear. The same hideous picture invades their heads. The twins murdered, lying half-buried in a trench.

Whenever the phone rings Jack answers, the others hang about drooping with dread. Jack lifts his hand to still them and then dramatically he drops it. 'It's not them,' he says.

On the fourteenth day of their disappearance the phone rings and it's Wodonga police station. They've picked up two boys, twins, a Michael and a Mathew, and they think they might belong to a Jack and Martha Wheatley.

'That's right,' says Jack. 'That's bloody right.'

'They all right?' Martha sobs.

'They're fine,' says Jack. 'I've got to go up and get them,' he says. 'And then I'll kill them.'

Jack brings them home. They are caked in dirt, their hair is dusty and stuck flat to the sides of their heads. Their necks are patterned in sweat trails through the grime.

'You look like a pair of Abos,' says Jack.

'And you've grown.' Martha inspects them. There's no meat on their bones, their filthy trousers sag at the bum but their bodies look pulled and stretched.

They have slept in lanes and railway sidings. The first week they hung around the tracks and railway stations.

'What did you eat?' Christine is looking at their caved-in bellies.

'It's amazing what you find in bins on the station,' says Door.

'Amazing,' agrees Mouse. 'Sandwiches with meat in them. Apples with only one bite out of them.'

'You disgust me,' says May.

The twins start to talk in earnest about the trains, the bogies, the engines, the signal boxes they'd seen.

'You'd think you've been on a bloody holiday,' Jack says.

They've hitched rides with tattooed truckies and wandered about small country towns. A farmer took them in one night. They'd chopped his wood and he'd fed them on lamb stew. They'd climbed to the top of a giant silo and watched the grain pouring into a train's carriers. They'd stood on the metal platform inside the silo and breathed in the dust. Each of them knew exactly what the other was thinking. Their feet felt the hard metal edge. They stood straight, their arms flat to their sides, two divers about to perform a pike.

'They'd never find us,' Mouse had said.

'That's for sure,' agreed Door

Martha looks at her two boys. They've grown wild she thinks. She asks, 'Where did you think you were going?'

Simultaneously they shrug.

Jack wonders if he should give them a thumping or yell at them or send them to bed. What's the point, he thinks, nothing seems to go in. At least they're as peculiar as each other, he thinks. He does go up to the school. He sits outside the principal's office and reminds himself that he's not in trouble. He goes in, his shoulders are squared and his jaw juts out, but there's no need for confrontation. The principal agrees and the twins are put in the same class.

May has grown into a beautiful young woman. And like Johnnie, she has an inordinately long line of suitors pursuing her. She chooses them as if they are mannequins wearing the next season's creations: she decides if she likes the appearance of them first. 'It's all about looks,' she says. She calls it a once-over and it gives her a good sense of their shape. 'They've got to be in proportion,' she says. 'And their faces are important, of course. They have to be desperately handsome.' Then it's how they carry themselves. 'What's the point of a beautiful piece of clothing if it falls like a bag?'

The phone rings and now when it's not for Johnnie it's for May almost always. There are boys from her high school, the cream of them, and boys from private schools, who Christine thinks look chiselled from stone. And Catholic boys who saw May at their school dance.

Martha is impressed.

'Catholic boys are very well behaved and extremely polite,' she says.

May rolls her eyes and thinks of the hands of these good Catholic boys and how they poked at places they shouldn't have poked.

'Yes Mum, very polite,' she says.

Christine watches May as she prepares to go out. May's long, immaculately filed fingernails fascinate her. Emery boards litter the house. She paints on layer upon layer of pearl varnish and she jams wads of toilet paper between her fingers until her nails dry. Then she cleans up the edges. The fumes from the nail-polish remover make Christine's eyes smart.

May's tools of trade are displayed on the dresser before her. There's an eyebrow pencil and eye shadows in shades of sparkling blue. There is mascara and a gadget that creases May's eyelashes so that they sit up like a startled-eyed doll's. There's foundation. It turns May's face orange, Christine thinks. There are lipsticks lined up and ready and always applied last. Christine leans in close, her mouth drops open in concentration. May squeezes a line of white glue from a tiny tube onto what looks like some spidery creature, which she expertly sticks on her eyelid.

Christine marvels at May's confidence as she colours and shapes her face and gathers her hair in clips and combs and bobby pins. She knows exactly what to pluck, how a blouse needs to be tucked, what bra gives her the right lift, what length her dress should be. And it's all achieved on a tight budget. May babysits and her pay is already committed to the next stick of makeup or to some fabric that she will make into a dress.

Jack continues to find May's beauty an agony. The long, lean, beautiful young men that come courting his daughter do not impress him. 'They look as if they've got sticks up their arses,' says Jack.

While May prepares herself to go out he comes into the small bedroom that May and Christine share. 'You might as well take off that dress because you're not going anywhere,' he tells her. May ignores him. He goes out but a few minutes later he's back again.

'You can forget trying to straighten your hair, young lady, you're not going out.' May ignores him some more. He goes and immediately comes again. Almost in a frenzy now. 'You can bloody well take that muck off your face because you're not leaving the house!' May continues her preparations. Sometimes she hums while he raves at her. She appears absolutely unfazed by Jack.

When the doorbell rings she meets her immaculately dressed beau at the door and invites him in. She introduces him to Martha and Jack. Usually Jack is still raving and the perplexed boy awkwardly withdraws his hand, which remains unshaken. One clean-cut young man she introduced had the misfortune to be named Karl. Jack clicked his heels together and called, 'Heil Hitler!' as he gave the German salute. He then goose-stepped around the lounge room. May quickly put her arm in Karl's bewildered one and led him to the door. 'I'll see you later, Mum,' she said.

Jill never brings boyfriends home. She does not think of them as boyfriends. She never gives her phone number to the men she goes with. She rarely goes out with the same one twice. It's not that she doesn't think any of them are nice. Their niceness is something she never considers. Every now and then one of them wants to see more of her, to call her his girlfriend perhaps, but Jill laughs him off. Martha worries sometimes that Jill might feel jealous of May. 'Someone will turn up for you, Jill,' she says trying to reassure her. Jill laughs. 'Gee, thanks Mum.' She smiles, shamming a pitifulness.

Jill has an enormous hunger for fucking. She goes at it with the same intensity as she did her study. She has plenty of men at her disposal because she is not at all interested in anything else but fucking them. She meets them at work and they fuck in lanes and in the back of cars, in the picture theatre, in the factory toilets, in the pub storeroom, on the beach, outside her house on the nature-strip. Sometimes she goes back to where they live and they fuck quietly so that their mothers won't hear.

She's taken to nightclubs, to jazz clubs, to illegal gambling joints, to clubs where women are really men. She goes with men who are twice her age, a couple who are three times her age, she goes with boys no older than sixteen. She goes with men with tattoos, with gold teeth, with hair in pony-tails, with married men, with men who usually fuck only men.

She arrives home in the early hours one morning. Jack is waiting for her.

'Where do you think you've been?' he hisses at her.

'Out and about,' she says.

There's a plumpness to her lips, a flush to her cheeks, the hair on the back of her head is matted. And Jack knows. She looks him straight in the eye, she wears a faint smile. She is brazen, fearless. Her look is saying, What more could you do to me?

'It's nice of you to wait up but I'm going to bed,' she says.

Jack almost lets her go, he is overwhelmed by her audacity. Then he grabs her hair as she walks past. He turns her and slaps her face. She holds his hand to her head to stop her hair from being wrenched out. She slaps back at him but can't reach. He calls her filth, and slut, and cheap. He pulls and pulls at her hair.

Johnnie appears. He is sleepy and confused, but only for a second. He tackles Jack and brings him down. With Jill. Their father's hand is still attached to her head.

'Let go of her!' Johnnie screams. He's got Jack face down.

'Let go of her!' he screams again.

Jill squeals when Jack pulls harder. Johnnie thumps at the hand that holds Jill's hair. Jack won't let go. Again Johnnie thumps. He's loosening Jack's grip. On the third thump Jack lets her go. Johnnie, not quite sure what to do with him now, grinds his face into the floor.

'You think you've got me?' Jack wheezes.

All Johnnie's weight presses down on him.

'I've got you,' hisses Johnnie.

'Not on your life. You'll never get me.' Jack struggles to get the words out.

Johnnie pushes Jack's body hard into the ground.

'I've got you,' hisses Johnnie. 'I've got you.'

Thirteen

'When you're little,' says Martha, 'men always carry your bag for you. Believe me, they don't help you when you're tall. No one's ever carried my bag.'

Christine is short. Very short. She's starting high school and her school uniform hangs like a dress-up. Her blazer is longer than the hem of her skirt.

'It doesn't seem right,' says Martha, arranging Jill's old grey straw school hat on her baby daughter's head. 'You're too little to be going to high school. You're too young.'

Christine's the right age, of course, but Martha's right, she is too young. She looks and acts about ten. Her brothers and sisters are constantly telling her to grow up. There is nothing that tempts Christine to grow, in height or in maturity. She likes being small. She likes being young. She thinks she's cute. Martha does too.

'Leave her alone,' Martha tells May.

Christine is crying because May's found an empty bottle of nail polish and Christine's doll is coloured pearl pink.

'She's a sook,' May says.

'She's not,' says Martha. 'She's young and you forget that.'

Johnnie teases Christine and when she pouts and whines he mocks her.

'Leave her alone,' Martha tells Johnnie.

'She's a sook,' Johnnie says.

'She's only little.'

'She's little but she's not that young any more, Mum,' says Jill.

Christine cries a lot. In a second she cries. Long and hard she cries. When she starts, her sisters and brothers groan and leave the room.

'Mum, Chrissie's crying again,' someone calls.

When Jack hears her he bursts into the room and looks around to clip the culprit across the ear. Most of the time Christine is crying about something so small she can't tell Jack. If it's too ridiculous he clips her ear and calls her a sook.

When Christine cries she really gets into it. She cries with the same intensity no matter what the cause. If Johnnie stands for a moment in front of the television and blocks her view she cries, and as loud when Mouse and Door take one arm each and give them Chinese burns.

The other five gang up on her.

'It's for your own good, Christine,' Jill tells her.

They've cornered her in the kitchen while Martha's down the shops.

Johnnie says, 'You've got to stop being a baby.'

May says, 'You've got to stop crying all the time.'

'Stop being a –' starts Door.

'. . . sook,' finishes Mouse.

'And stop telling on us all the time,' says Johnnie.

'The thing is, Chrissie' – Jill again – 'you're getting too old for it.'

'It's got to stop,' May says.

When Martha comes home, Christine wails at the top of her voice: 'They're picking on me!'

Martha looks accusingly at her bigger children. Christine is crying huge and bulging sobs. The others silently stare at Christine. They collectively sigh and leave her weeping in Martha's arms.

The tears are not all sook tears. There are many that fall quite legitimately. Often Christine is racked with growing pains. Her bones ache and she rocks herself in a ball of misery in bed at night.

'You must be growing,' says Martha.

'No!'

'It's only natural,' Martha says.

'No!'

Christine hugs herself and whimpers. Her body feels like it's about to split. What Martha doesn't know is that Christine has her great hoofed friend pressing within her, demanding to be let out.

There are many things apart from her size and the copious tears she sheds which make Christine appear young. Christine never knows anything. It's like she's cut off. She doesn't connect things. She doesn't connect that when they run out of food it's because there's no money.

'I haven't got any change,' says Martha, as an excuse not to pay the baker.

'Why don't you go to the bank?' Christine asks.

She doesn't connect the lack of money with Jack. She doesn't notice when Jack is not going to work. She never sees that Jack is never without smokes and drink but Martha's toes stick out of her shoes. She doesn't connect that her brothers and sisters always go out when their father comes home. She doesn't realise that the sinking feeling in her own stomach is because Jack's car has just pulled up on the front lawn.

She believes anything anyone tells her. Johnnie tells her outrageous stories. He tells her stuff that scares her out of her wits.

'Mrs Knox across the road is one of the walking dead,' he says. The Phantom is a friend of his, he tells her. 'And he told me Mrs Knox needs to suck the blood of someone young.'

Christine builds herself up to hysterical screams at this one: 'I heard Mum and Dad talking. I'm sorry to be the one to tell you but they've decided they can't afford to keep you, and they're going to send you away,' he whispers, all sappy-voiced in her ear.

Christine still believes in Father Christmas. She talks freely about what he's going to bring her. She writes lists for him and leaves sultanas out for a treat. This is not entirely her fault – everyone has kept her from the truth so that they can still enjoy the Christmas rituals.

She believes in god. She goes with a friend to an enormous mansion in the next street where some missionaries have their church. They talk of taking the Lord to the natives. There's even a native they've brought back with them to prove that they're telling the truth. Christine can't look at him. His blackness frightens her. She is escorted to the altar, where she is instructed to invite Jesus into her heart. Later she is rewarded with delicious pastries and a card in the shape of an apple. Inside, the bright red apple shows its white flesh with a small brown spot. Christine opens the card further to find a nasty worm at the centre of the apple.

At home every night she asks Jesus to come back because she knows he took off during the day. She waits for May to fall asleep and then quietly slips out of bed on to her knees and prays.

'I promise I won't keep asking you,' she whispers in the dark. 'I promise I won't need to because from this moment on I will never again do anything wrong.'

'I thought that was what you were up to!' interrupts May. The light and May glare over her. Christine crawls creature-like back into bed. 'Don't be ridiculous. Who do you think you're praying to? There is no god. For god's sake grow up, Christine.' May is contemptuous.

'I know,' says Christine's muffled voice buried beneath the blankets, which hide the deepest blush. She is secretly relieved that she doesn't have to bother with god any more.

Nearly everyone in the family hates god.

'What's he ever done for us?' says Jack.

Every now and then Martha packs Christine and the twins off to church. 'The thing with god is you just never know. It's good to leave your options open,' she says.

They're a motley lot in their ill-fitting clothes and mismatched socks. They just don't scrub up well enough to fit in with the patent-shoed, ribboned-hat, squeaky-clean children of Brighton who regularly attend the congregation. Martha forces them out of the house wielding a straw broom. The twins always put a penny in the plate and take out a shilling.

Christine comes home one day to find a strange man in the lounge room. He and Martha are on their knees, their heads bowed.

The sun through the venetian blinds casts a dusty, almost hallowed light. Christine stands gob-smacked at the door. Martha gives her the eye and gestures for her to kneel. The man resumes his prayer. On and on he goes, and Christine sneaks a look at Martha. Martha crosses her eyes at her and Christine's mouth drops open, aghast. Door and Mouse come in and collide with each other at the door. Before they can retreat Martha nabs them. In comes May and she too is brought to her knees. She crosses her arms, looks straight ahead and fumes. Jill turns up and Johnnie too and in they come and stop dead in their tracks.

'What the hell?' says Jill.

'Shit, what's this?' Johnnie too is amazed.

Martha's searing look makes no difference. She cannot make them obey her. Jill and Johnnie scream with laughter and run out of the house.

'If I'd been there I'd have tossed the bastard out into the street,' Jack says later. 'Parasites, that's what they are.'

He holds the stack of small envelopes the minister has left behind for Martha to put money in each week. 'If they can't get you there, they try to get you here.' Jack slaps his back pocket where he keeps his wallet. He throws the envelopes into the fire.

Christine still doesn't know how to tell the time. She can't see the point. She waits for someone to go into the kitchen, where the only clock in the house ticks five minutes slow. She calls from her room for the time, all innocent and busy-like. They gang up on her again when her ruse is revealed.

'You've got to be able to tell the time, Chrissie,' Martha says.

'Why?'

'So you stop asking us,' says May.

'Because you need to be able to tell the time.' Jill is appalled.

'Why?'

'So you will always know what time it is,' Johnnie says.

'I can always ask one of you.'

Jill tries, 'So you won't be late.'

'I don't have to.'

May loses patience. 'Oh for god's sake, Chrissie, grow up.'

'Why can't you tell me?' Chrissie begins to cry.

'You're not a baby,' Jill says.

'She is a baby,' says Door.

'A big baby,' says Mouse.

'I'm not!' Christine wails. Her mouth is stretched gaping and she turns to Martha.

'This time I'm with them,' says Martha.

Christine spends a lot of time on her own. There are no children her age who live in her street, and friends from school live too far away. She never plays with her brothers and sisters. They are always out. When they're not, they spend time in their rooms. Reading, that's all Jill and May seem to do. Christine doesn't like to read. She doesn't like to stay still for long and she is not interested in the fantastic worlds or the adventures that gangs of kids enjoy. May often draws but won't ever show her drawings to Christine.

'Don't touch,' says May as Christine picks up one of her pencils.

Johnnie listens to his crystal set or sleeps. He's almost always asleep, thinks Christine when she looks into his room and hears his gentle snoring from under the quilt.

Door and Mouse? Who knows what they do, but they do nothing with her.

These days it is a rare occasion when the children in this family do anything together. There are no family outings, no holidays off camping, no trips to the snow, most of the games have lost their pieces. When it is really hot Martha sometimes takes Christine on the bus to the sea. Now they're older the others go separately.

Christine wanders up and down the street looking for something to do. She's been hanging around Martha, whining about how bored she is. Martha has suggested that Christine help with the washing and that got rid of her.

Debbie isn't home, or that's what her mother says when Christine calls. Debbie is a little girl who lives a few doors down. She is four years younger than Christine and whenever they play together one of Debbie's toys gets broken. Christine doesn't mean to break them. She loves them. There are dolls made of porcelain and dolls in national dress. There are games and jigsaws and lovely little ornaments. There's a doll's house that has three storeys and tiny, exquisite pieces of furniture. In the lounge room there's a minute and delicate chandelier and when Christine tinkles it the tiny shards of glass come away in her hand.

Christine still always has war. It lives inside her. She doesn't include Debbie in her world of war. Debbie would not enjoy it. There's a level of seriousness that is difficult to explain. The world of war is for Christine alone. There is no contradiction for Christine that there is a place for dolls and Santa Claus and remaining small, and then a dangerous world of battlefields and espionage and camps for prisoners of war. She can play for hours with Debbie, putting on dolly voices, changing the baby dolls' nappies, until something comes over her and she makes a lame excuse and leaves. She is overtaken by the impulse to get a gun or to hide herself or to be ready for an attack.

On the street again Christine dashes from bush to bush. She throws herself over the nearest fence and lies on the front lawn until the sound of the tanks fades. She lifts her rifle to her shoulder and kills off Mrs Knox. She throws a grenade, and hits the deck, and Mr and Mrs Brown's remains are splattered across the street. She leads an army of men who trust her, who risk their lives to please her, who take her orders, who love her. They are always in Germany or France. They are always killing Germans. Christine rarely does battle with the Japanese. Germans are more glamorous and she likes the European settings best. There are times though when the Japanese do things better.

Whenever Christine is being tortured it is usually by the Japanese. She lays her head under the dripping tap. The drip must hit the middle of her forehead. She is staked out and the water drips, drips, drips, maddeningly onto the same spot. Her eye sockets fill with water so she has them shut. How long will she be forced to endure this unbearable torture? It's as if each drop weighs a ton and the sound of it when it hits is like a bass drum. She is unable to think of anything else bar the next drip. The cold water burns her skin. She has lost sense of who is around her, only vaguely aware that someone is inflicting this agony on her. She splutters and chokes and quickly pulls herself up away from the gushing water that pours from the tap.

'You never heard me. Never heard a bloody thing. I've been creeping up on you for about an hour.' Johnnie hoots with joy.

Christine gasps, water still up her nose. She gurgles and begins to cry. She's allowed herself to be ambushed. All that training and she's failed.

Sometimes Christine plays with a girl who is only two years younger and lives a few streets away. They play the one game. Horses. Her friend's horse is all white and Christine's horse is all black, of course. They groom them, take them over jumps, cross great plains on them, ford rivers, and race them. Christine loves the races. It feels so good to run hard and long, to feel her feet pound beneath her. Her friend is bossy with their game. She knows everything there is to know about horses. She has pictures of them all over her bedroom walls. She doesn't actually own a horse but she has bought a bridle and someone gave her a proper riding hat. And she's ridden them.

'I've ridden thousands of them,' she tells Christine.

Christine smiles. Well I've got a great raging stallion inside of me. Beat that.

Martha calls Christine into her bedroom and a streak of cold sneaks up her back. There is something about the way Martha is beckoning and smiling and looking nervous all the while that makes Christine feel sick. In the bedroom Martha gives Christine a small book called *Growing Up*.

'I want you to stay in here and read it,' says Martha, her quiet voice full of a terrible understanding kind of tone.

She shuts the door behind her. Christine knows it's a portentous occasion because no one's allowed to shut their bedroom door in this house. Jack says it looks sneaky. She doesn't want to read this book. She senses that it's about something that's going to change her life and she doesn't want her life meddled with. In the playground some girls once asked her if she knew the facts of life. They were sniggering, their heads were joined together in a cluster when they called her over. They asked her if she knew what her parents did to get her. Christine ran away from them and hid behind a peppercorn tree. She shook her head to clear their words from her ears. She is not curious, not even mildly interested in these things. Now her own mother has given her some horrible little book. On the cover a prissy young woman with her hair pulled up in a bun is standing in mist.

'I don't want anything to do with you,' whispers Christine.

Later Christine sits in the middle of the double bed and cries. She's not exactly sure why she's crying, because in fact she couldn't make sense of a lot of the book. The section on the rooster and the chooks went way over her head. It's the monthly periods that she understands only too well. She knows she doesn't want them. She decides then and there that she isn't going to have them. And that's what she tells Martha when she pops her head in to see how her daughter is taking it all in.

'You've got no choice, Chrissie. Every girl gets her period.'

'I'm not.'

'When you get it you'll feel fine about it.'

'I won't.'

'It means you're becoming a woman.'

'I don't want to be a bloody woman.'

'Its just part of growing up.'

'I'm not growing up, then.'

'Everyone has to grow up.'

'I'm not!'

Christine starts to cry like never before. She bawls and thrashes madly about in a spectacular tantrum. Christine's reaction to the idea of menstruation is clear to her: she cannot possibly take it on. She already has too much to deal with. She doesn't exactly know what it is that she's dealing with but she knows it is definitely too much.

Just before Christmas, Christine learns that her instincts are right. It is dangerous to grow up. She reads in the newspaper that an eighteen-year-old girl was on her way home from her work's annual Christmas party. She and another girl walked together to Flinders Street station where they parted. The girl took a train and got off at her station. Usually she would have rung her father to pick her up.

Perhaps she thought it was too late to disturb him. She walked. On the path flanking the railway line she met someone who murdered her.

In the newspaper there is a picture of the girl. Christine stares at her but cannot make her real. The newsprint flattens her features and cannot capture the life in her no matter how hard Christine stares at it. In another photograph the girl's handbag and shoes lie in the grass. The contents of the bag have spilled out and there's a calendar book. A rubber band holds open the date of her death. Christine thinks that there is something very eerie about that. The next photograph shows a detective holding up the girl's dress. It is the dress that the girl was wearing on the night. The description reads: *It was a shift with an aqua and white linen front which had distinctive red and yellow roses embroidered with green leaves down one side*. It hangs limply from his hands. Christine is disturbed that they have removed the dress from the girl's body. She thinks there is something not nice about that.

A man found her body early the next morning on his way to work. He noticed what he believed to be a bag of rubbish, until he approached it and saw it was a woman's body. During the night the girl's father had searched for his daughter and passed the place where she lay. Christine closes her eyes in dismay.

There's a photo of the scene of the crime. It is a wide view. Labels have been added to the picture. They say: *Station*, *Crossing*, *Footpath*, *Handbag and Shoes*, *Body Found Here*. Christine places herself in the scene. She walks the length of the station, stands at the crossing for a moment to make sure it's safe, crosses the road, follows the footpath to the place where the shoes and handbag with its contents are scattered in the grass. She continues on past a street to where the girl's body lies. She is about thirty feet off the path, face up, her underclothing disarranged, her skirt pulled up and covering her face. The newspaper offers Christine descriptions that enable her to see this young woman clearly. A part of her clothing is jammed in her mouth and there are bruise marks around her neck where the killer has wrung the life from her. Christine is captivated. She can barely take her eyes from that final image of the girl. She retraces her footsteps into that fateful night. She does so over and over again. She sees her body, her underwear, she lifts the skirt to reveal her face, the bruises around her throat.

A young man is found who was actually there. He saw the killer and mistook him for a dog. He actually spoke to him and watched him disappear over a fence. On the television the young man walks where he walked that night. He points to where the killer had been, to where he had fled. It is exactly as Christine has pictured it. They show a broken streetlight and suggest that the killer had smashed it so that the girl could not see him as he waited for her in the shadows. Each new detail enthrals Christine.

She had been a highly respectable girl, a keen worker, a very quiet and proper girl. Christine senses there is slight unease at the fact that she liked to dance, but it's clear she is truly an innocent young woman. Christine thinks, How unfair, such a good girl and to end up like that.

Christine is conscious of the level of her excitement while she pores over the newspaper pages. She knows that something in her is enlivened. And too much. She does not know the word titillation and that it might describe how she feels. She is aware that she should keep her excitement to herself. To think about the murder quite as much is not right, she knows, and especially not to hunger for the details as she does. The reports have given her entry into forbidden territory, an ugly and extreme and brutal and sexual world, and here it is in the newspapers delivered to her house morning and night.

Melbourne becomes a war zone. No woman is safe. '*Quite likely the killer is deranged and will attack again*,' say the police. This could happen to some other nice, innocent young girl. It thrills Christine. All this time she has thought the dangers were elsewhere, in some other time. And here in the suburbs of Melbourne, on her side of town, enemies are lurking, waiting for any opportunity to swoop.

All summer Christine concocts scenes where this loathsome murderer follows her. Behind every hedge he crouches, about to reach out and grab her and draw her in. A car pulls up with a roar and he throws open the door and drags her inside. Footsteps follow her, stop when she stops, cross when she crosses, all the time closing in. She lies in bed and sees him, squeezed between the wardrobe and chest of drawers, behind the door, she hears him breathing quietly beneath her bed. She works out ways to escape him, she talks her way out, she tells him she's married, she tells him she's got a disease, she fights like the toughest street fighter. She gouges his eyes, kicks his balls, butts his head. She is constantly on the alert. She will not become a woman.

Fourteen

'They've killed a bloody warder!'

Jack has the newspaper spread and his head buried in it. Christine has been waiting for him to finish reading it. She has come into the lounge room six times so she can grab it before anyone else does.

'They are in for it. They haven't got a chance in hell,' says Jack.

'Who?' she asks.

'They'll have every bloody cop in the country after them,' Jack continues. 'Mean as buggery, these two.'

'Who?' she asks again, a bit interested.

Jack rustles the paper in excitement.

'These are bloody tough men who've got nothing to lose.'

He drops the paper dramatically and looks toward the window.

'And they're out there, loose on our streets. Shit! I wouldn't want to bump into a pair like them.'

'Who, Dad? Who? What did they do?' Christine's hooked.

The world is becoming an interesting place for Christine. One day a girl is murdered and the next, two hardened crims escape from prison. She sits on the armchair beside Jack. The front page is filled with their escape. There is no sign of the young woman who lost her life only a couple of days before.

'Ronald Ryan and his mate Peter Walker, that's who. They climbed a prison tower using a homemade grappling hook and a blanket strip rope,' explains Jack. 'They forced a guard to open a gate. They took the bloody chaplain hostage.' Jack snorts. 'Put a rifle in his back and walked out of the bluestone fortress just like that. That's when the warder copped it. The poor sod was coming back from lunch. Then they grabbed someone's car and took off. The guts they've got!'

They look tough, thinks Christine. Their mug shots are on the front pages of the papers and on the television news. Ryan is older. He's got that Australian slit for a mouth. Christine can imagine him in an army slouch hat. Walker is young and handsome. Christine blames Ryan because she believes handsome can't be bad.

'They're both as bad as each other,' says Jack.

Ryan and Walker are called desperate and dangerous and have taken over the city. Roadblocks are set up on main routes throughout Melbourne and on country outlets. Every day one of them is spotted. A warder doing his Christmas shopping has seen Ryan in Swanston Street walking under the town hall portico. The city is cordoned off and policemen work their way through the crowds trying to spot a man in singlet and jeans. A linesman on the job is nabbed and later released. That afternoon Ryan is spotted in the Punt Road Bridge area; police cars rush to the site and buses are searched, but it's another man on his way home from work.

Johnnie's seen them too. 'I saw him,' says Johnnie. Ryan was on the bank of the Yarra opposite the Jolimont railway yards where Johnnie has his lunch. 'I asked him how's it going. And he offered me a smoke,' says Johnnie. He saw Walker on the train coming home. 'He got off at the same stop,' says Johnnie. He saw them having a kick of the footy down the park. 'That Walker, he takes a great mark.'

'Did you ring the police?' Christine asks.

'Nah, what for? They're good blokes. I invited them round for tea.' He can't stand Christine's wide eyes and gaping mouth any longer. 'For god's sake, I'm lying, Chrissie.'

It's reported that the two men have split up. Ryan likes to be a lone wolf, the police say. Christine loves the description. It makes him meaner, more dangerous. He knows that if he's going to survive he has to go it alone.

'He's as tough as they come,' says Jack.

Christine thinks that if Ryan were here now, Jack would slap him on the back.

'*The men will try to hide by day and make their moves at night*,' say the police. Nights become darker, more sinister, full of strange sounds and inexplicable movements. Christine lies in bed and is certain she can hear Ryan and Walker outside talking about breaking down their door.

Martha sends Johnnie to the shops to get milk, and Christine pleads with her not to let him go. 'It's not safe, Mum, they'll get him, I know they will.' Johnnie comes back, staggers over to Martha, slowly hands her the bottle of milk, and falls heavily to the floor. He strains to lift his head, and whispers, 'It was Ryan,' then falls back again as if dead.

Ryan and Walker are everywhere. They litter the city with stolen cars. One of them is spotted in a southern suburb.

'Near us!' cries an exhilarated Christine.

Ryan is identified as a man who had a drink in a St Kilda hotel. 'By god, I had a drink about a month ago in that same pub,' says Jack.

People call the police and report sightings of them in every suburb of Melbourne. A police officer calls them cheeky.

Christine says, 'They are really cheeky.'

'Bloody cheeky,' says Jack.

Like proud parents Christine and Jack can't help smiling. They discuss theories on where they are hiding, how they are surviving, how long before they are forced to give themselves up.

'They'll never turn themselves in,' Jack says. 'They'll go down fighting, those blokes.'

'Maybe they'll get away,' says Christine. She hopes so, life has never been so exciting.

Ryan and Walker hold up a bank in Ormond and walk with four thousand, five hundred pounds.

‘They’re on their way now,’ says Jack.

Christine is delighted. They might make it after all.

Cheeky is no longer the right word for Ryan and Walker. Now they are outrageous, they are audacious. Robbing the bank has elevated them to hero status. They are not two snivelling frightened little crooks hiding themselves away. They walk into a bank in the middle of the day and flaunt their contempt for the law.

‘Mustn’t forget the bastards killed that warder,’ says Jack a moment after he and Christine have been singing their praises.

Christine has long put the warder out of her mind. She and Jack look respectfully sorry for a moment.

Jack suddenly laughs. ‘They’ve got them running like chooks without their heads.’

A few days later Christine runs into the house with the newspaper. ‘*Escapees murder again*,’ she reads out dramatically.

‘By god, they’re in for it now,’ says Jack.

A man’s been found on Christmas Day, lying face down in a public lavatory in Albert Park. He’s been shot execution-style in the back of the head. Christine is disappointed in them. How can she stay on side if they murder again?

‘Bastards,’ Jack says. ‘Murdering bastards.’

Melbourne is under siege. Every member of the police force is on duty or on call. There’s talk of shoot-outs, of how they’ve nothing to lose. The police consider borrowing an armoured vehicle from the army. There’s an offer of a reward.

‘Someone will give them in,’ says Jack.

Christine whispers, ‘Better not, the dirty rats.’

Two young women are charged with harbouring Ryan and Walker. They kept her two-year-old daughter hostage, one of the women says. They stayed at her flat in Elwood and ate and drank and read about themselves in the newspapers.

If they’d asked me, thinks Christine, I could have hidden them in the shed.

The woman had brought around friends to help get back her child and one of them was the man that was found dead. Ryan and Walker didn’t trust him, the report says. Christine thinks that made it a difficult situation for them but that killing him was perhaps a bit extreme.

Ryan has a wife and two daughters. She's a class above him, the papers say. He's tried to contact her by placing an item in Missing Persons in the paper.

'He must love them,' says Christine.

'Looking for some cash, more likely,' says Jack.

Another sighting, this time in Broadmeadows; another in an Elizabeth Street theatrette where two men were sleeping. Ryan is spotted in Hay where he once was a shearer, and not far from where his mother lives. Walker has bleached his hair blond and is out and about in Melbourne driving in cars with pretty girls, or that's what's said.

Ryan's mum, an old white-haired woman who loves her son, is on TV. She says she's worried about him.

'So would I be, love,' says Jack.

The police seem as excited as Christine. They tell the public that some real action might be seen, that the net is closing. Christine and Jack give each other reports.

'They reckon they've just about got them,' Jack says.

'They say they've left the country,' reads Christine.

'They won't take them alive!'

'It's better that way.'

'For sure.'

Christine wonders. 'Will they make it?'

'Who knows,' says Jack.

'They've got to make it.'

They say Ryan and Walker must be feeling the strain, that they've created their own prison, holed up somewhere, not able to go out, eating tinned food, with nothing to do but turn against each other.

'They're trying to flush them out,' Jack thinks.

He talks to Ryan and Walker when their faces are flashed on the television screen. 'Just sit it out,' says Jack. 'Stay in, stay still, don't go out.'

'That's right,' adds Christine. 'Hold on, for god's sake.'

Finally the devastating news arrives. Jack wakes Christine. He's got the morning paper in his hand. Christine can tell that it's bad.

'They're done,' says Jack. He holds up the front page of the paper. *THEY'VE GOT THEM!* it says.

Christine groans. 'Oh no.'

'I'm afraid so,' Jack says.

It's all over. Seventeen days of high excitement have come to an end, and such an ignominious end at that. They were caught when they were picking up two young women. They were going on a blind date.

'What idiots!' Christine says. 'How could they be that stupid?'

'Got too big for their boots,' says Jack.

There's not the expected shoot-out, the grand finale that needed a tank – the capture goes off without a hitch. Ryan and Walker, spruced up for their dates, don't appear to suspect a thing.

'And they got them in bloody Sydney,' says Jack.

Ryan and Walker belong to Melbourne. It should have been Melbourne's catch. Sydney's always making Melbourne look like its poor cousin.

'Makes us look useless,' says Jack.

'You're right,' says Christine.

'The police were tipped off.' Jack's reading, filling Christine in. 'They walked into a trap. A hundred cops were waiting to strike. Six of them were up trees with shotguns.'

'They got them.' Christine can't yet believe it.

'That's that,' says Jack and continues to sit silently on the end of Christine's bed.

Now what am I meant to do, thinks Christine. School doesn't start for weeks.

Christine and Jack are depressed. Their lives feel empty, flat. The joy has gone out of them.

Christine still worries about Ryan and Walker every now and then. Jack drops them flat. He is not interested at all now they are captured.

'They're scum,' he says. 'I hope they both rot.'

There continues to be plenty to read about Ryan and Walker. The papers are still full of them. Christine laughs loudly at one report. Three thousand people watched along the roadside, applauding and waving to them on their way to the airport to be transported back to Melbourne. Women hung out of buildings and cheered the two men when they came out of the watch house.

She shudders when she reads about H Division where Ryan and Walker will now be housed. The H is for hell, so the prisoners say. They are in tiny cells for fifteen hours a day, where they are constantly watched. They have a bed, stool, plastic wash-basin and dish. They are not allowed to see anyone or speak unless spoken to, and then only to answer 'Yes sir,' 'No sir.' They will spend six hours a day in separate courtyards, smashing rocks.

'How can they bear it?' she asks Jack.

'It's bloody luxury, what they've got. You think they're doing it hard? They're not doing it hard. Believe me, I know,' he scoffs.

Christine drops them too. The holidays come to an end and she goes back to school and never thinks of them. At lunchtime one day she overhears an argument in the schoolyard and it all comes back to her. She stops to listen to two older students talking passionately about the evidence reported from the trial.

'Ryan didn't do it!' says one.

'Of course he did.'

'He didn't.'

'He was pointing the rifle right at the guy.'

'He didn't fire it.'

'People saw him shoot him.'

'They saw him holding the rifle.'

'The guy's a crim and he's trying to escape. Of course he killed him.'

'They say the bullet didn't go straight in. It went in high and down into his body.'

'What are you saying?'

'That it might not have been him.'

Her friends are way ahead and Christine runs to catch up.

Fifteen

Martha swoops into the lounge room. She's got a straw broom in her hands and she beats at the bodies writhing and heaving together on the floor.

'Stop it! Stop it right now,' yells Martha.

Whatever their age, it could be any one of her children clenched in rage. Often it's Christine in battle with one or other of her brothers or sisters, and she always ends up bawling. May and Johnnie often go at it hammer and tongs. Once in a while it's Mouse and Door down on the floor fighting. It is rarely Jill because she is hardly ever home. It wears Martha out. She says she wishes they never got the TV. That's what the fighting's about. Christine likes to watch *The Samurai* but May is watching *Kommotion*. The television gets flicked back and forth from station to station. Black-clad ninjas become teenagers dancing to pop. Johnnie, Mouse and Door sit on a screaming Christine and watch *The Three Stooges* to stop her from turning it over to *The Rifleman*. Johnnie gets scratches over his scalp where May grabs his head when he turns *The Lucy Show* over to watch *Hogan's Heroes*.

Martha comes in and turns the TV off. 'And it can bloody well stay off!' she says.

As soon as she leaves the room it's on again and so is the fighting.

They no longer eat their meals at the table. They sit with their plates balanced on their laps. For a few nights Martha sat at the table on her own, but now she joins them.

There are some programs where there is peace. It is accepted that Martha gets to watch the news. 'I want to find out about the weather,' she says.

She also watches *Peyton Place.* She makes a big thing about Christine being in bed. 'It's about adult things,' says Martha when Christine whines.

They rarely watch Channel 2 unless it's sport or a good film.

'I like the ads,' says Martha, 'so I can make myself a cup of tea.'

Martha tells them again and again to go to bed or to do their homework or the dishes. They promise her that they'll go after the next advertisement.

Martha watches films most nights. Christine is sent to bed and Martha pretends not to notice her when she crawls commando-style from the lounge-room door and lies behind the couch. She sets herself up to watch through the gap between the armchairs. There are many scenes that Christine witnesses through that gap that stay with her all her life, murders in showers, down spiral staircases, in convents in desolate places. She watches a film every night. Almost silently she sobs and laughs and sings along. She feels happy and snug and safe in her place between the chairs. She is especially happy when the film is about war. Her hands cup her head and shelter her from the dust after each bomb falls. She lies still when the Gestapo make a search and hopes they will not find her. She is inside tunnels digging her way out of prisoner-of-war camps. She's in the trenches throwing grenades or down low in the mud nursing a dying mate.

Jack is the biggest problem when it comes to the TV. He comes in and turns it off. No one says a word. He comes in and turns it over, usually to watch football, and leaves whoever was watching something else silent and fuming. He has no tolerance for films because he always comes in on them late. Once he interrupted Christine while she was watching *The Samurai.* She was so absorbed she didn't notice him come in.

'Turn that fucking thing off!' he yells.

Christine is up off the floor where she's been lying and has hit the button within a second. Jack is gone, out to the kitchen where Christine can hear Jap this and Jap that. She hugs herself for a while. How could she have done it? She knows what Jack feels about anything Japanese. She prides herself on knowing better than anyone else. He had told Christine he once entered a lift in a building in the city. When the doors closed he realised he was surrounded by Japanese businessmen. 'The hairs stood up on the back of my neck, I was drenched in sweat, my heart was beating like some bloody African drum.'

Christine waits excitedly all week for her favourite program, *Combat*. If Jack's home he insists on watching it and without fail he spoils it for her with his constant commentary.

'That would never happen,' he says.

Then he says, 'Bloody snivelling bunch of girls.'

'Shoot him, shoot the bastard, for Christ's sake!' he blurts out.

'Bloody Yanks! Would not have a clue.'

'Use your bayonet, you idiot!'

Many episodes are about the psychological well-being of the soldier. Christine is always absorbed. One night, Sergeant Saunders, a tough but very understanding soldier, is having great difficulty with one of his men.

'Kill that bastard. He's a danger to the rest of the platoon,' Jack snaps. He is about to burst.

Christine wishes Jack had had a few more drinks and would fall asleep.

During one episode a soldier stands on a land mine. If he lifts his foot it will go off. He talks to his mates, trying to fend off tiredness so that he won't release his foot. Christine is in tears. Jack huffs and puffs his contempt.

'Jesus Christ, lift your foot and put us out of our misery,' says Jack.

The soldier starts to cry and Jack is horrified.

'Bullshit! The bloody Yanks, they disgust me,' he says. 'They bleed everything dry.'

He cheers when finally the soldier is blown up.

When he watches the news Jack is always agitated. He leans into the screen as if he could take a step inside and wring someone's neck. He sighs. He groans. He hits his forehead with the palm of his hand. He stands up and bellows like some hurt beast. He drags long and hard on a cigarette and half of it disappears.

'Jesus Christ, Martha, get me a beer,' he says.

'*Melbourne's trains, trams and public buses will stop for forty-eight hours from midnight tomorrow in a strike by eighty thousand State Government workers,*' the newsreader says.

'Bloody unions! They'll break this country, they'll bring it to its knees.'

'*Power and gas are also expected to be hit hard in the strike. Your TV viewing will be rationalised,*' the news continues.

'Drag us down. Greedy fucking useless workers want everything they can get.'

A woman with a Yorkshire accent is interviewed about the introduction of the .05 blood-alcohol law that is to correspond with the pubs being open until ten. Jack squirms with rage.

'Whingeing Poms! They come here and think they own the place. Why don't you go home if you don't like it?' he says to the woman on the screen.

'*Aborigines living at Lake Tyers are protesting about carloads of local farm boys coming uninvited onto the community.*'

'Nobody waits for me to invite them to drive down my street,' says Jack. 'Jesus Christ, what next? They think they own the bloody place.'

When the news reports are about anti-conscription for Vietnam Jack holds his heart as if it's about to fly out. National Service had been brought in a couple of years before. There's an item about the discontent it has caused.

'It's the best thing that's happened to the country for years,' says Jack looking around to make sure that Johnnie has heard him. 'Young men today are soft. They wouldn't be able to fight their way out of a paper bag. They need direction, training. They need to know what life is really about. If you're called up, you're called up. There's nothing more to say about it.'

Christine holds her body stiff as if at any moment she might stand and salute. I'd do anything to be called up, she thinks.

The country is at war. Twenty-year-old men are to register their names with the Department of Labour and National Service. Numbered marbles, each representing two birth dates, are placed in a barrel and a certain number of marbles are drawn. Those born on the dates indicated by the marbles are obliged to serve. Part of this service means training, of course, and a year fighting in Vietnam. All have to register. Medical examinations decide each man's fitness and court procedure decides the sincerity of those who hold conscientious objections.

'Conscientious objectors! Cowards, Communists, should be shot,' says Jack.

Christine, like Jack, can't understand why all Australia's men can't go. Jack says, 'Call us all up, send us over and go and finish the bloody war.'

Jack watches a young man in a crowd holding up a burning registration card. Someone else swings a burning Australian flag.

'Oh my god,' says Jack. He sits down. He is staggered, shocked. 'I don't believe it,' he says. 'I just don't believe it.'

Melbourne's annual Moomba Parade, which fills the streets with thousands of people, is the next item. Spectators climb trees and traffic lights and sit on seats quickly erected on scaffolding and line Swanston Street. There are floats decked out in coloured paper, sculptured into papier mâché shapes. Mermaids and meter maids and the Queen of Moomba ride them. There are clowns on stilts and on bikes who shake kids' hands and tweak their noses. The businesses of Melbourne colourfully and gaily strut their stuff.

'*Anti-Vietnam demonstrators battled with foot and mounted police in a bid to disrupt the Moomba Parade today,*' says a very serious newsreader.

'Oh that's going a bit far,' says Martha.

The group of demonstrators jumps in behind the mounted police waving cardboard placards. *Vietnam is no festival*, one placard declares. *No conscripts for Vietnam*, says another.

'They have no idea,' Jack says. 'Haven't got a clue. They don't belong to the real world.'

The mounted police turn and ride into the group, hitting out at the demonstrators with their heavy leather riding gloves. Other police drag them kicking and protesting to the footpath.

'I'd have hit them with more than that. This sort of thing has got to be crushed,' says Jack.

In a final gesture of defiance the demonstrators sit down on the road and police grapple to remove them.

'What right have they got? Who do they think they are? Don't they know there's a war on?' The questions pelt from Jack's mouth. 'What do they want? Do they want the little yellow bastards to take us over? What do they know about anything?' Jack is beside himself. He sits for a while without speaking. He holds his arms down to stop them twitching.

'I just don't get it,' he finally says. 'I don't. I just don't.'

Jack takes Christine to a service at the Shrine of Remembrance. The day is bleak and the wind cuts through them as they mount the grey steps. This is Christine's first time and although she's driven past often enough she has never actually gone inside this magnificent building which smells of sadness. They pass the flame that never goes out.

'So we'll always remember those who were lost,' Jack tells her.

He gets a certain look on Anzac days and occasions like this. He's scrubbed up and Martha's ironed his suit. He looks taller, kind of dignified, Christine thinks. Like he's worth something.

This service is for the prisoners of war who died when a Japanese ship that carried them was hit. Unlike on Jack's ship, the hold was battened down and the ship sank fast, taking the lot of them with it. Jack's mate Davie was one of the men drowned and Jack has come to honour him.

The centre of the shrine is a dark and cavernous space. Christine stands with Jack and twenty other men in suits the same shade of grey as the heavy stone walls that surround them. There is one old woman dressed in blue slumped down low in a wheelchair. She looks confused and turns and talks to the man standing behind her.

'What's this for, John?'

'It's for Billy, Mum.'

'Billy,' she says in a whisper that becomes an eerie call for her dead son down the echoing corridors behind her.

Christine is wearing a summer dress and she shivers. She thinks of the eunuchs in a film she and Martha had watched, and how they were sacrificed and buried alive with the pharaoh in the pyramid. Above her, heads nod and offer muttered greetings. She is uncertain in which direction she is meant to stand and whether the service has begun. Beautiful flower wreaths placed in the centre form the shape of a grave. A man plastered with medals and badges booms too loud until he adjusts to a tone that immediately brings tears to Christine's eyes. He talks of courage and honour and country and how greatly the dead men are missed.

The woman in the wheelchair turns again. 'Take me home, John,' she insists. Tears have deepened the blue of her dress.

The man with medals continues while John awkwardly manoeuvres the wheelchair so that he can take his mother out. The man with medals calls for a minute's silence so that the dead may be remembered and it is then that Christine sees it. Light. It is as if it comes from nowhere. It touches the grey stone, and the flowers float eerily in the surrounding darkness. The light is unlike any Christine has seen. It scares her. She believes it's a sign, maybe from the drowned men. And they appear circling in and around the shaft of cold grey light, eternally swimming, trapped in the hold, looking for the way out.

'Lest we forget,' says the man with medals, and they chorus close behind him.

Christine sits in the car with Jack and she feels blessed. She thinks that the light and the grave of flowers have somehow purified her. They drive in silence for a while and then Jack turns into a familiar street. He pulls into the kerb outside the Club. Christine's heart sinks.

'I won't be long, Chrissie. I'll have one drink just to show my respects and then I'll be out,' says Jack.

*

Jack watches the news. Sydney roars an enthusiastic welcome home to Australia's 'Fighting First', the five hundred men of the First Battalion, Royal Australian Regiment, just back from the Vietnam war. A young woman, a twenty-one-year-old typist from Campbell-town, smeared in red paint, runs among the soldiers and rubs paint on their commander.

'Why would she do that? Why would she?' Jack is flabbergasted.

Johnnie thinks it's funny and snorts out a laugh.

'That's not funny,' says Jack. 'How does she think they feel? What they've been through and they've come home to that.'

'*The woman was later charged with offensive behaviour*,' the report goes on.

'I don't know what to do with a woman like that,' says Jack.

Christine echoes Jack. 'Why would she do that?' Christine is bemused by the act and by the fact that the woman was alone, that she had the courage, and that she felt that strong about . . . about whatever she was demonstrating about.

Sixteen

Jill's got a job at Prince Henry's Hospital in St Kilda Road. On the way to work on the tram she imagines she is a doctor and a huge line-up of patients is waiting for her to open them up. When she remembers what she really is employed to do, her stomach sinks. What are they going to do when they find out, she thinks. She's called a Trainee Laboratory Technical Assistant. In the interview they asked her if she had matriculated and she said, of course. When they asked her what subjects she'd done she said, without falter, physics and chemistry and maths. They said she should have brought her certificate in and she apologised and said she'd only recently shifted and her things were still in boxes. They asked her what school she'd gone to. She told them but then thought, Oh shit they're going to ring and check. But they didn't suspect such a respectable place to have liars and cheats. They sent her a letter and asked her to start the following week, and she was truly afraid. She hadn't expected to hear from them. She'd tried for the job on a whim, she was so tired of working in factories. The idea of hospital work appealed to her, but all the interesting jobs had demanded qualifications she didn't have. Going for the job at Prince Henry's was a joke. And she got it. But what if she couldn't do it?

She need not have worried. She does nothing but set up and clean for the technicians who test for bugs. She had hoped that the work might be engaging, that she might learn a thing or two or at least that it might lead to something more challenging.

May leaves school. How dare she, thinks Jill. They have a terrible fight. 'Why?' Jill demands. 'Why would you want to leave school?'

She follows May around the house. 'I mean it, May, tell me why, because I'm telling you it's shit out there. Shit pay, shit work, shit, shit, shit.'

'It's my decision,' says May.

'That's right. At least you can decide.' Jill wipes her tears on her sleeve. 'Please May, listen to me. I know what it's like, don't I? I'm out there doing it. Please May, stay at school.'

May starts work in a small factory opposite Trades Hall. They make underwear for men. She tests material for its strength. She bakes pieces of fabric in an oven. She clamps bits to see how far it will stretch.

'What about your pictures?' Jill says.

'It's only temporary,' says May.

'All those designs.'

'This job gives me an in.'

'All those beautiful clothes you wanted to make.'

'I'm going to do a course at RMIT next year.'

'But what if you don't?' asks Jill.

'I will,' says May.

'Go back to school, May, it's not too late.'

'You're driving me mad, Jill.' May rolls her eyes and walks away.

May and Jill travel to work the same time every morning. They sit at opposite ends of the tram. Jill remains furious with May and pretends she doesn't know her. May is pleased. She hates the way Jill looks and it suits her to sit as far away from her as possible. Unlike Jill, May is a snappy dresser. Jill likes sloppy joes and black tights. She wears desert boots and a duffel coat. She hates anything tizzy or tight.

She rarely buys clothes, preferring to wear things thin and until the colours are almost faded out. She thinks uniforms are a blessing, even if they are only lab coats, because she can wear whatever she likes under them. May pays Martha board and then spends most of her wage on Simplicity patterns (sometimes she lashes out and buys Vogue) and on remnants from Jobs Warehouse in Bourke Street. She's grown used to the two men in the store who fight all the time and sometimes throw things at their customers. She makes all her clothes. The regular passengers look forward to the moment she steps on the tram. She makes a pants-suit and causes a flurry when she gets on at her stop. Some passengers comment on its practicality, others tut their disapproval of a woman in pants.

Jill and another technical assistant at Prince Henry's, Louise, work on the public holiday, eager for the overtime. Jill still does nights at the pub now they're open until ten but most of her earnings still go to Martha. Jill and Louise are not as busy as they expect. Surprisingly the technician tells them to nick off for a couple of hours. They make a dash for the door before he changes his mind. They walk along St Kilda Road into town. It's sunny and it's a holiday and there are people everywhere. It's the day of the Moomba Parade. Jill looks at Louise, who is chatting easily beside her, and enjoys the warmth on her back and the way Louise grabs at her arm when she wants to emphasise something she's saying. Jill hasn't made any friends since leaving school. She liked some of the girls she's worked with, but once she left the job she never kept contact.

They squeeze in to look from the bridge down onto the Yarra where the water-skiing championships are in full swing. Six pink shaggy-capped women are pulled along, balanced in a pyramid formation, their arms stretched as if looking for something to grip.

'Look at those smiles,' says Jill and they laugh at the clenched teeth.

They push and jostle their way through the crowd along Swanston Street to catch the parade. Louise pulls Jill by the hand, winding and weaving around thick knots of eager spectators who have been there since the early hours of the morning and are determined to hold their ground. Louise takes out two white lab coats from her bag. 'I thought these might come in handy,' she says.

People who won't move are shoved and Louise shamelessly lies to them when they turn to shove back. 'Make way,' she says. 'We're First Aid workers.'

Their white coats gleam in the sun. Louise breaks through to the front of the crowd and pulls Jill out with her. 'Now we can see,' she whispers to Jill.

They can hear the beat of a bass drum and the squeal of bagpipes way before they come. Louise nudges Jill and points out a little girl who, wild with excitement, uses both hands to pull at her fanny. Her mother bends down and slaps her. Excitement becomes bewilderment and she buries her face in her mother's skirt.

All wearing the same neutral expression, policemen on huge horses lead the parade. The horses' gait is elegant and powerful. All of a sudden, Jill and Louise along with others in the front, are pushed through the barriers. Louise falls and skins her knees. A surge of people shoulder and elbow their way out onto the road behind the horses. Cardboard placards miraculously appear. One says, *I'm too young to die*. Jill glimpses another that says something about Vietnam. In those few seconds she wonders where this group was hiding. They stand out against the Moomba crowd so clearly. Their hair is long and messy and they wear jeans and torn shirts. Students, thinks Jill – but perhaps not, they are not all young. They are yelling things, but in the turmoil of children's cries and spectators' boos what they say is lost.

The mounted police turn and ride the horses into them. One man is pushed off balance by the enormous weight of the animal. A policeman, his face far from neutral now, bends down and slaps his leather gloves across a young man's head. Jill is shocked. The protesters scatter to avoid being trampled under hooves. A policeman on foot pulls a young woman kicking and screaming to the footpath. Jill is shocked again. It's a woman. For some reason she had assumed they were all men. But not only is it a woman, there is something familiar about her. It's Emma. Emma Lubransky, her old schoolfriend.

Emma is back on the road the moment the policeman releases his grip. She trips when another policeman tries to push her back through the barricade. When a spectator grabs her to break her fall she repays the favour by clouting him behind the ear. She is back again in the procession and she turns to the irate crowd. She stops. The sneer on her face dissolves into astonishment then into a smile.

'Jill!' she says.

A young man, his T-shirt almost torn in two, grabs Emma by the arm and pulls her along with him. She waves at Jill and is gone.

Jill is walking back to work and Louise is prattling on beside her. 'The protesters spoiled everything,' she says. 'What's it got to do with Moomba anyway?' Louise is perplexed. 'What do they think they're trying to prove? And look at my stockings, they're wrecked. Someone could have got badly hurt; there were small children there. Those people really should be locked up.'

Jill cannot say a word. She wants to laugh and cheer and whoop. She sees Emma's face, she sees Emma struggling to get back on the road again and again, how the demonstrators did not waver in the face of that angry crowd. There's something she's got to find out. And she's that excited. I haven't felt this excited in a hell of a long time, she thinks. And what's more, I don't even know why.

Louise says, 'What's your hurry Jill? Slow down.'

Jill takes the tram outside Prince Henry's and continues on through town into Carlton. She gets off in a hurry where the tram turns into Elgin Street, and she crosses Swanston Street and walks into the Melbourne University grounds. She follows a small street where there are buildings and walkways and signs that mean nothing to her. She wanders through cloisters and foyers and thinks she should not have come. She stands out, she's sure people are wondering what she's doing there, and at any moment they'll ask her to leave the grounds. She enters a building full of people. There's a cafeteria, there's groups sitting on stairs and against walls and in the middle of the floor. It is loud with raised voices, with shrieks of laughter, with emphatic speech. A man points his finger, almost jabbing at someone's chest, another is reading poetry to a rapt audience of three. Banners are taken down and others put in their place. There are posters everywhere, advertising meetings, inviting membership to clubs. There's music to hear, dances, films and theatre revues, so much to do. This is where I might have come, thinks Jill.

Jill is captivated by a poster of a ballet dancer who is balanced on one leg on the tip of her toes. The other leg points to the sky behind her. Her head is thrown back and her neck is arched. Like a swan's thinks Jill. She is certain she has seen this picture before. She knows it. The balance is delicate, the dancer exquisite, a marvellous capturing of daring and elegance. Where have I seen it? Jill wonders. And as if she has missed her step and fallen in a heap she knows. It is herself she sees there. A ridiculous parody of her in the schoolyard in her peculiar balancing posture, clumsy and oafish, and odd. And she knows she could never belong, even if she had won a scholarship as she had planned.

Trembling she sits to the side of some stairs. A group of ten or so students are scattered on the steps further down and they make no room for the people who are forced to thread their way through them to pass. Jill listens to their talk, about Menzies and how he was the worst Prime Minister the country's ever had. 'A war-mongering bastard,' one of them says. 'A pity he retired because he really should have got done,' says another who pretends to fire a gun. Talk turns to a film someone's seen, to where they should go for a drink, to whether the missing Beaumont children are probably dead. Jill is not envious exactly. She doesn't like them. She thinks their affected voices are silly and are projected in a way that assumes people hang off every word. She looks around her. She wants something. She tries to work out what it is.

Over the next few weeks Jill finds the library and the small picture theatre. She reads Zola and Flaubert and Tolstoy and Dostoyevsky, she sees *Battleship Potemkin* and *Ivan the Terrible* and *Gone with the Wind.* It takes her months to get up the courage to buy herself coffee from the cafeteria. She is less and less interested in fucking men. Once or twice she gets up from her cubicle in the library and nicks into the toilets for a quick one with some student or the janitor, and once with a law professor. Most of the time it's because of what she's reading and she mistakes her excitement as sexual.

She's lonely. She wishes she could have friends to laugh with, to talk books and films, to argue politics. She looks for Emma but never sees her. She thinks she hears her laugh during a film at the university's picture theatre but when the lights come up she can't see her. She reminds herself to phone Emma but never does.

What excites her most is the student newspaper. At first it was merely somewhere she could bury her head. Now it's like an obsession. She reads every issue with zeal. Sometimes she is almost faint because she forgets to breathe. The papers are full of the war in Vietnam. They call for an end to conscription; they implore young men to conscientious objection. They damn the government, damn the country, the shameful and unlawful presence of Australian and American soldiers in Vietnam. Jill is exhilarated. Her country is in the wrong. She can't believe it. What's happening is not right and people want to do something about it.

Jill catches the last tram. She walks miles from the stop to home but enjoys the quiet. Her head buzzes with ideas, half-baked, new, confusing and glorious ideas. Between the street-lights she lifts her arms and flaps them like wings. She dreads going home. Jack is a nightmare and always wants to fight her. She's tired of it. Shut your mouth and say nothing. That's Jill's new motto and she intends to stick to it.

Seventeen

Jill drops the tiny glass plates smeared with blood or pus or poo or some other gunk from who knows where. She misses her cup and her coffee shoots across the table into Louise's lap. The technician asks her twice to pass him some swabs and then, to get through to her, he has to shout. For about the tenth time she stops still in the middle of the room because she's forgotten what she was about to do. She goes to the toilets to take off her top under her lab coat. She is so hot.

She comes out of the front doors of Prince Henry's and crosses St Kilda Road. The cars are hurtling along and she is nearly hit. She sees the hundreds of people with paper American flags in their hands lining the street. They've come to see the President of the United States, Lyndon Johnson. He has been invited to tea at Government House. For one terrifying moment she thinks maybe no one else has come, that no one else is silly enough. She sees herself being torn apart by this happy smiling crowd. I'll be mincemeat, she thinks.

She takes a big breath and bends to pull a rolled up sheet of cardboard from her bag. She looks around her and shivers. 'Here goes,' she quietly says. She unfurls the cardboard and it curls back in a roll.

'Fuck,' she says and unfurls it again and this time she rolls it back on itself so that it stays almost flat.

She faces the road with her placard against her chest. A woman beside her leans forward and peers around at her sign. Jill watches her mouth the words, '*No Conscripts for Vietnam*'. She doesn't take it in straight away and when she does her mouth laughably turns in dismay. She whispers to her companion who reads Jill's sign and both of them move away.

Jill peeps over the top of the sign and stares ahead. She thinks of the young woman, Nadine Jensen, who a few months earlier had covered herself in red paint and walked out to meet the troops returning from Vietnam. Nadine, give me strength, thinks Jill.

She walks on to where the crowd has thickened a bit further along. She climbs a slope and looks down on their heads and sees other placards. Thank god, thinks Jill. These placards are feistier than Jill's. They say, *How Many Kids Have You Killed Today LBJ?* and *Hitler and Johnson – Two of a Kind.* The very moment Jill reads these words a policeman comes up and takes the placard from the protesters' hands.

She's happier on her hill, not far from this hub of protesters but not too close either. She holds her sign up a little higher. She's never seen so many police, on horse, on foot, lined up and down the street. There are men in grey suits standing alone or in twos. They don't look like fans and are certainly not holding placards in their hands.

'Why don't you go home,' says one of these grey men when he sidles up to her.

Jill's ears fill with sound and politely she answers him, 'Thanks, but I'm okay.'

There's a call of, 'Here he comes!' Instantly a cavalcade of cars appears and gathers in speed and sweeps past. Everyone is still, and amazed. Is that it, their faces appear to say. There are groans of disappointment. A young woman near Jill bursts into tears. 'I've been waiting to see him all day,' she says.

An angry rumble erupts and protesters push through the barricades and pour onto the street, calling and shaking their fists at the disappearing cars. Police rush in and try to push the protesters back. A policeman's hat is sent flying. There are violent scuffles where the police won't let go and the protesters struggle. Within seconds hundreds of people are on the road and mounted police push through, knocking people down as they pass, attempting to crush them under hoof. One man who wears a dog collar and holds a black flag is punched and kneed by the men in grey suits. Jill has been forced out on the road and her placard is wrenched from her hand. A couple of protesters are hauled off bucking and screaming, 'Troops out of Vietnam.'

Jill walks through the parklands that lead to Government House. On sunny days she walks here at lunchtime. She might walk as far as the Shrine but she never goes in. The hospital has its own smell of death and she had no inclination to draw in this mausoleum's breath. She feels naked without her placard and she wants something to identify her with the protesters. She reaches Domain Road where a large group is waiting for President Johnson to return. A young man sets alight an American flag and immediately the police converge and begin to punch him. He is left clutching his belly as the President's car is spotted. Jill stands in the thick of things as the car comes. A splash of blue makes its mark.

A bag of blue paint has hit the President's car. It almost obscures the windscreen and splatters over bodyguards and spectators and demonstrators alike. Seconds later another paint bomb follows and lands on the rear of the car and more agents are splattered, this time in red. It's a shock and Jill begins to laugh. She notices that others also laugh. She cheers when they too cheer. The culprit is searched for and caught. She walks shoulder to shoulder with other protesters as the crowd is dispersed.

Waiting for her tram Jill notices there's the smallest daub of red paint on the hem of her duffel coat, and she's glad. Then she feels a slight tug at her hair. She ignores it. Then another stronger tug draws her around – to face Emma.

'You are coming with me,' says Emma. A mock order.

Emma and Jill stand at the foot of a crowded table in a small restaurant. Mrs Lubransky is squeezed in at the other end.

'Mum,' Emma calls, 'look who I found.'

Mrs Lubransky screams. She can't get up at first but she pushes hard and the table actually moves. She leans over two of the seated people and grabs Jill. 'Sit,' she says and pulls Jill over.

She is hugged and welcomed and introduced. Plates and cutlery crash, chairs scrape and people talk and talk and talk. Jill listens to conversations that race around the table and are sometimes caught up in battle before they're let free again to be picked up and added to and changed, sent in remarkable directions. Laughter erupts and the tabletop shakes. The retelling of the events of the demonstration are enjoyed more than the plates of spaghetti which suddenly appear. They all have stories to tell, eyewitness accounts, opinions about the success of the demonstration, which are aided by great gulps of red wine from bottles hidden under the table.

'The paint was the *coup de grâce*,' says Mrs Lubransky – or Anna, as everyone calls her.

Jill is astonished. She hadn't realised that Anna had been there. Quickly she shuts her mouth. Why wouldn't she be, she thinks.

Anna is laughing about the shock on the agents' faces. 'They thought that they were covered in blood,' she says. 'The blue blood of the presidency.'

Emma catches Jill's eye and beckons her. She tries to introduce Jill to two men arguing furiously on either side of the table. There is a pause and Emma tries again when one of the men, the younger one, who is spitting with rage, stops suddenly and tells Emma to get him some cigarettes. Immediately he returns to the fury of the argument. Emma grabs her bag, takes out her purse and heads for the cigarette machine near the door.

The other man constantly wears a wry grin.

'All I'm saying is throwing a bit of coloured paint is not exactly violent.'

The spitting man says, 'Of course it's violent.'

'It's not going to kill anyone,' says the grinning one.

'The point is that it's perceived as a violent act. And any violent act will split the anti-Vietnam movement when what we need is unity.'

'Being squashed against a wall by a great fucking horse, now that's violent.'

'We must not resort to stupid and impetuous acts.'

'Being kicked by a couple of cops, now that's violent.'

'People will distance themselves from such acts.'

The grinning man stops smiling.

'Well, let them,' he says. 'Sometimes such acts are more important. They signify how hard people are willing to fight.'

'What a load of romantic bullshit,' spits his opponent.

Emma returns and he snatches the cigarettes from her hand.

Jill looks at her watch and realises she needs to make a run for the tram. She stands and waves goodbye to Mrs Lubransky, who throws her a kiss.

'Ring me,' yells Emma.

'I will!' Jill turns to rush out the door.

In the tram she sits back and closes her eyes. It's huge, she thinks. It's absolutely huge. She smiles, it's been a perfect day. This is peculiar because, although her heart still thumps madly in her chest, she's never felt so more at peace. Like there's been a bit missing and now she's found it she can relax.

The warmth of someone's breath on her face has her eyes open in a flash. It's the man with the wry grin.

'Hi,' he says, 'I'm Alex.' He plonks down in the seat beside her.

The tram travels the stretch of street where Jill had stood that day with her placard in her hand. Alex starts talking to the other passengers on the tram.

'You know why the President of the United States has come, don't you? He's not here to enjoy our beaches or our windswept plains. He's come sniffing around for our support. He wants more of us in Vietnam. He needs us. Nobody else is stupid enough to help him. Nobody else wants to join forces with a country that has started an illegal war. Oh, but Australia does. Good old bloody stupid Australia goes where it's told.'

Jill watches the faces on the tram. A couple of them pretend that it's not happening and continue to read or stare out of the window. One man is spluttering and writhing with anger in his seat. Others scowl at Alex. Someone else laughs as if Alex is some poor fool. There's not one that agrees with him, that's for sure.

Jill pulls herself up higher in her seat. She speaks: 'It's true. It's true what he says.' Silence overcomes her then and she thinks she might never speak again.

Alex sees her words of support as an invitation to continue to talk to her alone.

God, he can talk, thinks Jill, as she and Alex walk along Hampton Street. They've walked for miles since they got off the tram and Jill is glad that she is nearly home. The day has exhausted her and it's cold and damp. Jill looks at Alex and he's still talking. She's stopped taking it in.

He works the tugboats bringing the ships into the bay. He tells Jill about the secret qualities of seawater until she too is captivated by its swells, its strange eddies, its peculiar calm. He's from a long line of seamen.

'The salt water is in the blood,' he says.

All his family are unionists. 'We're union,' he says. 'But we fight. My father thinks unions should stay out of politics.' He laughs.

At the corner of her street she manages to interrupt him. 'This is my street,' she says. 'How much further do you have to go to get to your place?'

'My place? Oh, I live on the other side of town.' Alex grins.

'What did you come with me for?' She's suspicious now.

'You've been talking so much I got disorientated,' he says.

They laugh. Jill has barely said a word. They continue along Jill's street and he talks about when next they'll meet.

'You know,' he says with his smile, 'we should do this more often.'

Jill is anxious now. She is afraid of the shadows, she feels exposed under the yellow lamp outside her house.

'You know you can't stay,' she whispers.

'No, he certainly can't,' says a voice from the dark.

Jack steps off the verandah. He drags at his cigarette and his face lights up. Jill thinks, he's mad. He really is mad.

'Do you know this bloke?' Alex asks her.

'Of course she bloody knows me,' says Jack.

'He's my father,' says Jill.

'Who are you?'

'Sorry,' says Alex. 'I'm Alex O'Connor.' He goes to shake Jack's hand.

Jack ignores the gesture and says, 'It's three in the morning.'

Alex begins, 'It's been a very exciting night and . . .'

Jill thinks she is going to be sick. She knows that this man who can't shut up is going to tell Jack about the demonstration, about the paint thrown at Johnson, about their celebration.

Jill is in her room. She thinks, how come Jack didn't go berserk? She is uneasy. What's going on? Jack had waited for Alex to stop talking, which took quite some time. Alex had finished and there was silence until finally, disquieted, he said, 'See you,' and again tried to shake Jack's hand. Jack turned and walked inside, and she followed him. To her surprise he was not waiting for her by the door. He was not in the kitchen, nor was he in her room. He's gone to bed, thought Jill. But still she is not able to relax and undress and hop into bed. She listens but there's no sound other than the murmuring through the wall that comes with Johnnie's dreams.

'My god!' Jill says out loud. 'He's not going to do anything?'

In the morning she wakes suddenly to see Jack beside her bed. He's very quiet when he says, 'You can take this bag. You're to pack your clothes and go.'

Jill sits up and looks at him. He meets her eye. He speaks without the expected fury or threat. He is resolute. 'You understand,' he says. 'This morning. Out of the house. And you're never to come back again.'

Jill looks at her father and nods her head.

Eighteen

'An eye for an eye and a tooth for a tooth,' says Jack.

The people of Melbourne are on tenterhooks. The battle over the question of Ronald Ryan's sentence is raging. Will he be hanged by the neck or not?

'I'm glad they want to bring it back,' says Jack. 'Why should my taxes keep the murdering bastard housed and fed?'

Bolte, Victoria's Premier, is intent on hanging Ryan. He'd be the first person to die by capital punishment in Victoria for sixteen years. Christians are appalled, politicians cross the floor, unions march and send in delegations to knock on Bolte's door. A thousand people keep up a vigil outside Pentridge Gaol. Ryan's poor old mother appeals to Bolte to forgive her boy. Ryan's lawyer takes the matter to England to see the Queen, hoping she may intervene. The Pope is asked to support the commuting of Ryan's sentence to life. Melbourne University students face fines because they ignore a by-law that prohibits leafleting. The secretary for the Victorian Anti-Hanging Committee resigns from his teaching job. He will not be on the payroll of such an unprincipled government. Petitions are signed and sent and letters to editors are continuous. Jurors have gone to the press. They didn't realise they could recommend mercy for Ryan when they decided on his guilt. They had assumed that capital punishment was something of the past. And it had been. Until Ryan. There is a stay of execution and many think it's over, that the barbaric act will finally be put to rest. But a new date is set. The Victorian Cabinet is acting like a court of law to decide Ryan's fate. Bolte in particular is intractable when it comes to Ryan. He wants his death. New evidence is revealed. An ex-prisoner who had been in Pentridge the day of the escape had seen a warder in one of the towers shoot down into the street. Bolte and the Cabinet refuse to speak to him. They do not consider the evidence worth taking back to court. Ryan is to be shown no mercy.

'Who is he?' says Jack. 'He's a bloody crim who has done someone in. He's scum. Why should he get all this attention?'

It is as if Jack hadn't championed Ryan the year before. It's as if he had never heard of him. The protest, the vigils, the laments annoy him.

'Is Ryan going to be hanged?' Christine asks the day before his execution.

'Where have you been, Christine?' groans May.

Christine doesn't know where she's been. She hasn't looked at the newspaper for a long time. Once Ryan and Walker had been caught, there had been little to interest her. Every now and then, if the paper happened to be in front of her, she looked for reports on the murder of the young woman by the railway siding, but it was an old story. She sometimes watched the news on television but nothing went in.

With Christine it also took a while for Jill's absence to sink in. There had been no tears, no screaming, no fighting to herald her departure. She just sort of disappeared. Everyone was in shock, it was like the wind had been knocked out of them. Christine thought it was the right decision. She didn't like that Jill had betrayed Jack. How could she go and demonstrate, Christine thought. Yes, it was best, for her, and Jack.

Christine is stunned to learn that Ryan is to be hanged. For a moment she feels great sadness, but this feeling is soon waylaid.

'What about Walker?' she asks suddenly.

Walker should be hanged too. She thinks it's not fair that it's only Ryan. Walker had killed the man in the toilets: he should be hanged along with Ryan. And if they could find the man who killed the girl in the railway siding they could string him up as well.

At half a minute to eight on the morning of Friday the third of February, 1967, Ronald Ryan is hanged.

Christine does not think of Ryan that morning. She's going shopping with Martha for new school shoes. 'Nothing else grows except your feet,' says Martha.

School starts the next Tuesday and Christine is keen to return. She spent this summer again wandering no further than her street.

The following week, in assembly with new shoes on her feet, Christine sings the school song. Barely anyone knows the words so only the choruses surge. The flag gets stuck and refuses to be unbound until its rope is slapped. The boys salute and the girls lay their hands on their hearts. 'We love god and our country, we honour the flag . . .' It's a drone.

Christine and her friends find the classroom, charge to the desks closest to the windows and open them to let the hot air escape. They have English. When the new teacher enters the room they are instantly silent. She is young with long blonde hair, wears a short skirt and has bare legs. She drops her books from a height onto a table and the sound booms.

Sweat drips from the woman's nose onto one of the book covers. Christine thinks it's a tear that's dropped, but then she sees the teacher is barely in control of a raging fury.

'Last Friday,' she says, 'an unspeakable crime was committed.'

Christine is transfixed. She can't imagine what the crime could be.

'Here. In Australia. In our very own city,' says this young woman, with powerful timing. 'A huge injustice was served. A man – was hanged – by his neck.' She spits out this last sentence word by word and leaves a dramatic pause.

'And who is guilty of this despicable crime?' She pauses again, long enough for Christine to think she might accuse her. 'The state,' she says. 'The elected government of the State of Victoria, that's who. We should all be deeply ashamed.'

She calls for a minute's silence, a show of respect for Ronald Ryan.

There's a buzzing in Christine's ears as she lowers her head. She likes this teacher with her long blonde hair who talks to them in a way they have never experienced. Already it's clear that this teacher is unlike the rest. Christine has never felt this kind of fear before. She knows that this woman is a threat. She is dangerous. Christine senses she will take them into unknown territory, to places that will disturb their hold on the world. Christine's own face is wet with sweat now. She digs her fingernails into the palms of her hands. For sixty long seconds her heart pounds and her chest swells and she thinks she is about to split.

The young teacher immediately swings into action. Sitting on the table she points to students and asks for reasons for and against capital punishment. She points to Christine.

'A reason for . . . ?' she asks.

Christine is unable to speak. The teacher points to someone else. The class excitedly call out their responses.

'Get out your books,' she says, 'and write. Capital punishment. An argument for, or against.'

Christine writes. She wants to impress her new teacher, to show she feels deeply about things. She attempts to use the arguments against capital punishment that have been discussed. A tired list of points limps across her page. She wants to subdue Jack's fervent and passionate whisperings that call the bastard to account. 'Shut up,' she whispers. 'I can't think.'

The phone rings and Martha, a saucepan of burning stewed apple in her hand, answers it. She doesn't recognise the voice.

'Who? Who is it?' she asks.

It's the next-door neighbour of Martha's aunt Agnes.

'Oh yes, yes I know. How are you?'

The heavy saucepan tilts in her hand and stewed apple drips onto the phonebook and the floor. Agnes has had a fall.

'Oh yes,' says Martha, her voice thin. 'And is she all right?'

She puts the saucepan on the floor and wipes her sticky hand across her dress. Agnes has died during the night.

'Oh,' says Martha. 'Thank you for telling me.'

Martha leaves the steaming saucepan on the phonebook and goes to the kitchen to put the kettle on. When it boils dry she fills it up and it whistles its cry until dry again.

Christine comes home and finds her leaning against the sink.

'Aunt Agnes is dead,' says Martha.

Christine starts to cry, but stops to look at Martha – who hasn't moved to comfort her. Christine tries again. 'That's so sad,' she wails.

'Stop it!' Martha turns and snaps at her. Her eyes are dry and mean and she glares at Christine, who immediately stops.

'I'll make you a cup of tea,' says Christine, pleased she has thought of something she can do.

'Leave it. I'll do it.' But Martha doesn't move.

Christine escapes into the dining room. She waits for the others to come home and tells them first thing. 'Aunt Agnes is dead,' she says and bites her bottom lip to get the tears up.

First May then Johnnie and then the twins go to Martha. Very quickly they return. They all do their best, but the truth is they are afraid. They do not want Martha to be so strange and quiet. She's their mother and their mother doesn't do this. It unnerves them. They feel close to resentful. Not one of them can find a way to take her hand. They remain in the dining room. They are still, listening, waiting for their mother to do something, anything at all.

In the evening Jack is in the garden dragging on a smoke. It's his third in a row. Martha's silence rattles him. He waits for her to cry and when no tears come he feels awkward as if she somehow blames him. He looks at the back door every now and then and finally stubs out his butt and goes in.

'Come on, Martha. Come and sit in the lounge room.' Jack takes her by the elbow.

'No,' says Martha. 'I don't want to go in the lounge room.' She holds tight to the sink. A small spider runs frantically around the bowl, maddened by the high pitch of the kettle's keening.

'Where do you want to go then?' Jack rubs his hand over his face. He needs to come up with something better than this, he thinks.

'I'm fine right here, thank you very much,' she says, all light and tripping.

Jack moves to turn off the kettle.

'Leave that!' Martha snaps.

'Come on, Martha.' Jack tries again. 'Come on, love, come and have a lie down.'

'Why would I go to bed at this time? I've got far too much to do before I can go to bed.' She stays defiantly anchored to the sink.

Jack comes out and his nervous brood look at him expectantly. They suddenly annoy him. 'Leave her. Go on. Off to bed.' He shoos them away.

I'll go back in and make her come out, he thinks. I'll make her feel better, make her get on with life. He sneaks a look into the kitchen and sees that Martha hasn't moved. Her body looks bristled. And the confounded kettle is still whistling. He decides against it and goes to bed.

It's almost 2 a.m. when the cold gets to Martha. Her legs ache and the aluminium kettle is melted through. She leans over the sink and cries. She hugs herself and groans. She retches until she's sick. She wipes her mouth on the tea towel and talks quietly to the night outside the window.

'I want Jill,' she says.

'Do you want to die?' Jill is at her wits' end. 'Do you think Dad will love you then?'

Johnnie flinches as if he's been hit. 'No! It's not that,' he says. 'I don't feel the same as you, that's all. I'm doing what I think is right.'

Shit, I've lost him, thinks Jill.

Jill and Johnnie sit on the rocks at the end of St Kilda Pier. They meet every couple of weeks. Jill prefers it out there on the pier. Her tiny box of a room at an old private hotel on Beaconsfield Parade is sending her insane. When Johnnie comes they go out. They dare each other to walk along the pier's edge, they carry along a swag of hot chips and sit and scoff them on the rocks. Johnnie often brings her stuff from home, sneaks it out, 'Under the old man's nose,' he says. He brings Jill letters from Martha and food she's made her, like scones.

Jill misses Martha so much she goes to the beach at night and talks to her. 'Come,' she says. 'Come see me. Please come see me.' The water laps at her feet and the darkness swallows up her sad conversations. Often all she can manage to get out is one word. 'Mum,' she says. 'Mum.' The silence wounds her. Christmas Day hurts. She cries most of the day. She rings Martha a lot at first and then she gets caught and Jack tells her not to ring again.

She misses her brothers and sisters and feels guilty because she's left them alone with Jack. She worries about Johnnie. Jack no longer takes Johnnie on since that time his oldest son showed he had the physical strength to beat him. Now he leaves Johnnie dangling with a kind of camaraderie that's never amounted to anything. 'Remind me to take you out and buy you a beer,' he'll say, but he never does. He'll thump Johnnie on the back, too hard, and make some joke about the twins, and Johnnie colludes, then feels like a shit. Jill knows Johnnie wants something from Jack he's never going to get.

Surprisingly Jill worries about Christine too. Christine's secret worlds are not as secret as she thinks. Jill knows Christine's lost in battle fatigues and gun smoke. She knows Christine also wants something from Jack. 'She thinks he's something he's not,' says Jill to the waves one night when the ache to be home with her family is too great. 'Wanting something from Jack is the worst place to be,' she says.

When Door and Mouse get jobs at the State Bank, Jill visits them at their branch in Malvern. They wear the same cheap suits except one's brown and the other is grey. Jill cries when she sees them, she thinks they look so grown up. Their heads are down intently, they're counting wads of money. She notices how quiet it is in a bank. How everyone whispers. It's something about money that does that, thinks Jill. It kind of puts you in awe. She calls out softly to them and they look up in fright. Both of them see Jill and quickly look behind them. They are afraid to come over to the counter. She smiles and waves and leaves then and runs when she sees her tram.

'Useless. Both of them,' Jill says when the tram passes the bank. 'Absolutely useless.'

Her stuff disappears from her room. She changes locks almost every week. Sometimes she comes home to find a stranger in her bed. At first she had long conversations with her fellow tenants, but soon she grew tired of the endless dramas and the repetitive stories. People knocked on her door any time of the night, someone desperate for a match or a cigarette, wanting to borrow money, wanting to get into her bed. She learned quickly not to answer her door and to appear bad-tempered if someone wanted to tell her their life story.

Jill thinks she might die from loneliness. She thinks of Emma many times but can't find the courage to ring. I'm no fool, she thinks. Emma and I do not share the same world. She still has work, she continues to haunt the libraries and the picture theatres but she has to come home some time. One night she is lying on her small bed listening to the usual drunken fights, the insistent screams of a baby, the half-remembered song of an old soak. She gets up and puts on her duffel coat over her flannelette nightie and goes to the phone box down the street.

Emma shouts, 'Get in a taxi now. I'll pay this end.'

Emma shares a house with her boyfriend, Tim, and six other students in Faraday Street in Carlton. Jill arrives and there are people scattered outside the house and on the street. Some are dancing; others are sitting with their feet in the gutter sucking on bottles of beer or on fat cigarettes. She can't find Emma. As she makes her way to the door a man rushes past her, on his way to be sick.

Emma is whirling in circles in an almost empty room. She looks gorgeous, thinks Jill. Her hair is long with ringlet-curls. She wears a top cut low and her cleavage runs for inches. Emma opens her eyes and sees Jill and screams. She pulls her into the centre of the room and they dance, arms outstretched in circles. Jill's nightie billows in a tube below her coat.

Dizzy from dancing Jill staggers into the kitchen at the back of the house. Alex and another man sit opposite each other at a small table. Jill thinks she's experiencing *déjà vu*. Here is Alex wearing his wry grin, and this is Tim again, all hot and bad-tempered, spitting words at him.

'It's going to split the peace movement. That's all!' Tim yells.

'All I'm saying is I have nothing against sending money to the Vietcong. It's like putting your money where your mouth is.'

'We want Australian and American troops out of Vietnam. It's not our business to finance a war,' says Tim.

Emma dances in and rubs herself up and down Tim and he ignores her. She bends down and kisses the nape of his neck.

He turns and snaps at her. 'Fuck off, Emma!'

Emma flinches and dances out of the room.

'The money we'd make is like a piss in the wind. It's more a symbolic thing,' says Alex.

'Symbolic my arse! It's divisive.'

'It's saying we're on their side.'

'It's ridiculously provocative.'

'Nothing like a bit of provocation,' says Alex.

Jill moves outside into a tiny concrete backyard. There is only a single lemon tree and three men piss on the ground beneath it and create steam. She turns to go back inside and finds Alex in the doorway.

'Did you have to dress up so fine? You put me to shame,' he says.

Jill throws back her hair. 'Well, I am from Brighton after all,' she says.

'Let's see, let's look at the full elegance of this gown.' He undoes the toggles on her duffel coat and pulls it open.

'How divine. Such lovely fabric.'

Alex puts his hands inside her coat and pulls her to him and feels her body through the flannelette.

'Satin, is it?' he whispers. 'Or silk?'

When Jill tells him that Jack has kicked her out he says he feels responsible and thinks that it is his duty to come to St Kilda and be with her every night. They cuddle and kiss, slung low in Jill's tiny single bed. They make love. Jill beats at Alex when he groans too loud.

'Shut up, for Christ's sake shut up. They'll hear us.'

Someone in one of the many tiny rooms cheers.

Jill has been with a man who wanted her to lie still and let him fuck her in peace. She has been with a man who pushed her away because she rubbed her groin against his leg. She's been told she kissed too hard, she was a sex maniac, a slut, a nymphomaniac. She has felt some men recoil in disgust at her appetite. Alex is not particularly adept at lovemaking, he's lazy and clumsy sometimes, but he makes Jill feel that her desire is a glorious thing. He sinks back into her when she nuzzles in and grinds against his bum, he smiles at her ardency, matches her passionate kisses.

And Jill matches his passion for politics. They argue. All the time. They curse each other while they tug at the blankets, shivering in the cold nights. They scream at each other because neither of them will ever admit they're wrong. Alex thinks she has adopted the politics of the spoilt-brat students who know nothing of work and the real world. Jill says he's anti-intellectual and backward and afraid someone who doesn't wear overalls might tell him something he doesn't know. They talk into the night about Aborigines and land rights, about the White Australia policy, about the war in Vietnam.

She lies squashed against Alex and soaks in the heat of the man and smiles. 'Oh my god,' she says quietly. 'I knew it. I just knew that there was more to life.'

But then one night there's someone knocking at her door.

'Go away,' she calls in a hissed whisper. The knocking stops and there's whimpering instead. Jill is up out of bed, wrenching open her door, to find her sister damp and soggy standing there.

'May?'

May cries loudly now.

'What?' says Jill. 'Is it Mum? May, is something wrong with Mum?'

'No, it's me,' wails May.

Jill takes May downstairs to the communal kitchen, which is lined by cupboards with locks protecting cans of soup and caddies of tea. She lights the oven and leaves the door open. They sit with their cold feet inside it. They succumb to the fatty and burned-pastry flavours of the warmth.

'Can you talk yet?' Jill asks May.

She nods. 'I'm pregnant,' she says and gulps back a sob.

'Shit!' says Jill. 'How many weeks?'

'Maybe twelve.'

'Shit, shit, shit.' Jill inwardly thanks god for the Pats at the paper-bag factory.

Emma has had two abortions and her bloke can fit May in. 'I told him she's a friend of mine so he'll do her quickly. He and Mum have known each other for years,' says Emma.

Jill waits for May in the tiny dingy front room of a neglected Victorian terrace. They had stopped outside long enough for May to ask, 'I'm not going to die, am I?'

On the other side of the room sits a woman with her daughter weeping beside her. The woman drags hard on a cigarette and ignores her. Above the mantelpiece hangs a mirror. Someone has written Good Luck in the dust.

Afterwards, Jill and May walk slowly and silently up Church Street and down to St Kilda Junction. Having begun in a usual Melbourne kind of grey gloom, the day is now bright and warm. They pass the Astor Cinema, a poster for *The Graduate* catches Jill's eye.

'Give us a call,' Jill tells May at the bus stop. 'Let me know if you're okay.'

'I will,' says May, light and cheery, busily not looking at Jill.

Jill thinks she should hug May but her sister stands as if she's clenched. Jill looks for an opening, a soft place where she can swoop in and grab hold of her, but the bus pulls in and May is up the steps before Jill gets the chance.

Jill looks at Johnnie and thinks he's the most beautiful person she's ever seen. The wind off the bay chops the sea and sends up spray. His lips are blue and tremble slightly. His eyes perfectly match the blue. There is a delicacy to his face none of us others has, thinks Jill, and she feels no jealousy. He is too beautiful and she believes that somehow it's a danger to him.

Johnnie is rabbiting on about work, telling exaggerated stories as usual and making Jill laugh. He still works at Jolimont railway maintenance depot. They fit out all the red rattlers, they make their own tools, they fix the bogies, they wash all the trains inside and out. Johnnie is proud of his work. 'I'll be there till I retire, I reckon,' says Johnnie. 'There will always be jobs with the railways.'

He tells Jill about Gordon, a man who took Johnnie under his wing when he started as an apprentice. He has featured in many of Johnnie's stories. 'He died at his bench and no one noticed him,' says Johnnie. 'Not till the end of the day.'

'How's your love life?' Jill asks him.

'Can't complain,' he says.

Johnnie has been in love a lot of times for a young man.

Then, 'I don't know . . . ' he says. 'I just can't seem to make the feeling last.'

Jill leans over and takes a handful of his sleek black hair.

'What's the old man think about this?'

'Fuck him,' says Johnnie.

'You won't be able to have it if you're called up. It'll be short back and sides. No more pretty-boy locks then.'

'Give it a rest will you, Jill,' says Johnnie.

'You don't have to register. It's not your war. You can take a stand.'

'It's got to be pretty serious if they're sending us there to fight.'

'Muhammad Ali won't enlist. They've stripped him of his World Boxing title but he refuses to go to Vietnam.'

'Well, that's him.'

'This time we're in the wrong, Johnnie.'

'I find it hard to believe that.'

'Why? Because we're Australian? And they're Asian?'

'They're Communists.'

'So what? What's that got to do with us?'

'It stands to reason they'll be coming after us next.'

'Oh bullshit, Johnnie. That's so much bull.'

'If Australia's in it there must be a good reason. And I am going to register, and if I'm called up, I'm going to Vietnam.'

*

Jack comes into the pub. Jill is drying glasses at the bar. He's very drunk. She stares at him. I hate your guts, she thinks.

'Thought I'd see how you're doing,' he says.

'Bullshit,' she says.

'Well, that's nice,' he says in a slur. 'I've been worried about you.'

'Bullshit,' she says.

'Come on, Jill,' he says.

'Come on what?'

'Come on.'

'What?' She stands with her arms crossed.

'How about a beer?'

Nineteen

Thigh against thigh the twins sit on the couch. They smile awkwardly at Martha, who pulls a face of fearful anticipation. Two letters tremble in her hand.

'You read them, Mum,' says Door.

'I can't. I can't,' says Martha. She thrusts the letters towards Mouse.

'Don't give them to me,' he says and shudders.

'I'll read them,' says Christine, who is eyeing the letters enviously.

'No, not you,' says Martha. 'That wouldn't be right.'

Jack has come home and is calling Martha.

'We're in here,' she says.

He comes to the door and pulls up when he sees the twins and Martha all aflutter. 'What's going on?' he asks.

'Letters for Door and Mouse have come,' she says. 'From the Commonwealth.'

'Jesus,' says Jack and comes into the room. 'And?' he says.

'We haven't opened them.'

She offers Jack the letters and he tentatively takes them. Martha holds her face in her hands.

'Jesus,' whispers Jack.

Johnnie comes in and, like Jack, hesitates at the door. 'What's this?' he asks.

'The letters for Door and Mouse are here,' says Martha and a little squeal escapes her.

'Jesus,' Johnnie says. He comes in and sits in an armchair. His legs have gone wobbly all of a sudden.

Jack slaps the letters against the flat of his hand. He slaps again and then quickly opens one and reads. '*Mathew Dudley Wheatley, you are hereby called up for national service with the Military Forces of the Commonwealth.*'

They are silent. He opens the second letter, although they all know how it will read. '*Michael Samuel Wheatley, you are hereby called up for national service with the Military Forces of the Commonwealth.*'

'Jesus,' everyone says, including the twins.

Mouse and Door look at each other.

Jack is out the door, gone to the Club to give them the news.

'I'll miss my boys. What'll I do without my boys?' Martha cries.

Johnnie crosses the room and thrusts out his hand to shake Door's. Door doesn't know what to do with it. Mouse has had time to interpret the meaning of Johnnie's gesture but he mistimes it and their hands clumsily collide. Johnnie quickly disappears out the door.

Christine's body heaves. She erupts and stomps her feet. The glass in the windows shakes. 'It's not fair. It's not fair. How come they get to go and I don't get to go and I'm the one who should be going? It's not fair!'

Martha gives her bum an almighty slap and shoves her through the door.

Christine immediately puts her tear-stained face back in and yells, 'What's the use of them going? They'll be no bloody good.'

Martha threatens another slap and Christine quickly withdraws.

Johnnie rushes across the back lawn into the woodyard. He buries his face against the privet hedge. He hugs his body and cries. He'd missed out on the call-up a couple of years earlier. Jack had clapped him on the back and they'd gone to the pub to celebrate but he knew that Jack was disappointed. He thought that a stint in the army would do Johnnie good. They'd had the one beer and it didn't taste quite right and then Jack had said he had an appointment to keep and had left. Johnnie tries to subdue a heaving sob. It would have been good for me, he thinks. Toughened me up a bit. Got me fit. Maybe then the old man could bear to spend more than two minutes with me.

Door and Mouse are left alone in the lounge room. They watch a film they don't know the name of because they missed the credits in all the commotion. They have never been separated and as long as they're in it together they don't really mind.

'Might be all right,' says Door.

'Might,' says Mouse.

'Yeah, I reckon,' says Door.

They watch the TV screen and their fingers inch across the space between them and interlock.

Jack is bought a table of beers. They surround an ashtray littered with butts. His back is slapped, his hand shaken again and again. His mates are pleased for Jack. 'Congratulations, mate!' they cry when they hear the news. 'Jack's boys are going to Vietnam.' Jack acts subdued and he solemnly nods his head. It's a serious business, sons going to war.

When Jack comes home he can't get the key in the lock and Martha finally opens the door for him. He falls in onto his hands and knees and she pulls him to his feet. They stagger one way and then another until she drops him onto the bed. 'Jesus, Martha . . .' The words become furry and Martha can't understand what he says.

'What, Jack? What is it?' she says.

'They haven't got what it takes,' he says.

'Who?' she says.

'Door and Mouse.' Jack cries a drunken, moaning, tearless cry. 'They won't make it, Martha.' He pulls his head up from his pillow and grabs at her sleeve. 'They won't,' he says and falls back asleep on the bed.

Martha sits down and rubs the chill creeping up her arms. 'Damn you, Jack,' she whispers. 'Damn you.'

'You can't stop them, Jill,' says Alex. 'There's nothing you can do.'

'You don't understand. Door and Mouse, they just don't stand a chance.'

Johnnie had brought Jill the news. He'd stood silent and knotted up when his older sister lifted her head and screamed.

Jill goes home. She doesn't care if Jack is there. I hope he is, she thinks. 'Because I'd like to kill him.'

She feels strange inside the house. She's forgotten the tattered and worn-out carpet, and the nicotine-tinged walls. And the smell of it. The smell of home. She and Martha stand inside the lean-to kitchen and there's barely room to move. Martha's voice is high and light and it shakes uncertainly. She greets Jill as if she's been away on holidays and has come home. On any other occasion Jill would have sunk into her mother's arms and drunk her in. How many times had she closed her eyes and wanted Martha's touch, or cried bitterly from hunger for her? But this is not the time for a reunion with Martha. She steps away from her mother and hits the sink.

'Where are the twins?' she says.

'Now, Jill . . .' Martha begins.

'Where are they, Mum?'

Coarse grey hairs dominate Martha's hair and Jill feels her guts twist when she notices how old Martha has grown.

'They're in their room,' Martha answers finally, her voice down low now.

Jill turns and is about to go to them when Martha's words turn her around. 'Don't upset them, Jill.'

'Upset them?' Jill is confounded. 'Upset them, Mum? I want to save their lives.'

Christine is lying in wait for Jill. She must not let Jill get to the twins, she must stop her at all costs. She is the only one there to save them. Jack is at the Club, has left his post, thinks Christine. It is her duty to protect the twins. If she had a hand grenade, she thinks, she could hide it under her top. She is willing to sacrifice herself for her brothers and her country. She thinks of a bayonet, of knocking Jill out with a rifle butt. She thinks of booby traps, of land mines, of rolls of barbed wire. A tank, that would stop her she thinks. Her sister, her own flesh and blood, is the enemy, a spy, someone from the other side.

Jill comes out of the kitchen. Christine swings into action and blocks her path.

'You're not meant to be here,' she says.

Jill smiles. Christine is not taken in by her treachery.

'You're not,' she says. 'Jack will be home in a minute.'

'Good. Let him come.' Jill continues to smile.

She's tough, thinks Christine, she's not afraid of anything.

'I reckon you should go,' says Christine and is instantly ashamed of her limp tone.

Jill's smile has gone. 'Get out of my way, Chrissie.'

'I need back-up forces,' Christine murmurs.

'What?' says Jill.

'I think you should leave Door and Mouse alone. They're all right. They don't need you.'

'Oh yes they do,' snarls Jill. 'They need me. They need me more than ever. And you know what? So do you.'

Jill pushes past Christine and into the twins' bedroom.

Christine screams, 'I don't need you!' Jill closes the door.

Jill looks at her brothers sitting side by side on the lower bunk, smiling up at her.

'Hello Jill,' they say.

'Hello you two.' Jill sits on the bed opposite them. She laughs at the absurdity of the idea of the twins with guns in their hands. They're young and dumb and as peculiar as all hell, she thinks.

'We heard you coming,' says Door and he makes a guffaw.

'We sure did,' says Mouse. 'We're not sure what's all the fuss.'

For a moment Jill's at a loss for where to start, and then she plunges in. 'I don't want you to go to war. I don't want you to go to Vietnam. I don't want you to be hurt or to die. I don't want you to hurt or kill anybody.' Jill begins to cry. The twins sit in silence and watch her. She wipes her face and she begins again. She talks about the government and how Door and Mouse are nothing but cannon fodder. 'They think you're shit,' she says. 'They bow down to whatever America says. They couldn't care less what happens to you.' She talks about American imperialism, about communism and capitalism. She says, 'They've got no right to be there, we've got no right to be there, it's nothing to do with the Yanks or us, it's not their country, if the people of Vietnam want to live under communism that's to do with them, they work it out, don't think the Yanks are there to help anybody, they're there because communism scares the shit out of them and do you know why, because communism is about equality and capitalism is about how the rich have it all and everyone else is shit.' She takes a breath. Door and Mouse are glazed over but still she continues on. 'Have you heard about draft resisters?' The twins shake their heads. 'What about conscientious objectors, have you heard about them?' Again their heads shake. 'It's a bit late to resist the draft but it's not too late to conscientiously object.' She tells Door and Mouse how they don't have to go if war is against their beliefs. 'You're pacifists, aren't you?' They raise their brows. 'You want peace, I'm sure you do. Everybody wants peace,' Jill says. 'And you won't have to go to prison, me and Alex will hide you. Some people have been in hiding for years and they've never found them.'

Door and Mouse look like rabbits in a hunter's sights.

'So, what do you think?' says Jill.

Together the twins lower their eyes. 'We'll be all right Jill,' whispers Door. 'Yeah,' says Mouse. 'We'll be all right.'

Christine is running around in frenzy. It's as if the ship she's on is going down and she doesn't know whom to save first. She runs into the kitchen and yells at Martha, 'She's in their room. Do something!' Martha looks back at the custard she's making. Christine runs out to the jacaranda tree and is about to scale it. 'What's the point?' she says. 'The enemy has already got in.' She imagines Jill with bloody hands standing over the mutilated bodies of her brothers. Or that the twins have joined forces with her sister, made a pact and are about to go underground. She runs back inside so she can stop them and stands panting at their bedroom door. 'You leave them alone!' she yells. She dashes out the door and into the yard. If I had a rifle I could shoot her in the back, she thinks when she looks through the window and sees Jill stand.

Jill musses Mouse's hair, and then Door's. She can't speak. She smiles weakly at them and they smile weakly back. Missiles pelt thunderously against the window and Jill and the twins jump.

'Leave them alone!' Christine screams, and she pitches another handful of small, hard green apricots.

Christine's body aches. It aches so bad she rocks and moans and cradles herself in a ball, her knees up hard against her chest. The pains are excruciating, her bones strain in their desire to lengthen. Her body feels it's about to explode. It will grow. There is nothing she can do about it.

'I will not!' cries Christine, hugging her pillow.

Martha takes her to the doctor and he says perhaps she's about to have a growth spurt. He's amazed when he learns she's in her fifth year of high school.

'My god!' he says. 'She's so small.'

Christine is valiant in her battle. She shows extraordinary courage in the face of the most bloody and virulent attacks. She is a fighter of great skill and daring but she is finding it more and more difficult to control her body. It rages unrelentingly against her.

Her resistance to growth is well fought. She maintains a small group of friends who keep her safe. These are good girls who wear their skirts at regulation length, do their homework, rule their pages up in red and make neat, colourful headings. They never answer back and they never play truant, even from sport. Angela the Mormon plays the piano and gets good marks. Pretty Debbie and Jenny who are little, like Christine, and a bit silly, actually very silly, giggle almost all the time. Jane is a big girl who has large front teeth and is smart but never gets the joke. They are young-for-their-age girls who do what they are told, who secretly play with dolls, who can cut themselves off from nasty thoughts.

Angela the Mormon and Jane have got big breasts. They are breasts that belong to women in their sixties, not to sixteen-year-old girls. Their breasts give them trouble with the box-pleat tunics because the pleats buckle and will not sit. These girls have both got their periods and are constantly checking the backs of their skirts. They carry bulky packages in brown paper bags into the toilet with them. Christine's body remains defiantly flat, without curve. She feels irked by her friends' abdominal pain, their pimples, the way they sit-out at sport. The stench of smouldering pads from the overloaded burner in the girls' toilet makes her retch. It adds resolve to her body's resistance to the idea that it should bleed. Even the silly girls show no restraint and menstruate! Although they never talk about their periods openly there is something clubbish in their shared experience and Christine definitely knows she does not want to be a member.

Of her group there is only one who's rich and that's Jane. Her mother drives Jane to school in a maroon Jaguar and sometimes they pick Christine up on the way. 'We're more like sisters, aren't we, Jane? Rather than mother and daughter,' her girlish mother says.

Most of Brighton's rich kids go to private schools. The suburb's littered with them. Jane would have gone to one of them, she tells Christine and her friends. 'If I'd been a boy,' she says without any resentment whatsoever.

At lunchtimes they meet always in the same place. They have pulled two heavy concrete seats together and they sit and sing sweet pop songs.

There are attempts to flush Christine out from her daggy little group. Marion discovers Christine in art. Christine takes to a block of plaster of Paris and coarse sand with a bread knife and chisel. Alternating tools, she watches the shape grow definition. Features emerge as if she is unwrapping a parcel and with each layer the present is closer to revealing itself. When she stops she rubs her hand across a man's bent back, his head buried in his own muscular haunches. It is rough and powerful and when Marion sees it she is breathless.

'He's magnificent,' she says.

Marion loves to slap on thick paint, to throw colours together that are vivid and that aggravate. She slowly and meticulously scrapes away the oozing paint and gradually tones down the colours until her painting is still and flat, and dull. She reads poetry and knows all about the poets' lives and in particular their loves. She talks endlessly of love. Her entire body shivers in anticipation of one day feeling pleasure. Marion takes to Christine. She believes Christine is as desperate as she is for life out there, anywhere, away from Brighton. Christine loves her, loves her incessant talk of desire, how she stands up in class and outrageously flirts with both male and female teachers. But she has to make a run for it. Marion wants too much of her, she wants to spend their weekends lying in each other's arms on a rug on the lawn talking about colours and matching them with emotions. Marion's world disorientates her. If she spends more time with Marion she will lose her grip. She has to let her go.

Larissa is another potential hijacker of Christine from her girly mates. She sits next to Christine in Australian History. She draws figures on every spare space of paper. Her folders, her margins, her headings are crawling with bug-eyed naked creatures which stare gargoyle-like up at Christine. Larissa never uses a pen. 'I don't like their scratchings,' she says, preferring to write in pencil so that her urge to draw is not interrupted. She comes from a family of artists. There is no question of what she will be. She already makes figures in wax and has had some dipped in bronze. Christine is attracted by the certainty of her destiny.

Christine visits Larissa's home by the sea. Her mouth drops when she comes to the gate and wonders if she has got the number wrong. There's a circular drive and three storeys to the mansion, with a tower above it. The garden is littered with large-thighed bronzed women appealing to the gods. Christine had no clue that Larissa came from this paradoxical world where rowdy children run wild through their sumptuous house. Washing lies in piles. Dishes too. Larissa's mother, a baby on her hip, grunts at Christine and takes off after one of the kids. It seems a mile through numerous birch trees to the studio in the backyard. Larissa's father calls Larissa a half a dozen names before he finds the right one. He smiles at Christine but doesn't see her. There are no rules, they eat at odd times, sleep when they're tired, Larissa gets to school late in a uniform that's always unironed. Christine is overwhelmed by the disorder. And by Larissa's anarchic thoughts.

'What you are is prejudiced,' says Larissa furiously one day at school.

'I am not!' Christine is frustrated that Larissa cannot be rational.

'It's ridiculous. It's stupid. It's mean, and it's racist.' Larissa's hand punctuates her accusations with whacks on the desk.

Christine is confused. She can't imagine why Larissa would not agree that Aborigines are less intelligent than white Australians. 'They haven't had the same education as we have, that's all,' she says. 'I'm not saying it's their fault.' Christine believes Larissa is being deliberately obtuse, that her ideas come from the eccentricity that comes with her class. I can't afford to think like her, thinks Christine.

Christine and her core of friends never argue, not really argue. There's a bit of competition over who sits next to whom, and every now and then there's a tiff over something small but it's never serious. They rarely read newspapers, or watch the news on television. They don't talk about worrisome things. Christine is comfortable with this.

Christine never invites her friends home to her house. When Jane and her mother who is more like a sister give her a lift she insists they drop her at the corner of her street. She is afraid. She is ashamed. She does not want them to see her house and she does not want them to see Martha who is not at all like a sister. Her mind does an almighty swoop if she thinks they might ever meet Jack.

Once they drive past Martha in the street. Bulging string bags and a basket weigh her down and like uneven scales she lurches from side to side in an unbalanced gait. Christine slinks low in her leather seat as they pass.

Christine and Angela the Mormon end the year with their bare bottoms breaking the surface of the water, not at all dolphin-like as they imagine, on holiday at Bon Beach. They lie about in the hot sun on the hot sand and their skin snaps tight when they throw themselves in the sea. Christine thinks they will remain friends forever. 'Let's stay like this,' she says and suddenly duck dives and swims between Angela's legs.

Twenty

'You're looking good, Michael, real good.'

'Yeah, thanks, I feel it.'

'Looking the best I've seen you,' Jack continues.

Families of conscripts lie about on tartan rugs in a dusty paddock. There's cold chook and corned beef and meat pies, great attractions for a million flies. It's the first time they've seen their sons in months and the families surround their boys and look at them with pride.

The Wheatley family can't take their eyes off Mouse. He is almost unrecognisable with his short back and sides, his body taut and toned in his smart khaki uniform. Martha has cooked his favourite dessert, apple slice, and he hungrily scoffs three large pieces.

'You look smart, Michael,' says Christine a little reluctantly as she pats down the wayward epaulette on his shoulder.

'You're almost handsome, Michael.' May seriously scrutinises him. 'If it wasn't for your snoz.'

'You reckon?' smiles Mouse.

'Why are you calling him Michael?' Door's voice is low and trembling.

'You look fit, Michael.' Jack claps Mouse on the shoulder. 'You've filled out. A bloody truck would bounce off you.'

'I don't know about that.' Mouse bobs his head. He feels a bit at a loss. This is about as much attention as Jack has given him in his entire life.

'Mouse. You call him Mouse. You always call him Mouse. Why are you calling him Michael?' Tears well up in Door's eyes.

'But what's with the walk, son?'

Christine can't believe her ears. She's never heard her father refer to his children in a familial way.

'I might be fit everywhere else but my feet are killing me. They've given me boots two sizes too small.'

While everyone stares down at Mouse's boots, Martha leans over and pats Door's hand reassuringly.

'It's all right, Door. We know it's just our Mouse but it doesn't seem right to call him Mouse while he's wearing his uniform.'

'I can't tell you how much it hurts,' says Mouse.

'What's wrong, Mouse?' asks Door and he wipes his identical large nose on the back of his hand.

'Just told you, Door. It's me boots, they're too small.'

'No, I mean what else, what else is wrong?'

'Nothing. Why?'

Jack is on his knees, unlacing Mouse's boots.

Christine can't believe her eyes. Mouse is a king and Jack is paying his respects. There's no way Jack would bend before her. She looks for a moment down at her own lonely feet and pouts.

'That's bloody useless, that is. How in hell are you meant to train with boots too small for you?' Jack shakes his head in disgust.

'Tell them,' says Martha.

'I've told them,' says Mouse.

'You're not talking to me,' says Door.

'What?' says Mouse confused.

'For Christ's sake, it's not bloody good enough. Surely they can find you boots that fit!'

'You're not talking to me,' repeats Door.

'Yes I am. I'm talking to you, Door. I'm talking to everyone.'

'But that's it, Mouse. You're talking to everyone.'

'And you too. I'm talking to you.'

'It's an absolute disgrace.'

Jack eases Mouse's boots off. His woollen knitted khaki socks are stuck to his heels. Jack slowly and with tenderness peels them off and reveals suppurating and bloody sores. Everyone stands silent in sympathy. They have all experienced the misery of hand-me-down shoes, the big toe jammed up hard against unyielding leather, and raw and stinging heels. There's no reaching first base with a pair like that on your feet.

'It's a crime, that's what it is, and I for one am not going to put up with it.' Jack slings the boots over his shoulder and heads back toward the camp.

Mouse pulls himself to his feet, brushing his heels on the blanket as he goes. He winces. 'I'm in for it now. He'll get me chucked out,' he says. The red of his birthmark suddenly deepens to puce. May and Christine simultaneously shoo flies attracted to the meal on Mouse's heels. He winces anew and sings a little moaning song.

Now Jack is gone Door sobs loudly. 'I miss you so much, Mouse.'

Mouse forgets his heels and looks at Door. 'I know you do, Door, and I miss you.'

'It doesn't feel like you do.'

'I don't know what to do about that, Door.' Mouse controls a quiver on his lips. 'I really don't.'

'It's me, Mouse,' whispers Door.

'I know it's you, Door,' Mouse whispers back.

'It's me.'

'I know. I know it's you.'

They lock desperate eyes but Door cannot find the comfort he's looking for. He takes off. He clumsily climbs through the strands of a once-taut wire fence, snags himself on the barbed wire and tears the crotch in his pants. He crosses the paddock and heads for nowhere in particular. His flat feet slap the dusty ground. He turns and shouts across at his brother.

'Michael!' He chews his name mockingly. 'Michael!' He does a poncing sort of dance. 'If it wasn't for me fucking feet I'd be with you, don't forget. And they'd be calling me Mathew.' He runs towards a stand of gums. He skids in the dust and turns once more. 'And I wouldn't forget you, Mouse,' he calls, 'I wouldn't fucking forget you.'

Silently Martha packs the picnic basket while May and Christine fold up the rug. Mouse breathes deep to keep back his tears. They walk slowly toward the barracks. They stop every now and then to wait for Mouse who drags his miserable feet and walks as if each step could break through ice.

Mouse shows Martha, May and Christine his bed and locker. 'You were never this neat at home,' says Martha.

'How come Johnnie didn't come?' Mouse asks.

They are quiet. They had waited for Johnnie to come home that morning but he hadn't turned up. Jack had cursed him, calling him a selfish prick again and again all the way up the Hume Highway.

'He said to say hello, Mouse. He was sick as a dog this morning and couldn't get up,' lies Martha.

Jack walks in, sadly shaking his head. 'No luck with the boots, son.'

There he goes with that son stuff again, thinks Christine.

Then Jack makes a big show and reveals a new and bigger pair of boots. 'What do you think of your old man?' says Jack. 'Clever or what?'

'How did you do it?' Mouse asks.

'I know your sergeant. I've known him for years. He's another POW.'

There is no other place Christine would rather be than at the dusty camp at Puckapunyal, training to take her part in the war in Vietnam. Oh to be one of them, she thinks – square-shouldered, strong-jawed, and prepared to lose her life for her country. Everything in its place in her locker. Her body trim, taut and ready for battle. Her mind disciplined, focused, clear. She longs to pull back the grey blanket from the bed tucked so tight and lie in it, in a Nissen hut with fifty men sharing the same dream. She feels her life has been wasted. She watches the parade and the line-up of khaki-clad men in their spit-polished boots. There is no place for her among these young soldiers who wear the straps of their slouch hats like scars across their chins.

It's as if someone's left open the door of the chicken coop, Martha thinks. She has just got used to Mouse not being around. Now Johnnie's gone too.

Dear Mum, Heading north, I'll let you know when I get wherever I get to. Love, Johnnie.

Martha is relieved. Johnnie and Jack have been at each other almost constantly for the last few months, growling and baring their teeth, and she doesn't like the look that stays on Johnnie's face way after they fight. She puts the note in her apron pocket and goes outside to bring the clothes off the line. There's an almost new pair of Johnnie's jeans, dry and flapping in the breeze. She snatches them off the pegs and runs along the side of the house out onto the street.

'Johnnie!' she calls, holding the jeans up high.

She stands still and stares, then folds the jeans neatly and places them over her arm. She puts them warm from the sun to her cheek.

'Oh my god,' she keens. 'Oh my god.'

Door is transferred to a branch of the State Bank in Clayton. He moves to a bungalow at the back of a house in Oakleigh. Jack drives him and his stuff there and later reassures Martha.

'It's really nice. He has his own lounge room and kitchen and shares the bathroom in the main house.'

'He'll be lonely,' says Martha.

'No he won't,' says Jack unconvincingly. Door and Mouse had no friends. Jack doubts that Door knows how to talk to another human being. 'It'll be good for him,' says Jack.

Martha had liked one of May's boyfriends named Paul. He was handsome and fun and very polite. Martha had been sure he was the one for May. He was the only one May was ever nice to. They seemed very much in love, Martha thought. Then he didn't come around any more. She asked May about him, 'What happened to that fellow

Paul?' But May didn't answer her. 'You know, the one with the lovely hair?' May shrugged. Martha had smiled. It won't hurt May to be the one who's dumped for once, she thought.

Now May appears to believe her latest, Laurie, is a stunner. 'He's perfect,' she says, though Laurie is a surprisingly plain and stocky man. And in the next breath she says, 'And his family's got plenty of money.'

Martha looks at May. She expects her to laugh or to give a cheeky grin, some sign that she doesn't mean what it sounds like she means.

When May first brought Laurie home Jack squeezed his hand hard when he shook it. It was so bruised it hurt Laurie for a week.

Sometimes Martha thinks she can't wait to see the back of May. 'Nothing is ever good enough for that girl.'

May complains a lot about the way Martha looks, what she wears, the colour of her lipstick. 'I wear it to stop my lips from going dry, May. And to give a bit of colour to my face. I don't care what shade it is and I'm not buying a new one because of you,' says Martha.

The house is an embarrassment to May. 'It's the carpet, it's got holes and the lino is cracked and the venetian blinds are broken and the walls are smoky and every switch in the house gives you a shock.' May nags Martha. 'How do you expect me to feel when I bring Laurie home?'

'I don't know what you want me to do about it, May. Give me the money and I'll get everything fixed,' Martha tells her.

May is next to go.

'At least I've got time to get used to the idea,' says Martha.

It's to be a small wedding. 'Well, relatively small,' says May when Martha looks astonished at the invitation list. It might be a relatively small wedding but it's a huge wedding dress. May designs it. It uses fifteen yards of satin she bought for a good price from the brothers at Jobs Warehouse. She stitches all of it by hand, though Martha helps with the beading on the bodice. Matching beads are randomly sewn on the veil as well.

May has finished a course in dressmaking and intends to open a small dress shop somewhere close to where Laurie works in the office of his father's trucking business.

Martha plans the wedding cake she intends to bake.

'You don't have to,' says May.

'I want to!' Martha replies. 'And I'm going to.'

Laurie's parents have met most of the costs. 'It's all taken care of,' May says when Martha suggests she and Jack make a contribution.

'It's not right,' Martha insists. 'I can help with the cooking, can't I?'

'Oh Mum, it's being catered for.' May sighs. 'You just do the cake.'

Martha makes a few more attempts, she offers to do the flowers, to have Jack drive the bridal car. May laughs and tells her it's all arranged.

They go together into town to look for a dress for Martha.

'I'm going to choose you a dress to die for,' May tells Martha.

'What I'll choose will be fine,' says Martha.

'Don't be silly, I don't mind,' says May.

Why on earth did I think I might enjoy this, Martha thinks.

They have an argument over shoes. May wants Martha to buy the satin stilettos and Martha wants to buy less expensive pumps, which she knows she could wear again. 'It's my wedding,' May says dramatically, through feigned tears.

Martha is resolute, she picks up the pumps and tells the salesgirl, 'These are the ones.'

May looks divine as she glides down the aisle with Jack. Jack's hired suit fits him well. He holds himself straight, his shoulders are broad and his chin is up, and he looks proud. Like he's a king, thinks Christine.

Martha thinks her middle daughter is so beautiful she wonders how she could be hers. She also wonders if she can get through the ceremony and not itch where the seams of the dress bite into her flesh.

At the reception centre Jack makes a beeline for the bar. May had pleaded with Martha to stop Jack from hitting the drink. Martha was smart enough to know one word from her would have him pissed before May and Laurie were hitched. She has to leave the matter to fate.

Jack hates but also reveres people with money. He speaks with a toffy voice most of the evening, which Martha finds a bit unnerving.

Christine sees Jack swallow a glassful of beer in one gulp and her eyelid develops a twitch. She nearly keels over because she forgets to breathe when Jack gives his speech. Luckily it is short and he welcomes Laurie into the Wheatley family as a son. Laurie's parents give them a house in Mordialloc as a wedding gift.

Christine is surprised and happy that Jack appears to have changed his mind about Laurie. Only that day she had heard him call the young man a dumb lug. Jack seems to have everyone at the bridal table enthralled. Jack does this. He can be charming, witty, have people in stitches. He pats Laurie's father on the back as if they are the best of mates. He tells Laurie's mother a joke and she grabs onto his arm because she laughs so hard. Christine catches May's eye. Their eyebrows rise.

Jill was not invited. After the ceremony Martha whispers, 'What a pity Jill isn't here.'

'She wouldn't have enjoyed herself, Mum,' May says as Martha helps her off with her veil. 'And besides, what would Dad be like? There would have been a scene.'

Later on in the night Christine can't find Martha. She looks for her on the dance floor and gets twirled around by Laurie's big brother until she's flung too wide and she escapes. She finds Martha in the powder room dabbing her face with her handkerchief.

'Are you crying, Mum?' Christine laughs.

'No, I'm not,' says Martha and she dabs at a tear that makes a run for it down her face.

'How come you're crying?' Christine knows people get soppy over weddings but is surprised at Martha.

'I'm not!' Martha shouts at the mirror. She arranges the stiff curls on her head and Christine follows her out.

It's time to cut the cake and the couple clasp the handle of the knife and plunge it in. The cameras flash.

Christine stands with Martha and sees that the tears have come again. Martha closes her eyes and the drops fall onto her gown. Christine holds her mum's hand and whispers, 'Oh Mum, don't worry, she'll be happy.'

Christine looks at the cake and thinks it's a pity to spoil it. She had helped Martha with the tiny iced pink petals of the rose buds and thought they were perfect. The cake looks magnificent. Christine doesn't remember it being that large and thought that there were fewer roses.

'Mum . . .?' Christine's mouth is left open.

Martha doesn't answer. Her smile is fixed.

'Mum . . .?'

'Shush Chrissie,' Martha's voice is choked.

'Mum, that's not your cake.'

'No, it's not,' says Martha quietly.

Twenty-one

Jill's long gone, but now the house is peculiar without Johnnie, the twins and May. Their rooms remain as if they might come home any minute. The beds are made up, there are clothes in their drawers. They still smell of them. Occasionally Christine goes to their rooms and smells. She doesn't miss them. It's peaceful now. It's almost as if they were never there. Her room without May is next door to Jack and Martha's and suddenly it feels too close. Christine moves out the back into Jill's old room but she's back in her own bed before the end of the night. The house is suddenly huge and full of strange noises.

Most of the time Christine sticks close to Martha. They watch film after film. They watch Bing Crosby and Bob Hope, Fred Astaire and Ginger Rogers, Nelson Eddy and Jeanette Macdonald. They laugh at one another when they both sob into their handkerchiefs watching *Mrs Minerva* or *Random Harvest*.

Martha never reminds Christine to do her homework. It's as if she's forgotten that Christine is still at school. Christine has never had so much of Martha. Sometimes Martha lets her sit on her lap. Often she holds Christine's feet.

'I've only got my baby left,' says Martha, giving Christine's feet a squeeze.

When Jack comes home before the end of the film Martha and Christine look at each other and groan. 'Quick, go to bed,' says Martha. 'It'll be on again some other time.'

Aunt Amelia comes for lunch every Sunday. Uncle Bob died two years earlier and Martha invites her because she can't bear to think of her on her own all the time. She and Amelia tolerate each other now. It's Jack who finds her difficult. He tells her she can only come if she limits herself to one glass of beer, and there is always an argument.

'You've had your glass,' says Jack.

'I bloody well have not.'

'You have. I poured it myself.'

'Where is it then?'

'You drank it, you silly old –'

'Prove it,' yells Aunt Amelia.

Amelia still doesn't like Christine. The thing she likes the least is that Christine is smaller than her. When Christine speaks Amelia puts her fingers in her ears. 'What kind of girly voice is that?' she calls out. If Christine leaves food on her plate Amelia is on to her. 'Eat it you little sneak. Trying to starve yourself, I know you.'

Jill rings Christine once in a while. She rings when Christine comes home from school.

'Are you all right?' Jill asks her.

'Yes.'

'I've got a flat now. Come and see me.'

'Yes, okay.'

'When?'

'Um . . . Soon. I'm a bit busy with schoolwork. I will be for a while.'

There's a long pause.

'Okay. I'll ring you again in a while. Put Mum on, would you.' Jill's voice is curt.

Christine does not want to see Jill. She thinks it would be disloyal. She thinks Jill has acted selfishly and has been mean to Jack. 'After all he's been through.' The words echo from somewhere way back.

Every now and then there's a postcard from Vietnam. Mouse never writes much.

He says, *Hi, I'm fine. Hope you're well, Love from Michael.*

He says, *Hi, slept all day. It's very hot here. Hope you're well, Love from Michael.*

He says, *Hi, haven't heard from Door. Tell him to write. Hope you're well, Love from Michael.*

He sends Christine a doll. It's a Vietnamese peasant woman and it's made of soft plastic. The large breasts beneath the blue traditional dress have been squashed in on the journey to Australia.

Christine is outraged: 'A doll! What does he think I am? A kid?'

Christine sneaks into Martha and Jack's bedroom and switches on the light. Electricity bites into her like a savage dog. The shock literally lifts her off her feet and throws her onto the double bed. She lies there and concentrates on breathing; machine-like her chest expands and contracts as she takes in great shafts of air. The current has entered her fingertip and burnt through the heel of her palm. The smell of burnt flesh lingers in the air. Aunt Amelia and her grandmother stare at her from the photograph on the dresser. Amelia sneers, it seems, and her grandmother with her sad eyes commiserates. Christine's resolve is jolted. She knows that she can't hold back much longer. She has been switched on.

She often comes in here to visit the full-length mirror. She spends a lot of time in front of it, just looking, reassuring herself that nothing has changed. Nursing her hand now, she gets up off the bed and stands before it. She can see no difference, but later she is sure that it was in that moment she began to grow.

It is the first of many shocks that reverberate through her body and make it difficult for her to keep it under control.

Christine begins to walk with Lorraine on the way home from school. She has never been in the same class as Lorraine but she knows her. She and her friends have talked about this girl many times. She is loud and hikes up her skirt and conveniently loses the top button of her summer school frock. She's got this tremendous laugh, which echoes across the quadrangle. It rankles some teachers so much they have told Lorraine to put a stop to it. Christine finds her laugh infectious and often when her friends are scoffing she finds herself chuckling.

One day Lorraine shouted across the street at Christine: 'Hey! Don't you live near me?'

Christine's heart raced as Lorraine joined her. She is too much flesh and bones, too wild, thought Christine. But by the time she left Lorraine at the end of her street that day Christine felt she was a different person, as if some of Lorraine's courage had rubbed off on her. She feels it in her stride, in the swing of her arms. She giggles when she thinks up Lorraine's laugh, how loud it is, how shocking.

For months they talk on the corner of the street where they part, until finally one afternoon Lorraine invites Christine to her house.

Lorraine's mother is in bed. 'Is that you, sweetheart?' she calls out from her bedroom.

In that one call Christine knows. There is something inexplicable in the tone. She feels her chest expand and her heart lightens. Lorraine's mother comes out of the bedroom. She wears a nylon nightie and it sticks to the insides of her skinny legs and outlines her barrel-like frame. Her hair is peroxide yellow and a cigarette is jammed down low between her fingers. She stops when she sees Christine and with a trembling hand she pats down a disobedient curl.

'Who's this, darling?' she says. 'I didn't know you brought someone home.'

'This is Christine, Mum. Why don't you go back to bed?'

Lorraine's mother looks jealously at Christine. 'Orright darling,' she says. 'Nice to meet you, Christine.' She staggers a little towards Christine as if she's about to hit her and quickly rights herself. 'Will you bring me something to . . .'

'Yes!' Lorraine says. 'I'll get it for you in a minute.'

On the way home Christine skips. She can't believe it. She laughs out loud. 'I've found someone,' she says. 'I've finally found someone.'

Christine invites Lorraine to her house the very next day. Jack is home but he's only slightly drunk. Christine is unnecessarily disappointed. As soon as Lorraine sees him she turns and looks at Christine and laughs. Christine laughs back.

'What's so funny?' Jack frowns at them, instantly annoyed.

'Sorry,' Lorraine says. 'It's just that you remind me of someone.'

They spend hours talking at the corner. Every day after school they talk. Lorraine clears up a few things for Christine. She calls her mother and Jack alcoholics and Christine is shocked again.

'Dad's not an alcoholic,' says Christine. She is horrified and thinks it is too serious a claim. 'He just drinks every day.'

'Christine, wake up, what do you think alcoholics do?' Lorraine laughs.

Lorraine tells Christine she's had sex. 'I lost my virginity years ago,' she says. 'You should consider it. It's a huge weight off your shoulders. Once you get rid of it you don't have to think about it any more.'

'I will never let any man urinate in me.' Christine says it adamantly.

It takes Lorraine a long time to stop laughing. She finally explains that when men have sex it's some other fluid that comes out and that's the fluid that makes kids.

'That's the gunk you should be worrying about,' says Lorraine. 'Not piss.'

Lorraine teaches Christine how to kiss. She pulls her inside a bush. She pushes her mouth over Christine's and slips her tongue in.

'Yuck!' says Christine because she thinks she should.

'Get used to it,' says Lorraine. 'That's what you're in for.'

Lorraine visits and a cantankerous Jack waylays her. He has taken to grabbing at Lorraine when she comes round, giving her too hard a hug or clipping her lightly behind the ear. There is something he likes about Chrissie's new friend, she's feisty and he wants to let her know that he always wins. Lorraine tries to get past him. He spars with her, pretends a playfulness that doesn't fool Lorraine. Christine senses the danger and an uneasy laugh quietly rides her breath. He throws a punch and it lands with a thud on Lorraine's shoulder. She becomes a windmill of flailing arms. She catches Jack off balance and sends him over onto his bum. Lorraine continues to fume and Jack, taken aback, laughs. Christine is astounded at how much he laughs and in relief she joins him. Lorraine doesn't crack a smile.

Later Lorraine tells Christine, 'Your dad's an arsehole.'

Christine is shocked because for a moment she knows that Lorraine is right.

Christine and Lorraine befriend Eleanor, a new girl at school. She and her sister have come to live with her father and stepmother. They had been living with their mother in an outer suburb when she suddenly died. 'He pissed off with a woman half his age and they thought they'd be fancy free. But Mum died, didn't she? And they inherited us, didn't they? And now we're meant to play happy family, aren't we?'

Eleanor is dry and perceptive and she smokes cigarettes and wears thick eyeliner on the lower edges of her eyes. 'My step-mummy hates it,' she explains.

Their house is a battlefield. Christine dodges as Eleanor's thin-lipped stepmother, who looks not much older than Jill, grabs at her stepdaughter and tells her to take off her jeans. 'You're not going out of the house looking like that!' she says.

Eleanor swears at her and smiles infuriatingly. 'You're not my mother,' she says with pleasure.

Having made a run for it Christine and Eleanor laugh at the corner of the street. 'It's much worse,' says Eleanor, 'when she tries to be my friend.'

Christine feels exhilarated when she's been witness to these spats and scrimmages. Once the two of them fight the entire length of the hall. Eleanor cries and Christine tries to comfort her but Eleanor will have none of it. 'She's such a bitch!' she spits and through her tears looks at Christine and laughs.

Christine thinks she has never seen any other family in disarray. In fact she has seen many families in disarray but not openly like this. She never thought for a moment that there was fighting or yelling or ugly outbursts in anyone else's home but her own. Until she went to Eleanor's. It is such a relief. In the tidy and almost identically decorated homes of her other friends she knows there are uncomfortable and strange tremors. She'd seen Jane's mother smile too wide and offer a hard powdered cheek to Jane's father when he'd come home late. She noticed Marion's mother's voice, how brittle it was and unkind and yet how she smiled when she spoke. She's sat up at dining tables covered in white damask cloths with candles and flowers and sumptuous meals, and wondered why no one spoke. She has walked past doors and heard sharp words under breath. She's felt the icy cold from underneath the veneer of warmth. All under, bitter undercurrents, underlying resentment, undertones that confused her, all horribly under control.

Christine's departure from her old friends is not confrontational. The first time she doesn't turn up to their lunchtime rendezvous and hangs out with Lorraine and Eleanor instead, they surround her at the lockers. 'Where have you been? Where were you? What happened?' They've been worried about her. They don't suspect anything because Christine is an expert in maintaining a double life. 'Something came up,' she says enigmatically. Soon the old friends see the new, and realise they have been replaced.

Christine, Eleanor and Lorraine spend lots of time laughing at nothing much. They say shocking things for the sake of it. They swear outrageously. They surround Christine's old friend, Angela the Mormon, and won't let her go until she says the word fuck. They tell each other who they hate. They walk along the pavement and take up all the space. The world's theirs for the taking and they're going to take. Christine is exhilarated to have found two such fine fighters. With them on either side of her she knows she's safe.

It is wonderful, their laughter. Silly, tear-spilling, wet-your-pants, out-of-control laughter and each of them goes home refreshed, happy even. And somehow more resilient.

Christine's uniform is pinned together, it is frayed, it shines, it has been worn by both Jill and May, and to death. Teachers pull Christine aside and ask her where her hat is, why she has on the wrong shoes, where is the belt for her box-pleat tunic. They ask her time and again. They appear never to guess why it might be that Christine does not have all the bits. It is as if it's beyond them. For years Christine has been afraid of these interrogations. She's been afraid that what she is will be revealed. And it is only lately that she can name it. She's poor. And lately she feels her body pull itself up tall when she's confronted with their blundering questions.

This not seeing, deliberate or not, is a malady from which many of the teachers suffer. The twins were strapped by their physical education teacher every Friday of the school week until the day they left school. He strapped them with great vigour because they continually refused to bring their sports clothes. They didn't have any sports clothes to bring.

Most kids at the high school are neat and clipped and ironed and heeled and polished and shiny-haired and have watches and pencil cases and no ladders in their stockings. They take music lessons and go on holidays to beach houses on the Peninsula. Some have been on trips abroad. They are taught swimming and tennis and have extra tutoring. They go out to restaurants, to the theatre, and to the ballet. They've been to the museum and the zoo so many times they don't want to go again. They own all the volumes of the *Encyclopaedia Britannica*. They get more than one present for their birthdays. Mothers with elegant hair-dos driving expensive cars drop them off at school.

There are the kids from the housing commission flats who are marked as though a sign reading *POOR* is pinned to their backs. And there are kids Christine can pick because she knows what to look for. Their uniforms are impeccable but their shoes are worn flat. They run out of paper and write on the backs of folders. They have sloppy tomato sandwiches for lunch. They are asked to stand up in class and in front of everyone explain why their school fees are not paid. It is both obvious and not. It is not talked about. The struggle to find the money for excursions, for fees, and for fares, is hidden.

With Lorraine and Eleanor at her side Christine no longer pulls down the sleeves of her blazer to cover her frayed cuffs. Lorraine and Eleanor are not poor but their uniforms are untidy or stained, or have bits missing. Teachers constantly tell Lorraine she's not presentable. 'So what?' she says to Miss Harris, a woman who viciously prods students in the back. Eleanor is told by the head prefect to put on her hat. Eleanor tells her, 'Why don't you go and get stuffed?' Christine marvels at their audacious retorts, she smiles expansively, she feels herself taking up space.

Lorraine and Eleanor are often at detention after school. Christine is asked to join them when she splutters with laughter and can't stop. Christine is amazed at her new friends because they don't care. 'It's a load of shit,' says Lorraine. 'They can all get fucked,' Eleanor concurs.

This is Christine's sixth year at high school and she has never finished a book. *My Brother Jack* by George Johnston had been set for English. Jill reads all the books on Christine's book list and she rings her.

'Read it, Christine, just read it. I've never read anything like it,' she says excitedly.

The novel is set in Melbourne and is written by an Australian novelist who'd grown up in a suburb not far from them.

'It's like it's talking to us,' says Jill. 'It's like it really is, not all this hero stuff. It's about men who have been to war but it doesn't slap them on the back. And the family is like ours, full of fighting and shit.'

Christine reads it and finishes it but doesn't know what Jill is excited about until one Sunday Jack storms into the lounge room looking for her. He holds the novel up in the air, a mad preacher standing in his underpants.

'Who belongs to this?'

He stares at Christine, full of fire and damnation, ready to curse her and send her shamefaced from his house. 'Is this yours?' he roars.

'Yes,' says Christine.

'Where did you get it?' He looks at her as if she's something he's caught.

'We're doing it at school,' she says.

'You're what?' Jack can't believe it. He slaps his forehead as if he's been shot.

He smacks the cover as if it's the hand of a naughty child. 'The bastard who wrote that has never faced anything in his entire bloody life. What does he know about being a man? What does he know about war? How would he know what it was like? That snivelling little coward has got no right. I've never read such shit!'

He throws the book of the devil with all his might through the open window of the lounge room and it flies out into the street.

'I never want to see that book in my house again, do you hear?'

'Okay.' Christine shrugs.

Christine is shocked. Jill's right, she thinks. It must be good, and immediately she bites her lip.

Christine who never reads chose English Literature as one of her subjects. She was given the task of writing an essay on the symbolism of the green light in the novel, *The Great Gatsby*. Mr Collins, her English Literature teacher, holds her essay in his hand. Christine is shocked as she watches it waving high in the air. She is already fearful of Mr Collins because there is a rumour that he fucked one of the students last year and it unsettles her to be in a class with a man who knows no boundaries. The knowledge has also given him a visceral quality that she never associated with a teacher before and it makes her nervous. He does not reveal the owner of the essay but she knows it's hers because she recognises the heading that she took some time decorating in coloured pencils.

'You cannot get away with rubbish like this,' he yells. 'This is nonsense. Full of gobbledygook. If this is an example of the standard of your work then I can see there's some growing up to do.'

Christine struggled to make sense of her essay. She didn't know what a symbol was. She found it hard to grasp that there were layers of meaning, that a thing, an object, an animal or whatever, might mean something else. Christine had struggled to read the book. How can I explain to him, she thinks, that I can't, I just can't take anything in?

Mr Collins talks on passionately, he sprays the class with spit, he gets up and waves his arms about, he twists his body into curious contortions. 'There's Gatsby,' he says, 'a most peculiar character, standing in the night, entranced, looking out across an expanse of water, gesturing across it, and all that is there is a minute green light. But it's not a bloody light he's entranced by, is it? No, it's the light at the end of the dock where Daisy lives. The light is Daisy. The light is his love that still burns for Daisy. The light is the hope that he will be with Daisy again, it's his dream to reconstruct the past.'

Christine is in shock. She feels her head might burst as the idea that things might not be as they seem expands in her, and she seems to grow then and there, in the middle of the class.

At night Christine continues to grapple with her recalcitrant body. The familiar restriction in her chest is changing. There is some other strange sensation there. She has begun to develop ridiculous bumps, which quite quickly become more like mounds, and round.

'Oh my god!' Christine exclaims and snaps the elastic in her underpants shut. There is hair under her arms and now pubic hair too.

A fighter from way back, she continues to resist. 'I will not, I will not, I will not bleed.'

Twenty-two

Christine hears things she's never heard before. All of a sudden her ears have become unstuck. With her brothers and sisters gone, the house is almost empty and she wonders if it's the echo she hears.

She hears Jack.

No matter where she is in the house she hears him. His voice sneaks through the rooms and finds her out. His voice is a perpetual shout. It shouts for Martha. She hears him shout for Martha because his dinner is cold. He shouts for Martha because she's forgotten the salt. He shouts for her because he can't find his comb. He shouts at her to bring him toilet paper. He shouts because she is taking so long to come when he calls her. He goes to bed and he shouts for Martha to join him. He is so loud Christine covers her ears with her hands, she sings a little tune to drown him out. What's wrong with him, she thinks. Why all of a sudden does he feel he has to shout?

'Shut up, just shut up,' she mutters quietly under her breath.

She sees Jack. It's as if her eyes have for the first time come into focus. He's like a big kid, she thinks when he bellows, 'I can't find my socks.' She sees him eating ravenously, throwing beer down his throat, dragging hard on every smoke. Just a big greedy kid.

There is something in her about to bust and she's not sure what it is but it's definitely about Jack. And it frightens her. She senses that there is a battle lurking, a battle like no other she has ever imagined. A huge thunderous battle, and she wonders if she is equipped, if a lifetime of training will be enough. Her up against Jack. She thinks of his fights with Jill, and she pulls her jaw up and looks for a moment remarkably like him. If she can do it so can I, she thinks. Immediately her jaw quivers and drops.

She avoids being in the same room with Jack. She no longer draws him into discussion about the war. She imagines him on the raft, his knuckles white with holding on, desperately holding on, and she lets him release his grip and drop down below the surface of the water. Gone, just like that.

She does not stay to watch their usual shows on the television. She makes up an excuse to leave the room the moment he walks in. She cannot keep eye contact with him and once her back is turned her lip peels into a curl.

From her bedroom Christine hears Jack drunk and raving about someone who has done him wrong.

'Come on, you bastard, I'll take you on.' Christine pitches her voice low and menacing as she rehearses. 'You stupid, poor old bastard, you won't know what hit you,' she intones in a gravelly voice slightly coloured with an American accent. 'I'll fight you. I'll fight you and set Mum free.'

She sees Martha in a way she's never seen her before. Jack has Martha captive, thinks Christine. All tied up. Her sisters and brothers have deserted their mother and Christine alone is left to save her.

Jack too appears to find the house large and empty with five of his six children no longer at home. There is no one to talk to any more, that's what he thinks. No one to share a joke. Martha's there but she's usually dithering around, cooking or some such thing. And Christine, she's too young.

It's ages before Jack notices that Christine has grown. If someone had asked him how old she is he'd say that she's about twelve or thirteen. If he were asked what year she was doing at school he wouldn't have a clue. What he does notice is that she's not on side.

He's very good at picking up enmity and he senses that his youngest daughter is carrying a bundleful.

He looks closer and he sees a stranger, a silent young woman who is always making a beeline for the door. When she stays they sit in uneasy silence. Neither of them has a word to say to the other these days. Sometimes he sits there and looks at her and she tries to look back. He could stare down a snake, she thinks. She breaks her gaze and walks out and goes directly to find Martha.

'I hate him,' she tells her mother.

'Don't talk like that.'

Jack is shouting for Martha to bring him his lunch. 'Why don't you tell him to get his own fucking lunch?'

'Don't swear like that!'

Jack is shouting for Martha to bring him a bottle of beer. 'Why don't you tell him to get up off his arse and get it himself?'

'That's enough of that!'

Jack is shouting for Martha to hurry up. 'Why don't you tell him to shut up?'

'Why don't you?' Martha turns on Christine. 'Why don't you bloody well tell him?' Martha shouts.

Christine is in shock. She is frozen in fright. 'Shush,' she says. 'Shush.'

Jack is shouting, 'What's the hold-up?'

Christine finds it difficult to go out at night. She does not want to leave Martha. She'll be alone and Christine can't bear that. Or worse, she'll be alone with Jack. She leaves Martha prey to the enemy if she goes to a party with Lorraine and Eleanor. It is her duty to stay with Martha. Boys have begun to notice her and want to take her away from her post. Perhaps it is because she is no longer surrounded by good girls and she stands out. Perhaps it's because she has those mounds on her chest.

She goes because she doesn't know how to tell them no. Her first kiss is full of spit. Another boy's kiss has her retching. His tongue was stuck way down her throat. Lorraine's kisses had not prepared her for these. Her body is not ready for their clumsy groping fingers that hurt. She constantly pushes their hands away. She feels the desire, all right, but it is caught somehow and unable to come out. In the back of a car or jammed up against a fence she grapples with his and her own desire, but the most heightened feeling she feels is guilt. She should be home looking after Martha.

Christine is happier at home and finds comfort in the sound of Martha rattling pots. If she can't hear her she searches for her. 'Mum? Mum? Mum?' She yells at the top of her voice.

'What? What do you want, Chrissie?' Martha asks, exasperated.

'I just wanted to know where you were,' Christine says, hurt.

'Well I'm here,' Martha snaps.

When Jack walks into the lounge room the hairs on the back of Christine's neck rise. He's drunk and snarling and looking for a fight. Christine gets up and faces him. She loses courage and tries to get past.

'Where are you scuttling off to?' He bars her way.

'I've got homework,' she says.

'Too high and mighty to speak to your dad?'

'No. It's just I've got homework to do.'

'Stuff your homework and sit down and talk to me.'

Christine folds her arms and sits.

'Come on then,' says Jack. He sits forward on the edge of his chair.

Christine doesn't say, I hate your guts, or You're nothing but a drunk, or You should be ashamed to speak to my mother like you do, or any of the countless other retorts she's tried out over the last few months. She is silent.

'I'm waiting,' Jack says. He wants her to make a move.

Now is the time. Christine's mind races. Tell him. Tell him what a shit he is. How there's no excuse for what he's like. No fucking excuse. That's right. No fucking excuse. He'll make mincemeat of me, she thinks. So what? Let him. At least he'll know. At least then the war will be declared loud and clear. Just get it over and done with. Do it. She squares her shoulders, looks at him straight and takes a big breath. He stares at her and slowly smiles. Her eyes slide and she exhales a pathetic hiss.

'I thought so,' he says. 'Nothing to say to me. Nothing at all.' He gets up then and takes out his keys. He slams the front door as he goes out.

Christine remains still and hears the Holden start in a roar and die down suddenly and then whine in reverse. Martha comes in carrying a tray with a steaming meal. Wide-eyed she chews at her lip. 'What's up? Has he gone off in a huff?' She puts down the tray and does an odd little nervous dance. She looks out the window. 'It was the bloody gas jet. It's blocked. Blast!'

Christine summons up all the passion Jack uses when he tells Martha what an idiot she is. 'Jesus Christ, Mum, don't be so bloody stupid!' she says. And the rest pours out like a molten stream. 'Why do you let him talk to you like that? How can you put up with that? Why don't you ever tell him you're not going to stand for it? Why don't you leave him?'

She stops. 'Why don't you leave him?' she asks, slowly this time, really asks.

Martha has been standing with her eyes shut and she finally opens them. 'Why don't you mind your own business?' she says.

And this is how it is with the three of them. Jack walks into the room. Christine's hackles rise. They circle one another, snarling and sniffing and stretching their claws, just dying to let rip. Their jaws are set. They stink with a scent exuding warning. Martha enters with a cup of coffee for Jack. Jack wants tea and he snaps at her because by bringing him coffee she's suggesting he drinks too much. He growls and badgers and harries her and tells her how stupid she is. He drives off to get well and truly pissed. Then Christine turns on Martha and shouts at her. She insists she be told why her mother puts up with him. She tells Martha how stupid she is.

Christine comes home from school and groans because Jack's car is parked up on the lawn. Usually she has a few peaceful hours with Martha on her own. She can hear Jack shouting through the wall. It's like the boards of the house have responded to the years of his bellowing with their cracked and peeling curls of paint. She passes beneath the kitchen window and sees her mother staring out and smiling. Christine smiles back, eager to be conspiratorial against the raving Jack. Martha does not see her. Martha is smiling at a small bird, a grey and dusty-looking thing that is perched on a bending twig chirping while it swings. Christine looks back and sees that Martha is in a tower and Christine knows she must save her.

She walks through the back door and lets it bang shut. She throws her bag down and skittles some glass jars stacked waiting to be filled with stewed apricots. She doesn't stop when Martha comes out of the kitchen to greet her. She moves fast through the house into the lounge room. She knows Jack will be sitting there, probably smoking, probably having a beer or eating a meal, complaining that there's no ashtray or not enough salt or his beer's flat, shouting at Martha, telling her that she's useless and stupid and can't do one bloody thing right. She rushes up to Jack's chair and she leans over him.

'Why don't you just shut up for once. Just shut up!'

Jack lifts his head and stares at her.

'What? What did you say?' he slurs. His head drops back, his eyes shut and the venetian blinds rattle to his snores.

In bed in the dark Christine holds her arms tight around her body. She hasn't stopped trembling since she uttered those pathetic words to Jack. He won't even remember them when he wakes, she thinks with contempt. He won't remember them, will he? Her tremors accelerate as her fear sets in. She weeps. She can't fight Jack, now she knows that. She can't save Martha, there's no hope up against Jack. Christine lets go. She wakes to find she has bled in the night.

'We saw him from the kitchen window,' says Jane.

'I saw him too. On the golf links,' says Angela. 'I fell off my bike.'

Christine feels the heat rising and she knows her neck is tellingly red and the blush will spread up and across her cheeks.

'He was enormous! Maybe seventeen hands or more, I'm sure,' says Jane. 'And black, entirely black.'

Oh my god, he was black, thinks Christine. She secretly runs her fingers in a line from her neck down between her breasts.

'I fell off my bike,' says Angela again as she remembers the fright she got seeing this massive animal crossing the green.

'They say his hooves cut up the turf,' says Eleanor.

'I saw that,' says Jane. 'He reared up again and again. He was wild. And then he disappeared, just like that.'

'How could he?' Eleanor asks. 'How could he disappear just like that?'

'He did,' says Angela. 'He was there charging across the links, his tail out behind him, and then I fell off my bike and he was gone.'

Christine, her hand flat on her chest, concentrates. He's gone, she thinks, he's escaped.

'He might have been one of the horses from the dairy,' says Eleanor.

'No!' say Jane and Angela together.

'He wasn't a draught horse,' explains Jane. 'He was an Arab.'

'That's for sure,' agrees Angela.

Christine presses her hand harder against her chest. The bell rings and the others scatter, grabbing for bags and hats. Christine remains still. She dare not move. She couldn't have let him out. She couldn't. It isn't possible. There's no ache across her rib cage, no tenderness at all. She had neglected him for a long time now – but she would know. Surely she would know.

Twenty-three

Christine sees her brother walking along the street and doesn't recognise him. At first she thinks it's Door with his hair cut until she sees the splash of colour on his face and then she knows – it's Mouse.

She sees he's changed. It's in his walk, as if his heels still hurt. It's in the way he holds his head, as if it's heavy like lead.

She runs inside. She doesn't want to greet him alone. She yells: 'Mouse is home! He's walking along the road!'

Martha and Jack and Christine run out. They meet him on the path. Martha hugs him and Jack shakes his hand.

The excitement simmers down and Christine asks, 'Where's your uniform?'

'They suggested we didn't wear it,' he tells her. Christine is perplexed. 'A lot of people don't feel very friendly towards it,' he explains.

'When did you get in?' Jack asks.

'This morning around nine o'clock.'

'I'd have picked you up,' says Jack.

'Of course, Mouse, why didn't you give us a ring?' Martha asks.

'They didn't want any fuss when the train came in,' says Mouse. 'Told us it was best to make our own way home.'

'What fuss?' asks Martha. 'We would have loved to be there for our boy.'

'They wanted to avoid trouble with demonstrators, I think,' says Mouse.

'So you have to sneak in.' Jack's mouth is a violent slit.

'That's about it,' says Mouse.

Jack stands bellowing in the street. 'That's the fucking Australian army for you, full of officers who are nothing but cowardly shits. Weak bastards who let a bunch of poofta demonstrators tell them what to do.'

Here he goes, thinks Christine, and she sneers.

'You fight for your country and you're given no respect.'

'Now Jack. Now Jack,' Martha punctuates as Jack speaks.

'You put your life on the line and they treat you no better than a bloody criminal.'

Mouse is looking at Jack but he doesn't see him. He has disappeared way off, thousands of miles into some unfathomable space.

Jack suddenly grabs his bag. 'Jesus Christ, let's get you inside.'

That night Jack takes Mouse to the Club. He and his mates line up the beers and they give three cheers, they jab playfully at Mouse, they tell him jokes, they pull him in, close to hugging him, they dance around him, they muss up his hair and each of them asks him, 'How was it over there?' All the while Mouse stands silent, downing beer after beer. It's not a sullen silence. It's empty. As if he's not there. Jack fills in the spaces and prattles on. Sometimes he gives Mouse an encouraging nudge and says, 'Come on,' but he grows tired of trying to cover for Mouse, and he too becomes silent like his son. The mates soon become uncomfortable and move on.

Jack takes Mouse home and props him up against the wall, and Mouse immediately slides down onto his haunches and rolls over onto the lino floor.

'He's as drunk as a skunk,' says Jack.

'I can see that,' says Martha.

Christine comes looking for Martha and when she sees Mouse sprawled out in front of her she begins to laugh. She stops because Jack and Martha don't notice her. So intent are they on the body that lies, out cold, at their feet. It's like he's died, thinks Christine, they're that sombre. And Jack is sober. She's amazed. The Club must have run out of beer.

The following afternoon Jack stands in Mouse's room. Mouse has not got out of bed the entire day. Jack stands and stares at Mouse who's gone again somewhere far away. It dawns on Mouse that there's someone there. He slowly turns his head and sees Jack peering down at him.

'What?' he asks.

'Nothing,' says Jack and remains staring at his son.

'What?' Mouse asks again.

'You all right then? I mean, you're all right, aren't you?'

'Yeah, I'm all right.'

'Good,' says Jack. 'Good.' He offers Mouse a cigarette. Together they light up and inhale.

In silence they smoke until the filters burn acrid and black. Jack goes to leave, but as if some bee has bit him he turns and says, 'You're laying it on a bit thick, aren't you, Mouse?'

'What!' says Mouse.

'You heard me.'

'Why don't you go and get fucked,' says Mouse.

Jack's hand rises up in a fist but it rests unpunched in the air. Mouse has gone again, his eyes staring at some other place. Jack backs out the door.

Mouse lies on his childhood bunk. There's no bulge from his twin brother's body in the wire bed-base above him. He lights up and blows smoke rings at the striped mattress ticking and they dissolve into a haze.

Door has not come to see Mouse. He is living in Ferny Creek in the Dandenong Ranges. He still works for the State Bank, at the Ferntree Gully branch, at the foot of the mountains.

One morning Christine gets out of bed and finds Martha staring at the phone. 'I think Door might have a girlfriend,' she says.

'Who'd go with Door?' Christine doesn't believe it.

'It is a bit hard to believe,' says Martha. It is seven o'clock in the morning and a woman had answered the phone.

Martha rings Door again that night. 'I was wondering when you were coming to visit your brother,' she says. 'He's been home a month, Door. He'd love to see you.'

'I've been busy, Mum,' says Door. He says no more.

Martha says, 'Hello? Hello, are you there?'

'I'm here,' says Door.

'Oh Door,' says Martha. 'Too busy for your brother?'

'I've got to go, Mum,' Door says.

Martha puts down the phone and Mouse says, 'Who was that?'

Martha squeals. 'Oh god, Mouse, you frightened the life out of me.'

'Who was that?' repeats Mouse.

'That? That was May,' says Martha. 'She rang to say she won't be able to come on Sunday. I don't know why she bothered. She hasn't come for Sunday lunch in the last six months.'

Jack pulls up. There's a hand-painted number five on a sign nailed to a tree. He peers through the thick bush and sees glimpses of an old timber shack. He walks down an overgrown drive and along a path intruded upon by ferns, which saturate the legs of his pants. He knocks but no one answers and there is no sound behind the mildew-spotted door. He follows the house around to the back and in the yard he sees Door and a young woman sitting together on a fallen log looking down into a gully. Jack can hear the trickle of water echo up from a hidden creek. The young woman has long hair and it falls like a shawl over her back. They are not in pajamas but there is a lack-adaisical way to their dress, which suggests to Jack that they have just got out of bed. The young woman laughs and, for a moment, leans against Door's shoulder. Door bends and kisses the top of her head. Jack is caught, as if he's wandered into the yard of people he does not know. He watches them. They are easy with one another, comfort-able, unafraid of silence. Jack has never seen Door as relaxed with anyone before. Except of course with Mouse.

There's a mattress on the floor and Jack stands on it and spills his tea as he tries to make it to the only chair in the room. Lenore has pulled on an overcoat and she talks with Jack, all the time looking around for Door who is now nowhere to be seen.

'Took me hours to find the place,' says Jack.

'No, it's not easy,' says Lenore. 'You're our first visitor.'

That'd be right, thinks Jack. He has taken in Door's abode in a single glance. He doesn't want to look too close, doesn't want to see anything that might upset him. There are posters on the wall, record covers strewn on the floor, books in piles, the mirror on the mantel has some kind of poem written across it in lipstick. He doesn't want to know how Door lives. If it hadn't been for Mouse he would never have come.

Door comes in newly dressed. He sits down to put his shoes and socks on.

'I've got to go with Dad,' he tells Lenore.

Lenore is surprised, but not as surprised as Jack. All the way up the winding mountain road he had geared himself for an attack on this twin, had passionately practised remonstrations against him. He was brimming with words like unbrotherly, and traitorous, and slack-arsed shit.

Door hangs his head out the car window. 'I'll be back,' he yells at Lenore.

'Mouse?' Door whispers at the entrance of his old bedroom. The curtains are pulled and he can see the shape of his brother lying on the bunk. He sees it rise up like a grey ghost and fly at great speed to greet him. He feels the vibration on his face as the door is slammed shut.

An hour later Door returns and tries to open the door. He knows there is no lock. But Mouse has put something up against it and it won't budge. 'Mouse,' Door calls. 'Open up.' He rattles the doorknob. 'Come on, Mouse, will you please open the door?' For another hour he stays there and calls his brother's name. He leans his head against the door and calls and calls. There is something soothing in his calling. It waylays an awful feeling that churns down low in Door's guts and threatens to erupt.

Martha makes Door come away from his vigil and he slurps down her barley soup and toast. In the bathroom he washes his face and glimpses himself in the vanity mirror. The awful feeling surges up and out and he quickly bends his head and is sick in the sink. Mirrors had played no role in Door and Mouse's life. They needed only to look at one another to know what they looked like. Door had forgotten that. Now he doesn't recognise his reflection. And he had forgotten Mouse. For a year now he has fitted into the curve of Lenore's body, their limbs coiled around each other in a tight clutch. No one had dared intrude upon them, nothing had diluted the potency of their union. Door had felt true happiness – but at a price. He had let go of Mouse.

He returns to the door and he smashes his fist against it. 'Open the fucking door, Mouse. Or I'll break the fucking thing down,' he screams. He attacks the door, kicks it, rams his body against it. Exhausted, he breathes heavily up against it and he hears Mouse breathe in synchrony on the other side.

'I'm sorry, Mouse,' he whispers.

Jack is in the lounge room. He leans forward, cigarette in hand, and listens to Door shout. 'That's the way,' he says. 'That's the way.'

Door pushes away a straggly bush and thumps hard on the glass of the window but it doesn't smash. He bends down and picks up a piece of brick and brings it up when the curtain is pulled aside and Door and Mouse are face to face. Mouse is full of uneven stubble, his hair is matted, a cigarette hangs out of his mouth. For a moment they stare, and all the ferocity of what they feel is held at bay. They let each other sink in. Door puts his head in his hands and sobs.

Mouse is out of the house and charges Door from behind. He throws him down on the buffalo grass. He pins him down, his knees digging hard into Door's arms. 'What are you crying for?' he spits and slaps Door's face. They roll in a tangle of flailing arms and kicking legs. They grab and slap and punch. Mouse bites Door on the arm to make him release his grip. Mouse is strong, his muscles well defined but the way he fights would give no suggestion that this is a man recently home from war. They stop when they run out of breath. They sit side by side, their legs outstretched. And rest.

In a while Martha comes out and asks, 'Do you boys want a cup of tea?' And together they answer her, 'Yes please.'

Later they walk along Hampton Street until they reach the railway crossing gates. The rhythm of the trains and gates and traffic are comfortingly familiar and Door and Mouse sit together and watch. When the last train rattles past they linger on.

'I can't talk, Door,' Mouse says. 'I can't talk.'

'You don't have to, Mouse,' says Door. 'You don't have to.'

Twenty-four

More than seventy thousand people rally in Melbourne's city streets. Jill is pregnant and, on the way in on the tram, she and Alex work out what she should do if the demo turns nasty.

'We'll keep to the edges as much as we can and if anything happens you can run into a shop,' says Alex.

In the first few minutes Jill loses Alex in the crowd. She is too taken up in the excitement to give her big belly a thought. She buries herself in the masses of people. The sensation of being a part of something as grand as this is euphoric. She and thousands of others have taken the city's streets. She carries a slogan in her hand demanding troops out of Vietnam. There are no outbreaks of violence. No unruly mob is this. They march with resolution. 'We'll have no more to do with this immoral and shameful war!' someone beside her shouts.

Jill knows that she is part of something powerful. The country is on the move. It's about to shed its former self. Over twenty years of conservative government is close to coming to an end and the crowd feels alive, they have taken their destiny in their hands. Most have never marched before and they are exhilarated, renewed, high on the feeling resistance brings.

After the rally Jill and Alex's small flat in Elwood cannot contain the party. People spill out onto the park opposite. They chant, 'One side right, one side wrong, victory to the Vietcong.' Some go to the beach and, despite the weather, throw themselves into the sea but they cannot cool the heat from their ecstatic bodies. They hoot and shout and scream. They dance until the very ends of their hair drips sweat. They hug and laugh and pick each other up and fall elated together to the ground. They are inspired, energised and ready to take on the world.

Christine knocks on the door. She is startled when Jill suddenly opens it wide and yells at her. Christine steps back and raises her arm over her face as if expecting a punch.

'It's you, Chrissie. Sorry, I thought you were my neighbour. She's always complaining.'

The walls are covered in posters, placards, photographs and album covers. Jimi Hendrix and Bob Dylan fight for space with LBJ, who wears a Hitler moustache, and a baby whose skin is melting off, screaming in its mother's arms. Jill's own Hugo sits in a high chair and suddenly lets go a shrill shriek.

Christine has not seen Hugo since his birth. She and Martha had visited Jill at the Royal Women's Hospital. They left Jack in the car. 'I have no intention of seeing the little bastard,' he'd said. When they were on the ward, cooing and taking it in turns to hold tiny Hugo, Jack had appeared and without a word to Jill had taken the baby from Martha. 'Here, let me hold him. You've forgotten how to do it.'

The three Pats had not told Jill about the pill, they would not have approved. Emma told Jill about the tiny liberating tablet and she was on it within a week. In a month her breasts had doubled in size and she had a brown stain on the side of her cheek. Hugo had snuck in when Jill was giving her body a break, as she had been advised to do. She and Alex had mulled over whether to keep it or not – and ran out of time. 'You're fucking mad,' Emma had yelled at Jill.

'Congratulations,' says Jill now and raises her cup of tea to Christine. 'Mum told me the news.' Christine smiles. She still can't quite believe it. She is going to university. She isn't really sure why except she's got in. She is more excited that she and Eleanor and Lorraine are looking for part-time jobs and going to move out of home. She says nothing of this to Jill because she hasn't told Martha. She's afraid her mother will learn how desperately she wants to get away.

'You must be really pleased.' Jill lurches forward suddenly and gives Christine a fright. Her hair covers her face as she leans over and wipes Hugo's nose.

'I suppose,' says Christine. The idea of more study makes her inwardly groan. She thinks it's quite likely that somehow they made a mistake when they marked her exam papers and that when she goes to university the truth will be exposed.

'You suppose?' says Jill. 'You must be!' Her voice is caught and sounds harsh. 'You bloody well ought to be.' Christine looks warily at her sister but Jill's voice is free again when she says, 'It'll be fantastic.'

Jill asks after Martha. She searches under piles of books and reams of paper for some photos of Hugo to give her. Christine wants to clear the mess and wipe the table clean. Instead she tells Jill how their mother took herself off to see the intermediate session of a film called *Cabaret.*

'On her own?' Jill stops searching.

'Yes,' says Christine, instantly guilty. 'She loved it. She said Liza Minnelli was wonderful,' she finishes limply.

Jill is crying. Christine is frightened by her face as she watches it fill with fury. 'He's such a bastard! She can't go to the pictures with a friend because she hasn't got any friends. He made sure of that. She has to go in the afternoon because he might come home, and watch out if she's not there with his bloody dinner all cooked and kept warm for him. She has to go alone. I'd have gone with her. But no, he made sure I couldn't do that. A bloody bastard, that's what he is!'

Christine is silent. She had thought nothing of Martha's outing to town, to the pictures. But she knows Jill is right and believes herself an accomplice in Jack's crimes against Martha. Jill blows her nose and Hugo gurgles appreciatively. A photograph on the table has been unburied and Christine picks it up. It is a picture of Mouse and Jill sitting in Jill's kitchen. The photograph includes the mother with her screaming melting child, which is taped to the wall, inches above Mouse's head.

'You've seen Mouse?' Christine is surprised.

'Michael? Yes, of course,' Jill says, wiping her face with a tea towel. 'He comes around a lot.'

Christine had thought that Jill would have been extremely unfriendly to Mouse, so unfriendly that she wouldn't allow Mouse into her home. She looks at the photograph and it has caught Jill and Mouse laughing at a joke.

'He says he's all right,' says Jill. 'But he's always lighting up a smoke, he drinks like a fish and he doesn't sleep. He stayed here the other night and whenever I got up for Hugo he was up smoking.'

Why wouldn't he be all right, Christine thinks. She has not given Mouse a thought since his return. She hasn't seen him much but when she does she doesn't know how to talk to him. She'd never known how to talk to him.

Jill and Christine lie on the carpet and whisper over Hugo sleeping, curled up on a bunny rug between them. The sun streams through the window and warms them. They are dozy, almost relaxed. Christine looks at Jill and thinks she barely knows her. If she were here with Eleanor and Lorraine she would be telling well-known secrets and rolling about the room shrieking with laughter. Christine isn't sure how to talk to Jill. She never guesses for a moment that Jill feels the same. There seem to be too many danger zones. Jill flares at any mention of Jack. She flares also when Christine talks about Martha because Jack is responsible for what Jill perceives as Martha's misery. They talk about May safely for a while. May had to close her shop, or boutique as she called it, because most of her orders remained uncollected and, more importantly, unpaid for. She now works for a tailor in Prahran and alters trousers.

'Laurie's business is in a bit of strife, I think,' explains Christine.

'Such a fucking waste!' fumes Jill.

Christine is not sure what Jill means but chooses to ignore the outburst. They speak of Alex and his job on the tugboats and his involvement in the union, about which Christine doesn't know what to say. Jill asks her what she thinks about the government and Christine reddens and squirms under Jill's expectant look. She knows nothing about the government. She knows that Menzies is no longer Prime Minister and that the next one drowned in the surf at Portsea and she thinks there were a couple after that but she can't remember the name of the current one with enormous flapping ears.

Soon they lapse into easier talk about Hugo and about the area and how nice it is to be living by the seaside. Christine does not know how to talk about herself, to tell her sister what she thinks about or what she feels. I don't know what I think or feel, she realises.

There is a moment when Christine thinks she could say something. It's something that has only recently trickled through and she's not sure she has the words for it yet. It's got to do with how things are not often what they appear to be, how a lot of it is a load of shit. Jill knows, Christine reckons, she's known since she was a kid.

Hugo stirs and Jill quickly comforts him back to sleep. Christine lets the moment pass. Some other time, she thinks, I'll tell Jill.

Jill reads from letters that Johnnie has sent her. Christine learns that Johnnie has been to every state in the country and has worked in jobs she never knew existed. He's worked the fishing trawlers, driven the big trucks at Mt Isa, cut cane and picked every imaginable vegetable and fruit. He's done farm work, mustered cattle, cut the tails off lambs. He's worked down mines and in pubs and factories. He's sold used cars. *I can get them to buy the biggest heaps*, writes Johnnie, *Even when I tell them they're heaps they still buy them.*

'Who knows what he's doing?' says Jill.

'What do you mean?' Christine is perplexed.

'Look at the postmarks. They're from the same place.'

'I don't get it.'

'When it comes to lying he's the best. What's clear is he doesn't want to be found.'

Christine takes the letters and checks each one. All but a few are marked Kings Cross.

Christine suddenly misses him. 'Do you think he'll come home?'

'Yes. When Dad's dead,' Jill says.

Hugo wakes and they bundle him into his pram. They walk to St Kilda and stand outside the window of a cake shop in Acland Street and drool. They walk to the bus stop, their furry lips perched over paper bags. They have chosen lamingtons over the glorious custards and cakes with cream and liqueurs.

'Come again,' Jill says.

They embrace awkwardly.

'I will, I will. Of course I will,' Christine says.

Jill pushes Hugo out along the pier and sits with her legs hanging over the edge. The sea swells up and sucks back, threatening to take her shoes. Hugo is asleep again. She has eaten all day but cannot rid herself of the emptiness she feels inside. The days are long now and here is one place she often ends up, filling in time. Some days this is the only place she goes outside of her flat. She no longer gets to the regular meetings she would normally attend with Alex, which means she goes less to the pub afterwards where they meet up with friends and talk and argue. She's tried taking Hugo but it's usually meant she ended up outside or going home early. People in passionate debate about politics have no tolerance for a crying baby and when she tried to quieten him and put him on her breast she was told very quickly to feed him elsewhere. When Alex is off work he goes to meetings and talks and there's no time for going anywhere together. Jill accepts that he is a political person through and through and admires his commitment and dedication, but lately she has felt something new to her. It's not anger exactly; she has no trouble in identifying when she feels that. Foolish is what she feels and she knows that some time she's going to have to find out what that's about.

'Next year,' Jill tells the gulls that collect greedy-eyed around her. 'Next year I'm going back to school.'

She notices a gull with only one leg and wonders what joy a shark would have got from so small an offering.

'Mark my words,' she says to the gull, 'next year. I am definitely going back.'

The gull looks at her with its hard little black eyes. 'I am!' she shouts and it tilts its head and appears to mock her. 'Shoo!' she cries and suddenly lifts her arms. The gull flies up to settle a little way off.

Jill rubs her belly. Her threaded hands cradle the gnawing emptiness. Suddenly she is sick. She wipes her chin with Hugo's nappy and hopes the lamingtons weren't off. Then another thought bites her and she almost yelps.

'Oh no,' she groans. She looks down at her belly. 'Oh no, it couldn't be.'

The woodyard looks smaller. Perhaps it's because the creeper and the privet hedge are overgrown and crowd the space. Christine stands where she would normally stand. She has not been in the woodyard for a long time and she can't make out what is so different about it. She has grown eight inches during the year and she hasn't realised yet that she looks down on the yard from a different height. The smell is definitely the same. She breathes in deeply and smiles. If I could make a perfume of this I reckon I'd be a millionaire, she thinks. Of all the reminders of her childhood, she would like to take the sweet smell of the cut wood away with her.

She and her friends have rented a house in Carlton near the university and Christine has packed her stuff. Martha has told her she can take her bed. When Christine told Eleanor she said that they would ask the removalist to stop off on the bridge and toss it into the Yarra. 'There's to be only double beds in our house and preferably with two people in them,' she said.

Telling Martha she was leaving was the hardest thing Christine had ever done. Mouse was already gone. He had moved into the house in Ferny Creek with Door and Lenore. Christine felt she had betrayed Martha, given her up to the enemy. She had stood at the lounge-room door and scrunched her eyes up in dread. Her mother had been watching a film on the television. She had a block of chocolate on the arm of her chair and without taking her eyes from the screen she would take a piece and place it in her mouth. Like a child she savoured the sweet creamy chocolate.

'I need to live close to the university and the library,' Christine told her mother. 'It's what all the kids do,' she added. 'They all live close.'

Martha's tears fell silently and she nodded. 'If that's what you need to do.'

She hugged her mother then. She felt only the need to run, to bolt, to travel great distances. Martha could not come.

Christine closes her eyes and breathes in the smell of the wood. She allows herself to sink into her body, to go deep. She listens. No heart-beat. She is still. No movement. Not a tremor. Not a twitch. Not the slightest sense of his presence. She moves her hands slowly across her solar plexus. They move up and over breasts. No pressure. Not the mildest push.

'He's gone, definitely gone,' Christine says.

Jack is in the garden. He takes the small shoots of the tomatoes between his finger and thumb and nips them off.

'More flowers is what I want from you,' he whispers lovingly.

He attends to the marrows next. There are small fruit, each with a bright yellow flower on its bum. He loves how fast they grow and the sound they make when he gives them a slap but he'd never eat the mush they become and won't have it on his plate.

Jack spends a lot of time in his vegetable garden. It is the one thing that gives him pleasure. He no longer watches the television. He cannot look at the news and hear how the country is falling apart, how everything decent is now something to be scorned or cast off. He doesn't want to know about any of it any more.

A pumpkin vine has self-sown and taken off along the back fence. 'It's gone mad,' says Jack when he sees it's run up the apricot tree. He admires its vigour and follows its trail up into the branches, noting the tough twine-like clutches coiled and holding onto small twigs.

'Jesus Christ,' he says. There's a pumpkin, a golden lantern hanging from the tree. 'Look at the size of that apricot,' Jack laughs. He turns and takes a few steps towards the house.

'Kids,' he calls. 'Kids, come and have a look at this.' For a moment he feels annoyed because there's no response.'Come on,' he calls and goes to call again but realises his folly.

'Martha!' he shouts and then remembers she's gone shopping.

He shrugs his shoulders and takes out a cigarette.